BRASKA

ALSO BY WAYNE D DUNDEE

BRASKA

BRASKA
BOOK ONE

WAYNE D DUNDEE

WOLFPACK
PUBLISHING
— EST 2013 —

Braska
Paperback Edition
Copyright © 2025 by Wayne D. Dundee

Wolfpack Publishing
1707 E. Diana Street
Tampa, FL 33610

www.wolfpackpublishing.com

Paperback ISBN 979-8-89567-069-9
Ebook ISBN 979-8-89567-068-2
LCCN 2025931226

BRASKA

PART ONE
HOMECOMING

1

WHEN BRASKA DREW REIN AND LOOKED DOWN ON the old place for the first time in six and a half years, his initial impression was that it appeared not to have changed much at all. But then his gaze fell on the gateway arch over the lane leading up to the main house and outbuildings. The Bar S brand emblem that should have been hanging there, suspended between the two tall oak bracketing posts he'd helped set in place a dozen years earlier, was nowhere to be seen. What hung there instead was the brand marker for an outfit calling itself the Cross T.

The corners of Braska's mouth turned down and the muscles at the hinges of his jaw bulged visibly. Unfortunately, this development didn't come as a total surprise. The tone of the last couple letters he'd received, and then the absence of any letters at all for the past two-plus years, had indicated plainly enough things weren't going well here. But the sight of a foreign brand marker hanging over the gate, indicating that this spread his father had taken so much pride in and had put so much back-breaking work into now belonged to somebody else—that still made for a bitter pill to swallow.

Braska reached inside his pocket, took out the makings, and unhurriedly fashioned a cigarette. After he'd snapped a match to flame and lighted the quirley, he exhaled a long plume of smoke into the crisp morning air. The sun, less than an hour old in a cloudless sky, would warm the morning quickly, and by noon, a blanket of heat would be laying heavy across these choppy, rolling plains of southern Nebraska. Though a long time past, Braska had known many such cool summer mornings and subsequent hot days on this very ground. Out of that, he'd made up his mind early on that staying and working on the Bar S wasn't how he wanted to spend his life. Yet now, seeing it gone and the land evidently in the hands of somebody else, he felt a curious sadness. He should have gotten used to loss by now, he told himself. But somehow, in some cockeyed way, he'd always had a feeling the Bar S would continue on.

After finishing his smoke, Braska took care to pinch out the coal and shred the remains of the butt before tossing them away. This place might not be in his family any longer, but taking precautions against a grass fire had long ago been deeply drilled into him. It was evident that spring hereabouts had been quite dry, leaving the surrounding grassy hills a virtual tinderbox.

The conclusion he'd reached while thoughtfully burning through his quirley was that, while the Bar S had clearly changed hands and he'd been absent from being able to do anything about it, he still had every right to go down and ask some questions regarding what happened. Considering there was some still-living kin—at least as far as he knew—to be accounted for, a body might even say he had an obligation to do so. Thus resolved, Braska gigged Savvy, his tall buckskin gelding, into motion and they started down the slope toward the gate bearing the brand marker that continued to nag him for looking like it damned well didn't belong.

Drawing nearer to the buildings, Braska was puzzled not to see some signs of activity. It was early in the day, true, but things tended to start plenty early on a properly run ranch. Yet, apart from the apparent lack of activity, everything else about the place—the trim and tidy main house, the bunkhouse and grub shack, the barn and various sheds, the corral fencing—all bore the stamp of a well-maintained operation. If anything, Braska had to admit grudgingly, the place probably looked a little sharper than when last he'd been here.

As he was considering all of this, one of the double doors on the front of the horse barn rolled back and a man emerged from the structure's shadowy interior. He was an elderly gent, slouch hat, gray whiskers, stooped shoulders. One out-cocked hip caused him to move in a kind of half shuffle, half limp.

He came forward a few steps in this peculiar gait, then stopped and canted his head to one side, peering up at Braska. After a moment, he declared, "About doggone time you showed up!"

It took a minute for recognition to sink in. When it did, a grin split Braska's face and he said, "Fossie! Dick Fosslinger, you ol' horn-dodger—is that you?"

"A-course it is, you scalawag," responded the

oldster. "Yer blamed eyes goin' bad on you or something?"

Braska swung down out of his saddle and reached out to shake Fossie's gnarled, calloused hand that proved still capable of a mighty firm grip. "It's just that, with all the other changes I saw ridin' up," Braska explained, "I wasn't expectin' to run across a familiar face from the old days."

"Reckon I'm that right enough—an old face from the old days," Fossie allowed. "Reckon, too, I had the advantage on account of havin' been *expectin'* to see you. Plus, I knowed it was you the minute I spotted you when you wasn't much more'n a speck sittin' your horse up on the crest of that slope yonder. Some men got a distinct way of forkin' their saddle. You're one of 'em. That's how I knowed right off it was you."

"I only know one way to fork a saddle," Braska said. "Never knew there was anything special about the way I did it."

"Didn't say it was special. Just said it's your own particular way is all."

Braska let that ride and instead asked, "How is it you say you been expectin' me?"

"Ever since word came you'd got out. The marshal in Piney Flats was notified and word sorta spread. Only thing is, that was quite a spell back. Thought I'd be seein' you sooner." Fossie paused, scrunched up his wrinkled, whiskery mug. "Don't know what took you so long, but I held on to the hunch you were bound to come home eventually."

"I came back," Braska corrected him. Then, cutting a meaningful glance over at the Circle T brand marker hanging above the gate, he added, "But it don't hardly look like this is home to me no more."

Fossie's mouth twisted ruefully. "Yeah. Sad to say, I got no argument against that."

"So what happened?" Braska wanted to know.

Fossie worked his mouth some more before abruptly jerking a thumb over his shoulder and saying, "There's some hot coffee on the stove in the grub shack. Follow me, we'll take a load off and I'll fill you in."

Both getting *filled in* and the promise of some hot coffee, inasmuch as he'd ridden out of a cold camp before sunup, sounded good to Braska. He wordlessly tied Savvy to a post and then followed Fossie into the grub shack. The latter was considerably refurbished since Braska was last here—a low-ceilinged, rectangular structure made of chinked log walls with a wood plank floor. There were two long tables with bench seats on either side of a center aisle. The lingering mixed smells of fried bacon and cigarette smoke hung in the air. Through an open door at the far end could be heard the clatter of pots and dishes.

Gesturing toward the door, Fossie said, "That's Cookie back in the kitchen, cleanin' up after breakfast. He won't bother us. He throws together a pretty good feed, but he's about as sociable as a green bronc with a boil where the saddle goes."

"Where's everybody else?"

"They rode out before sunup to move part of the herd to a high meadow pasture so's to fatten 'em good ahead of fall roundup. Don't expect 'em back 'til near evenin'." Fossie tipped his head. "Park yourself on a bench. I'll go fetch us a couple cups of mud. As I recollect, you take yours doctored up with plenty of sugar. Right?"

Now it was Braska's turn to give his mouth a rueful twist. "Not any longer. I take it black these days. My recent, er, accommodations were kinda short on amenities like sugar for your coffee."

Fossie paused awkwardly for a moment, like he wanted to say something. But then, deciding against it, he turned and disappeared into the kitchen. He was back in no time, bearing two steaming mugs. He placed these on the table and then lowered himself heavily across from Braska. "In case you're wonderin' about this hitch in my get-along," he said, slapping his bum hip, "you can thank your pa's prize bull Thunder for it. You remember Thunder, don't you?"

Braska's forehead puckered. "Not that I want to, but yeah. Hell yeah. I wasn't but about fourteen when Pa brought him home and unloaded him, and he scared the bejeebers out of me from the first time I laid eyes on him. He produced some fine offspring, I gotta admit, but I always sensed a mean streak in that big bastard that made me think he'd rather stomp the pudding out of some wrangler if he ever got the chance than diddle the prettiest heifer on the range."

"Well, I don't know if he passed up a pretty heifer or not," Fossie said sourly, "but I'm the wrangler who let down my guard and gave him his chance to try for some pudding stompin'. He lived up to his name sure enough, too—came at me like thunder and seven bolts of lightnin'. It happened not long after...well, while you were gone away."

Each man quietly took a drink of his coffee. Then Fossie continued, "Luckily, your brother Link and some other fellas were close enough by to hooraw ol' Thunder off before he finished me for good. Laid me up for six months, though, and when I finally crawled out of bed, I was this shufflin' crip you see before you now."

Braska frowned. "Don't run yourself down like that. You know more about ranchin' and workin' cattle than most men can hope to ever learn. A bum hip don't change that none."

"Thanks for the kind words, boy. I appreciate hearin' 'em," Fossie replied with a faint smile. "The new owner—Telford's his name, kind of a young squirt but pretty savvy about the cattle business his own self—asks my opinion on things now and then. I think it's more a courtesy than a real need, though. On account of, like I said, him bein' pretty sharp on his own. Mostly, due to this hip keepin' me from bein' able to sit a saddle for very long, he counts on me to take care of things close in around headquarters here—the buildings, corrals, nursin' sick critters and the like." Fossie shrugged. "Ain't a bad deal. Not like the old days...but then, what the hell is anymore?"

"Yeah. I'm findin' that out on a pretty regular basis," Braska said.

Fossie eyed him. "We came in here on the promise of me fillin' you in. Which I full intend to do, every bit I can. But I won't lie—there's stuff about you I'm hankerin' to know in return. If you've a mind to unload some of it, a-course. If'n you do, I got the ear of an old friend willin' to be bent."

"Stuff about you I'm hankerin' to know in return..."

Braska had figured for a long time that there'd come a day when he would have to—*want* to—tell somebody the whole story. He hadn't reckoned it would come this fast or happen here at the old place. But all at once, it was upon him. The time felt right to open up some, and Fossie seemed an appropriate person to hear it.

Only not right here, not with the anonymous *Cookie* within earshot.

Braska said, "Is Ma buried up on the hill with baby Alice and the others?"

"Indeed she is."

"Your hip stand a walk up there?"

"With nobody else left around to care, my hip has stood many a trip up there," Fossie answered. "Tendin' that little plot the way your ma used to is something I've sorta assigned myself apart from my other chores."

"Obliged to you for the consideration." Braska lifted his cup and drained it. "Let's take that walk."

Fossie downed his coffee too, then they quit the grub shack. Leaving Savvy still post-tied, the pair struck out across the dusty, hard-packed ranch yard.

The burial plot within which lay the graves of Braska's mother and infant sister was on the crest of a low rise off to the west of the ranch buildings. It was encircled by a low, wrought-iron fence to keep the cattle out, and at the northwest corner stood a sturdy cottonwood and a brace of thick pines to block the bitter winds out of the north. The spot was originally selected by Braska's parents as a final resting place for little Alice, who died from fever just short of two years old. It was anticipated they would both one day rest there beside her. Over time, a couple of loyal wranglers—one who was trampled in a stampede, the other who froze to death when a sudden, savage blizzard trapped him in an outlying line shack—were also laid to rest within the plot. Since they died in service to the brand and had no other known kin, Braska's father declared it only fitting they be considered part of the Bar S family.

As expected, the sun, now well above the horizon, was warming the morning rapidly. Part way up the slope, Braska could feel a thin film of sweat starting to form where the inner ring of his hat pressed against his forehead. Holding his pace to accommodate Fossie, his strides had a smooth, catlike grace.

He stood an inch-plus over six feet, his body lean, wide across the shoulders, flat-bellied and narrow-hipped. His flat slab of a face showed all of his near thirty years and then some. A somewhat hawkish nose, flinty eyes, and a thin-lipped mouth pressed tight and grim-looking much of the time made for a mug not likely to be called handsome, though not altogether unpleasant either.

His attire of levis and a panel-fronted shirt showed some miles of trail dust but were relatively new and of decent quality. A .44 caliber Colt Peacemaker holstered on his right hip hung there easy and natural, almost seeming like a physical extension of the man—a sign to anybody with a lick of sense that it was for more than just show.

When they reached the fenced-in plot, Fossie hung back while Braska pushed on through the swing gate. Removing his hat, he walked the few remaining steps and came to a halt before the stone markers.

BERNADINE SMITH

BELOVED WIFE AND MOTHER

1825—1871

ALICE SMITH

BLESSED CHILD, TAKEN BY GOD TOO SOON
1852—1853

TIMOTHY SMITH
INFANT NOW CRADLED IN THE ARMS OF THE LORD

Though nothing showed outwardly, slowly churning thoughts and emotions welled up inside Braska. Memories mostly. Good ones. It was hard to think of his mother without the thoughts being good. So gentle and kind and patient. Quick to smile, slow to stay angry or moody. God-fearing without being preachy. Mostly, even through the toughest times, she clung fiercely to the hope and belief that better times were just ahead. And as for little Alice, the two precious years she was part of the family, she was nothing but an adored, chubby bundle of happy, giggly joy...until the evil black fever visited and stole away all the brightness that shone from her.

The third marker, for Timothy, was a surprise and a puzzlement for which Braska would need to get a further explanation from Fossie.

Regrets joined the memories churning in Braska. The pain of losing loved ones never really goes away. And then, too often, regret isn't far behind. Regret over things one could have/should have done differently before it was too late. In the moment, there were two especially heavy regrets weighing on Braska. One, the glaring emptiness of his deceased father *not* lying here beside his wife and daughter as planned—due to him instead being buried at Gettysburg, where he fell in battle. Not that Braska lacked pride in his father for going off to war or that he wanted him dead at all, but, damn it, if he did have to meet his end, why couldn't it have been here at home so he could be next to Ma and Baby Alice where he belonged?

The other regret, more personal and thereby even more deeply stabbing, was the fact that Braska hadn't been present when Ma took sick and passed. Making it worse was the reason he wasn't able to be—because he'd been serving hard time in southern Colorado's notorious Hellstone prison.

Braska didn't know how long he stood there alone with his thoughts before he sensed Fossie move up quietly alongside him. The oldster had his hat removed too and was twisting it slowly back and forth in his hands. "Your ma was as fine a gal as ever there was," he said in a hushed voice. "Wasn't a soul who knew her who thought otherwise. For her funeral, folks came from Piney Flats and ranches and farms for miles around. Pastor Wiley said it was the largest gathering he ever held any kind of service for."

"Yeah," Braska said woodenly. "Everybody but me, her eldest son."

Fossie cut him a sidelong glance. "You had your reasons. Your ma knew and understood. And most folks, leastways the ones who count, have always had a pretty strong hunch about the truth as well."

Braska met his gaze. "They do, do they? How about you, old friend? You got a hunch about *my* truth, too?"

"I don't have to go on no hunch for part of it," Fossie answered flatly. "I was in the Buffalo Wallow saloon the night those Johnny Rebs got shot, saw with my own eyes how it went down. Your reasons for doin' what you did afterward, though, I can only guess at...but what I *do* have a hunch you was aimin' for, I'm afraid, went to a shameful waste."

"If you're talkin' about the waste of the Bar S, then it seems that brings us right back around to what you're supposed to be fillin' me in on."

Fossie nodded. "And you me on some things." He tipped his head toward the trees at the corner of the plot. "Let's step over in the shade and get on with it. We both got some throat clearin' to do."

2

JUST SHORT OF SEVEN YEARS PRIOR TO THE morning Braska and Fossie settled down to do their *throat clearin'*, there was a shooting one Saturday night in Piney Flats' Buffalo Wallow saloon. The Civil War was two years over. Like his father, Braska had joined to fight for the Union, though he had to wait out the first year because he was too young and, even then, finally lied his way in at only seventeen. Unlike his father, he came out of the conflict alive. His brother Link, three years his junior, remained behind to keep the ranch operating with the aid of Fossie and a handful of other hands too long-in-the-tooth to go off to war.

It had long been understood that Link was the son who had the savvy and the interest to make ranching his life and was earmarked to take over the reins of the Bar S one day. The job he did at its head during those war years, even though still in his teens, only reinforced that belief in him. The restless streak in Braska, on the other hand, had surfaced early on, along with his showing no reluctance to frequently state flat out that he had no intention of prodding cattle all his life. It was a disappointment to his father, to be sure, but at the same time Ira Smith was proud of his son's honesty and strength of will to want to pick his own life's path.

Through all of this, there had also been an understanding that Braska would never up and leave the Bar S in a lurch. He'd take his leave only if and when the ranch was on an even keel and he had a more clearly defined aim for himself. Which was why, when he returned from the war, he ended up sticking around for a while. Though the Bar S had endured those turbulent times—times when other smaller ranches in the area folded—it had hardly flourished. Braska felt obligated to help Link turn things around before he moved on. Plus he needed a spell in the familiar home setting to purge the lingering horrors of battle out of his head.

Two and a half years of dedicated hard work had the ranch thriving and positioned to provide good beef to a hungry, equally thriving market. During that time, Link lost his heart to a pretty neighbor girl named Linda and they were married. Only a few months after that, Linda broke the news she was pregnant. It was in response to this that Braska and Link decided a visit to town one evening was in order—to spread the news and do a bit of celebrating over it.

Bitter feelings about the recent war had never surfaced much in or around Piney Flats. This was due largely because Union sentiment had always run strong hereabouts and sympathizers for the Confederacy were either non-existent or had the sense to keep their feelings to themselves. When the conflict was over, a handful of ex-Rebels started drifting through and a few even hired on to local ranches. But they were soft-spoken, decent, hard-working types, so no trouble ever came from them being on the scene.

On the night Braska and Link went into town to do their announcing and celebrating of Link's pending fatherhood however, a fresh pair of ex-Rebel drifters also showed up at the Buffalo Wallow. And they quickly proved themselves *not* to be soft-spoken, decent sorts. Drinks and well-wishes were flowing freely when the pair first walked in. It didn't take long for their unsavory appearance and surly attitudes to start taking the edge off the good spirits. Both were heavily armed and wore filthy, sloppily patched remnants of Confederate army uniforms as if conveying a challenge to anyone seeking to question the cause so represented. The taller of the two wore a wide-brimmed Boss of the Plains hat, had cold eyes and a mean slash of a mouth. His shorter companion wore a battered kepi, had darting, nervous eyes and a weak chin that caused his neck to appear oddly elongated.

At first, the pair took spots at the end of the bar, somewhat apart from the throng surrounding Braska and Link. Once the initial wave of dourness the new arrivals carried in with them had passed, the celebratory mood within the throng started to pick up again.

It was when the tall hombre asked the bartender what the celebrating was about and got his answer that the beginning of trouble resulted. Turning to his long-necked pard, the tall one said in a voice purposely loud enough to be heard across the room. "Ain't it a cryin' shame, Duffy? After all the trouble we went to thinnin' out blue bellies in the war, everywhere we go these days, the stubborn devils seem hell-bent on poppin' out a whole new crop."

Duffy guffawed. "Ain't you been payin' attention to all this grassy empty we been ridin' through of late, Meade? What else is there for 'em to do but breed? And if the womenfolk are scarce, I bet some of the prettier cows start to get a little nervous, don't you reckon?"

This sent both men into a fit of braying laughter. When they were done, they found the saloon had gone quiet and a dozen sets of eyes were glaring at them.

"What the hell?" growled Meade. "Why all the the owly looks? Ain't you cow nursers got no sense of humor?"

"We do when we hear something funny," responded Braska. "But insults spewed by a couple no-account peckerwoods don't hardly measure up."

Scowling, sensing trouble escalating fast, the barkeep said to the two strangers, "You fellas have had yourselves a drink and your idea of a laugh. I think it'd be a good idea for you to mosey on along now."

"To hell with that!" snapped Meade. "I'll mosey when I'm good and ready—and not before."

Both Braska and Link rose from where they'd been sitting in the midst of their well-wishing friends. Several of the latter scooted their chairs back, allowing the brothers to stride forward toward the pair at the bar. At nineteen, Link was only a shade shorter than Braska, not as broad through the shoulders, whip lean and range-toughened. He packed a six-gun, but unlike Braska—who both before and since the war had demonstrated the skill as well as the willingness to succeed against another gun when forced—Link had never been tested to that limit. The look in his eyes that night as he advanced on the trash-talking strangers however, left little doubt he was ready to meet the test if need be.

"The man asked you polite-like to mosey and take your snotty remarks with you," Braska said to Meade. "I suggest you make yourself ready—and do it pronto."

"And I suggest you mosey to the hitch rail out front and kiss the hairy, sweaty ass of the horse I just rode in on. How about that?" sneered Meade.

But, beside him, nervous-eyed Duffy was looking like he wished his pal would ease up a bit on his belligerence. "Maybe we'd just as well shed this dump, Meade. Ain't nothing here worth—"

"The hell there ain't," Meade cut him short. "Maybe there wasn't before. Damn sure not that piss-warm beer or watered-down rotgut we just got served...but what's worth hangin' around for now is to teach these wet-behind-the-ears pups that it ain't smart to stick their faces up to two of the South's ruggedest who never surrendered and damn sure never turned their swords into no plow shares neither."

"The war's long over, mister," Braska told him. "Continuin' to pick at old scabs ain't ever gonna allow 'em to heal."

"What do you know about the scars and scabs of war? You ever been through the ground-down, burned-out South that was left in its wake? Where what little remained standin' is now bein' swarmed over and scrounged up by northern carpetbaggers? Appears to me like you nigger-lovin' Nebraskans with your grassy ranges and fat cattle got off mighty easy."

"The war took its toll on everybody," Braska grated.

"Including the life of our father!" blurted Link.

"Well, that's real heart-tuggin'," drawled Meade with a smirk twisting his mouth. "Tell me, sonny...

which battle was it your pa got killed runnin' away from?"

The whole saloon went dead silent now, smothered by a heavy layer of tension.

Until Braska said in a cold, raspy tone, "You got two options, you piece of crud. You can apologize and slink out of here with your tails tucked between your legs...or you can die with that filthy lie still in your throat."

Duffy looked very much ready to take the tail-tucking advice. But Meade was having none of it. His response was, "Get ready to join your old man, you blue-bellied brats."

An instant later, the roar of four tight-spaced gunshots filled the saloon. Powder smoke rolled and bottles and glasses on the shelves behind the bar rattled with a contrastingly musical tinkle.

Meade was first to claw for his gun, a converted Navy Colt worn for the cross draw on his left hip. But Braska beat him handily, his cutter leveling in a blur and spitting flame and lead before Meade fully cleared leather. Braska's bullet drilled square into Meade's heart and knocked him flat. As he went down, the tall man's trigger finger spasmed and his gun discharged a harmless round into the saloon floorboards.

Immediately adjusting his aim, Braska saw that Duffy was hopping away from his falling partner and was holding empty hands out to either side in a sign of wanting no part of the gunplay. Braska reacted in time to pull his second shot a foot wide of Duffy and instead send a bullet burrowing into the side frame of the front door.

But an over-excited Link also had his gun out by then, and he didn't allow for Duffy's empty-handedness. His gun crashed simultaneously with Braska's second shot—only Link's bullet slammed into Duffy's elongated throat just below the Adam's apple. Duffy staggered once, making a choking sound and spitting blood, then collapsed into a lifeless heap alongside Meade.

The saloon promptly erupted into chaos, with everybody chattering at once about what they had just witnessed. Despite a few exceptions who claimed it all happened too fast for them to be certain, the greater consensus was that each of the Smith brothers had cut down one of the troublemakers. At first, no mention was made about Duffy being empty-handed. And then, before such could be brought up by anybody else, none other than Braska began vehemently stating that *he* had shot the unarmed man and how much he regretted his carelessness. Not even protests by Link could curb his brother's insistence that it was *his* bullet that cut down Duffy and Link's that went wide. Braska repeated this claim so intently—almost threateningly—that by the time Marshal Elmer Coggins and his deputy arrived in response to reports of gunfire, no one, no matter what they'd seen with their own eyes, was willing to give voice in opposition to Braska's version.

Coggins had no choice but to put Braska in jail. The shooting of Meade was clearly self-defense. But blasting a man holding out empty hands, which was what happened according to Braska's own admission, was just as clearly something else.

It didn't take long, of course, before any number of people understood what was truly happening. Braska—single, restless, on the verge of moving on—was covering for his kid brother who was newly married, a father-to-be, and the future of the Bar S. Never once, not to his mother or Link or anybody else, did Braska ever admit this. But they knew all the same. Yet as long as what he *did* admit, to the law, was that the blood of unarmed Duffy was on his hands, no amount of counter confessions or pleas or behind-the-scenes whispers could sway what Braska had set in motion.

He stood trial for aggravated manslaughter and was sentenced to eight years in Hellstone prison. At his sentencing, the judge stated somberly, "The wounds of the late war are not, sad to say, fully healed. The behavior of the victims, Meade and Duffy, are unfortunate reminders of this. It is for that very reason, however, that your response to them, Mr. Smith— though provoked—can neither be condoned nor treated lightly. To do the latter would only signal to others who remain as embittered as those two that their feelings have a foundation and would thereby propagate more of the same. My harsh sentencing of you is meant as a counter to that, evidence that impartiality and not prejudice truly exists."

————

AFTER REVIEWING ALL OF THIS IN THE SHADE OF the graveside cottonwood, Fossie said, "Ol' Judge Sturnheim was a tough cookie, that's for sure. But apart from that overlong hitch he slapped on you, I think most folks found him not too unreasonable. All, that is, except for a fella named Breame. In the middle of a trial over in Benkelman just five or six weeks ago, this Breame got plumb pissed about how the judge was dressin' him down, so he pulled out a hideaway derringer and plugged Sturnheim smack between the eyes. They killed Breame on the spot, a-course—not that it did the judge any good, though."

"I hadn't heard any of that," Braska replied, frowning. "Damn shame. I was figurin' on lookin' the judge up while I was back."

Fossie gave him a sidelong look. "You wasn't thinkin' on revenge, was you?"

"Nothing like that," Braska assured him. "Quite the opposite, in fact. When I read over my release papers, you see, I found that one of the reasons I got turned loose after only six years instead of the full eight— besides playin' it smart and keepin' my nose clean behind those walls—was that Sturnheim had been checkin' up on me regular-like and recommendin' an early release if I *did* toe the mark. I wanted to thank him."

"Well, I'll be damned. I guess the old scoundrel really wasn't so unreasonable...say, do you reckon he knew all along the truth about who shot Duffy?"

Braska blinked innocently. "Sure he did. He sentenced me for it, didn't he?"

"Now, goddamn it—" Fossie started to say. But he stopped short and cast a guilty glance over at the graves. Scowling, he started over again, saying, "Sorry to cuss in front of your ma and sis, but blast it all, we said we was gonna come up here and level with one another. All this time I never said anything out loud to counter your story. But, like I told you before, I was there that night and saw what I saw."

"You also said you had a hunch why I did what I did afterward."

"So did a lot of folks. If that was how you wanted it,

we all went along thinkin' it was maybe foolish but nevertheless a kind of noble thing...all except, the way it turned out, for one."

"That would be Link."

Fossie nodded.

Braska dug out the makings and fired up a cigarette. Exhaling smoke, he said, "Which would also be the waste, as you put, that came out of what I did."

"Don't see no other word for it."

Braska took a hard drag and released another plume of smoke. "Okay, I'm ownin' up to what you thought, what you wanted to know. Yeah, I took the rap for Link because I figured he had hell of a lot more to lose than I did. Now it's time to hear the other side of it. Tell me how it all went wrong..."

3

It was the middle of the morning before Braska rode away from what was now the Cross T. After he and Fossie had finished their confab on the crest of the hill, they'd walked back down to the ranch yard, where Braska retrieved his buckskin and said so long to his old friend. Then he'd gone back up to the graves to spend a bit of additional time, alone, with his ma and sister, and nephew he never met or heard of before. Telling them goodbye for now, he assured them he'd try to come back around again if and when he could. Once more in the saddle, he pointed Savvy to the south and heeled him off at an easy lope.

After riding for a ways, he realized he was headed in the general direction of Piney Flats. Braska had mixed feelings about actually proceeding on to the town. After his talk with Fossie, he had mixed feelings about a lot of things. His head was aswirl with emotions that ranged from anger to dismay to confusion and back to anger again.

How could he—and a lot of other people—have

been so damn wrong about his kid brother? Link, who, since he was barely tall enough to stare at eye level with the stirrup on a saddled horse, wanted to be nothing but a cowboy, a cattle man. By age twelve, he could ride and rope as good as most veteran wranglers, and he just kept getting better. Braska developed those same skills at a comparable age, but for him, it was merely a rite of passage, an obligation he felt toward supporting his father's ranching dream until such time it felt right to strike out on his own. But for Link, every indication had been it was a passion rivaled only by that of Ira Smith himself.

It was for those reasons that Braska had made the decision that *he* should take responsibility for gunning the unarmed Duffy. All he had to risk was a chunk of his undefined life's aim spent behind bars and a stain on his reputation that he could wipe clean by moving far enough on after his release. What was at risk for Link was a life he had well planned and already set in motion with a wife and children and the future of the Bar S in his hands. Oddly, even though he'd never meant to remain part of it himself, seeing his father's dream continue on was still important to Braska.

So he'd made his confession, made his sacrifice, and left things—he thought—to the competence and dedication of his brother. But now, based on the stark evidence his eyes had beheld of the Bar S no longer existing combined with the details related as to why, Braska was left with the bitter realization that, to use Fossie's word, it had all been a waste.

As related by Fossie, in the beginning, after Braska was transported off to Hellstone, things had gone pretty well on the ranch. As expected. That first fall's gather and drive to market in Omaha delivered a good-sized herd of nicely fatted beeves who brought top dollar. A baby girl named Alicia, in honor of baby Alice, the aunt she would never know, was born to Link and Linda. Grandma Bernadine was ecstatic. But even during that period, Fossie noted a slight change in Link. Brief periods of moodiness and testiness like he'd never shown before. Making the adjustment, the old timer figured—what with Ira gone and Braska off to prison— of having the whole load of the Bar S now on his shoulders. Everything would be okay once he got settled into it.

Only that didn't happen. Things only got worse. Back-to-back severe winters and dry summers took a harsh toll on the herd. For those two years, the beeves the Bar S drove to market were scrawny and underweight and got passed over by the prime buyers and had to settle for lower dollar per pound offers from second-rate purchasers. In order to try and build up the next crop of cattle, Link was forced to take out a bank loan. During that same period, he grew steadily more sullen and ornery in his treatment of the crew. He began to argue frequently with Linda and had little patience when Alicia fussed and seemed to require, in his opinion, undue attention. He even snapped at his mother on occasion.

And he also took to drinking too much. Both at home and on regular trips to town. What was worse, on those trips to town, he began gambling. Heavily. He somehow got the notion that if he was able to come out ahead at the gaming tables he could apply his winnings to helping get the Bar S above water again. But Link was a lousy, reckless gambler and only succeeded in sinking deeper in debt. Nobody could talk sense into him. Not Linda, not his mother, not Fossie. When Fossie tried, Link threatened to punch him and told him to mind his own damn business.

In the spring of the fourth year after Braska was sent to prison, two things happened within a five-week span that had an even more devastating impact. First, Linda lost a second child, a little boy—Timothy, who died at birth. Shortly after that, Bernadine suddenly fell sick and passed away. Link seemed stunned into a wooden, barely functioning state. By then, his treatment of the hired help had already driven off all of the decent hands, leaving dregs and drifters mostly going through the motions to get a payday that would give them enough of a stake to move on. Only Fossie stuck, out of loyalty to the brand and hoping against hope that Link would finally snap out of it and start running things the way he damn well knew how.

But he didn't. Things only continued to get worse. Link seemed to quit trying or caring almost completely. Linda left him and she and Alicia went to live in town with her older sister. As far as Fossie knew, Link never made any attempt to get her to stay nor to visit her or his daughter once they were gone. Both the bank loan and property taxes were overdue and threats of foreclosure were getting more strident daily. Plus Link owed substantial gambling debts. Exactly how much, nobody but him and his debtors knew for sure. And the herd, by that point, was less than half of what Braska and Link had it built up to before the fateful encounter with the ex Johnny Rebs that night in the Buffalo Wallow.

Came the morning when Link called his ragtag crew together, paid each man the wages they had coming up to that point from money he'd somehow acquired, then told them they no longer had jobs because he was giving up the Bar S to the bank and the tax collectors. As for himself, he announced he was heading off somewhere unnamed and leaving the cattle business for *"some other poor dumb sonofabitch who thinks he can make a living bouncin' back and forth between cow horns and horseshit."* He was gone before sunset that evening, and, to the best of Fossie's knowledge, no one in or around Piney Flats had seen or directly heard from him since, not even Linda. That had been over two years ago. Then, to put an even uglier cap on it all, three or four months back, a growing number of reports had begun drifting up from the Four Corners area—where Colorado, Utah, Arizona, and New Mexico all connected—of a fellow who sounded an awful lot like Link riding with a pack of rough hombres raising hell in all four sections.

So there it was. Everything Braska had sacrificed for, hoped for, counted on...all turned to shit. Because the key to it all succeeding and being worth it—the dependable, dedicated, always-wanting-to-be-a-cattleman Link—let everybody down. And it wasn't like he'd tried hard and failed, been overwhelmed by a string of nothing but bad luck. No, he started folding as soon as a few breaks didn't go his way and then proceeded to worsen everything via a foul temperament and reckless, foolish decisions that drove away everybody who could have supported and helped him get through those tough times. Alienating his family, perhaps hurrying his mother to an early demise, turning to booze and gambling in an attempt to get out of the hole he'd put himself in but only managing to dig the hole deeper. And then, most unforgivable of all, running away like a coward with his tail tucked between his legs to ultimately, if there was any truth to the recent reports, head down the owlhoot trail.

A corner of Braska's mouth quirked wryly as this thought ran through his mind. There was irony for you. Him, an ex-con fresh out of prison, thinking low thoughts about his kid brother for *allegedly* riding the long coulees. But, considering everything else, damn it, it was hard not to give credence to such reports.

Everything churning inside of Braska built to a bitter bile that made him half sick to his gut.

It was an attention-demanding chuff from Savvy that stirred Braska out of his contemplative state and brought him to a fuller awareness of the present, of how much ground he and the buckskin had covered and what they were now approaching. Just ahead, a line of trees and underbrush, their brighter greenness standing out in contrast to the duller, brownish green, rain-deprived range grass he'd been traversing, told Braska these were indicators of a water course he realized had to be Piney Creek. The nearness of fresh water being the cause of Savvy's chuff.

What was more, as he appraised the layout more closely, Braska recognized the exact spot they were nearing. By a pleasant coincidence, it was a particular section of the creek he had visited often, all during his boyhood and youth and even a few times after he'd returned from the war. It lay just beyond the southern boundary of what used to be Bar S range, a short stretch where the banks spread back a little wider to create a sort of pool-like feature. At rare leisure periods and sometimes nearing dusk after a hard, hot day in the

saddle, he'd come here to swim, cool off, and just relax.
Link tagged along occasionally when they were
younger, but for the most part, Braska had grown to
consider this *his* spot where he could get away from
everything and everybody for a while. And now, lo and
behold, here he was again—feeling farther away from
everything and everybody than he'd ever experienced
before.

With the sun high and hot overhead, nearly at its
noon peak, and Savvy eager to get to the cool water,
Braska's decision to give the buckskin his head and tarry
here for a brief spell pretty much made itself. And then,
after passing through the trees and underbrush and
drawing rein on the edge of the pool-like area, he
revised that decision and instead concluded he would
do more than just tarry briefly—he'd make a day camp
and stay out the afternoon.

————

THE MORNING'S COLD CAMP AND MEAGER
breakfast made the notion of remaining here to cook up
a good lunch and maybe have a swim for old-time's sake
seem all the more attractive. And another conclusion he
reached before quitting the saddle was that he *would* go
ahead and pay a visit to the town of Piney Flats. It lay
astraddle the creek only a few miles to the west, so stopping here for a time still made it easily reachable by
evening. There were a few old friends there he
wouldn't mind seeing again, assuming they were still
around. But most of all, he meant to drop in on Linda
and see if she could add anything regarding Link to
what he'd already heard from Fossie.

4

In no time at all, Braska had Savvy stripped down and picketed at the edge of the creek where he could munch lush grass or sip cool, fresh water as he pleased. Then Braska got a small fire going and hung a pot of coffee over it to start cooking. While that was brewing, he stripped down himself and got ready for a dip in the creek. He took along a bar of soap plucked out of his saddlebags and laid a blanket from his bedroll on the grass to use for wiping dry afterward.

Somewhat to Braska's surprise, considering the dry condition of the surrounding range grass, the water level in the creek, which seldom ran more than five or so feet anyway, was only moderately lower. It was cool and refreshing, carried along on a mild current. He submerged himself, rolled over a time or two under the surface, came up, and let the current carry him a ways before swimming back to where he started. For a brief period, he almost felt like a kid again. But it didn't take long for that to pass, those days being long gone.

He scrubbed and rinsed himself thoroughly, climbed back onto the bank, and dried off with the blanket he'd laid out. After pulling on clean socks, then his pants and boots, he stayed stripped to the waist while he shaved. That done, he unrolled a fresh shirt from his bedroll and finished dressing and strapping his Colt back on. A meal of bacon and the last of some potatoes he'd bought three days prior from a farmer came next. He drank two cups of black coffee as he ate, then treated himself to a third one doctored up with some brown sugar while he stretched out on his upturned saddle to let the food settle.

Braska felt about as good as he was likely to feel for some time to come. He'd have to go after Link, find him, and hold him to account for the things he'd done. That was all there was to it. How long it would take, where it would lead him, exactly what he expected in the way of accountability, he wasn't sure. But he had to find out before he could move on to anything else.

He was tipping up the last, tepid swallow of his sugar-laced coffee when Braska heard a horse neigh from somewhere on the other side of the creek. He promptly set aside the cup, rolled over and up onto one knee, and leaned in behind the trunk of a birch tree that stood just behind his saddle. As if of its own volition, his hand swept down across his hip and slipped the keeper thong off the hammer of the Colt holstered there. It never hurt to take precautions, be ready.

Scanning the opposite bank, Braska saw nothing right away. When he glanced over at Savvy, he saw that his head was up and his ears were perked. He too had heard the other horse but didn't appear overly concerned about it. Braska swung his gaze back to the other side of the creek and, this time, saw a single rider materializing into view, guiding his horse through the underbrush and trees on that side. The horse was a sleek black mare, and the rider appeared tall and lanky, wearing a blue checked shirt and a flat-crowned brown Stetson. As Braska watched, the pair emerged the rest of the way out of the bushes and came to a halt on the grassy bank.

The mare was eager to drink, but the rider wisely restrained her until she had the chance to cool some. He dismounted, talking to her soothingly as he patted her neck and pushed her a couple steps farther back from the water's edge. When he had her sufficiently stilled, he began uncinching the saddle, preparing to strip it off and help the animal cool that much faster. In the process of doing this, something about the rider's mannerisms and movements, especially when he was bent over tugging on the cinch strap, gave Braska cause to look a little closer and damned if he didn't suddenly realize the rider was no man at all, but rather *a woman*! And if he needed further verification—on top of already noting how she filled out her jeans when bent over to work on that cinch—the way she filled out the front of her shirt when she swung around to deposit the stripped-off saddle onto the ground settled it pretty convincingly. No, not tall and lanky, amend that to tall and willowy. Hell, maybe downright curvy.

Now Braska found himself in an awkward position. A young woman out by herself for a peaceful ride in the country might very well be alarmed by a strange man stepping out from behind a tree and abruptly revealing his presence. If it alarmed her enough to make her flee and report it to somebody, like a father or brother from a nearby ranch for instance, and it resulted in Braska being identified—him a recently released ex-con and all —wouldn't that be a fine kettle of fish? Yet if he held back, tried to stay out of sight but somehow got noticed anyway, that could turn out even worse.

Shit.

And then, before he could make up his mind how best to play it, that turn for the worse didn't wait around. With the mare sufficiently cooled, the girl let her go on to the edge of the creek and proceed to drink. While the animal was thus occupied, the girl kicked off her boots, pulled the hem of her shirt out from being tucked into her jeans, and began unbuttoning it. It quickly became evident she wasn't just out for a ride— she'd come here with the intent of also taking a swim.

Braska swore under his breath. There went any choice he had in the matter. Much as he might enjoy such a show under the right circumstances, he'd have to step out and let the girl know she wasn't alone before she got undressed any further.

He straightened up behind the tree. But then, an instant before he started out around it, something in the bushes behind the girl caught his eye and he froze. A moment later, that *something* turned into the face of a man poking itself stealthily through the leaves and high grass to gawk blatantly at the girl. It was a broad, fleshy mug with its mouth stretched into a lewd grin and eyes bright with anticipation. Whoever it belonged to, he clearly had none of Braska's reservations about enjoying the show in progress.

Braska's first reaction was an even stronger urge to let the girl know she was far from enjoying the privacy she believed she had. But then, an odd, cautionary thought struck him and held him in check once again. What if this was some kind of peek-a-boo lover's game being played out between her and the man in the bushes? Braska had heard of such. After all, the hombre had shown up awfully quick. Kinda hard to believe he'd just innocently happened along at this opportune moment. On the other hand, Braska's presence at that same moment might seem equally dubious.

While Brasca was wrestling with indecision, the girl finished removing her shirt and, after draping it over the saddle she'd set aside earlier, began wiggling out of those tight jeans. This would leave her clad only in a flimsy article of clothing with pencil-thin shoulder straps that Brasca believed—but wasn't certain—might be called a camisole. The precise terminology for lady's undergarments wasn't one of his specialties.

Something he *had* become certain about, though, regarded the hombre in the bushes. No way he was there by prearrangement or with the knowledge of the girl. The beads of sweat popping out across his forehead and his ever-widening lecherous grin, with drool practically dripping from it, marked him plainly enough as nothing more than a lowdown peeping tom—or maybe worse, depending on the full extent of what he had in mind.

Braska's feelings of awkwardness and indecision gave way to anger and disgust. He wanted, in the worst way, to charge out and confront the goggle-eyed, gawking slob. Only the positioning of the girl—directly in between them—gave him pause. Should the gawker be armed and have the potential to react desperately if caught in the act, then the girl might be thrown into more danger than just being the victim of a peeper—or two, if you also counted the inadvertent viewing by Braska.

But then the girl, who seemed almost as eager to get into the water as her mare had been to take a drink of it, abruptly—though unknowingly—solved the problem of her being in the line of fire. Stepping out of her jeans as soon they dropped down around her ankles, she peeled away and discarded the camisole in a single smooth motion before extending out gracefully and leaving the creek bank in a flat, shallow dive that plunged her under the surface of the water.

Braska had seen naked women before. Had, in fact, undressed and bedded more than a few. Mostly during his Army days, mostly of the soiled dove variety. Some had been quite fetching. But never had he seen a female form more splendid than what had just been revealed on the other side of the creek. He probably should have felt guilty for viewing it in such a covert manner, he told himself. Especially since he hadn't looked away when given the chance. But damned if he regretted *not* averting his eyes.

Somebody far less regretful for what he'd seen, of course, was the peeper over in the bushes. What was more, he didn't hesitate to let this be known by suddenly and unexpectedly bursting forth to reveal himself. Out he stepped, bold as brass, still grinning broadly and clapping his hands together in slow, deliberate applause.

That was the sight that greeted the girl when her head and shoulders popped back up above the surface and her attention was immediately drawn by the sound of the clapping. Skimming both hands up over her face to clear the water out of her eyes and then slick back her shortish mop of chestnut hair, she swiveled her face to the man now looming on the bank. Since said face was turned away from him, Braska could only imagine the expression it wore.

But there was no need to guess about the angry tone in her voice when she exclaimed, "Marv Kenna! What the devil are you doing here?"

Braska held in place behind his tree. So the two were acquainted after all—though not necessarily in a favorable way, at least not where the girl was concerned.

"What I'm doin' here," Kenna responded, drawling the words through a nasty chuckle, "is havin' me a look at about the finest hoochy-cooch show I ever did see. That's why I'm applaudin'. I gotta tell you, though, Rosie darlin', you need to work some on slowin' things down considerable in order to give your audience an even bigger dose of enjoyment."

"I'm not your *darling*, you lecherous ape. How many times do I have to tell you that before you get it through your thick head?" The girl's voice now took on a frostiness that sounded damn near cold enough to put a sheen of ice on the water she was keeping herself lowered in. "And I sure as hell didn't come out here to put on a show for you or anybody else."

Kenna appeared wholly unfazed by her caustic remarks. He was a big man—a full six feet in height, thick through the chest and shoulders, gut running toward fat. His face might have been considered moder-ately handsome at one time, but nowadays, excesses of food and drink had made it too puffy and bloated to to retain that claim. Just north of thirty, he looked closer to forty. Hooking his thumbs in the shell belt hung around his waist with a mean-looking Remington revolver riding in the rig's holster, he curled his lips smugly and said, "Well, whether you set out to or not, a show is what you put on. And, like already told you, a right fine one it was...but not near as good as what I expect for Part Two, when you gotta come out of that water."

"You'd better get out of here, Marv. Right now!" the girl—Rosie, if that truly was her name—warned him. "If you do that, if you just turn and leave, I'll forget this ever happened and not report it to Marshal Coggins."

Kenna threw back his head and laughed. "Haw! Is that supposed to be some kind of threat? In the first place, anything that happens here'll boil down to your word against mine. Even apart from that, you oughta know ol' Elmer will lean my way. He damn well better —he counts on me too much not to."

Listening, Braska scowled hard at these remarks. Elmer Coggins had been the town marshal of Piney Flats back near seven years ago, when Braska was first jailed for the shooting in the Buffalo Wallow saloon. Elmer had been plenty old even then. It surprised Braska somewhat to hear the old law dog was still packing a marshal's tin. More than that, it troubled him to hear the implication that Elmer would be predisposed toward a particular side, no matter the truth of the situation. Whatever else, Marshal Elmer Coggins from the past had always played it square down the middle.

"I mean it, Marv. You've pushed this far enough," Rosie insisted, though Braska thought he might now be detecting a faint tremor—of fear?—in her voice. "Why are you so determined to keep pestering me anyway? You've got a dozen or more other girls in town willing to do your bidding any time you want."

"But they ain't you. They're too easy," Kenna snarled. "You're the one who stirs my blood—and have ever since the first night I saw you at the Palace. Twitchin' that fine ass, kickin' high, and smilin' that teasin' smile."

"I never teased! I made it clear to everybody that I was a dancer and that was all. High kicks and smiles are part of my job."

"Yeah? Well part of my job is givin' little teasers like you what it is they need and really want—whether they're willin' to admit it or not." The look on Kenna's face had changed. It was no longer just a lecherous gleam in the eyes and a drooling grin. It was a look of mad, intense lust. "I finally figured out what these lone rides you take two or three times a week are really about. You've been wantin' me to follow you—to find you here, like this, so you could release all the wild passion you've been storin' up. Release it in this wild place! So today, I finally took the hint and followed you, and now—"

"No! No, it's nothing like that at all!" Rosie protested stridently. "You're talking and thinking out of your head. You need to snap out of it, come to your senses!"

"I did come to my senses," Kenna replied. "I told you, I figured out why you kept ridin' out here. The only question now is: Do I come the rest of the way in there after you, or"—here he extended a hand in a dramatic flourish—"are you ready to quit playin' games and let me haul your pretty tail up here so we can commence with what it is we both want?"

"How about a third option? How about you keep your grimy paws to yourself and step back away from the water's edge—or is it gonna take some .44 caliber persuasion to help you decide?"

5

Braska's words cut across the width of the creek and knifed into Kenna, giving him a visible start. Eyes immediately narrowing under fiercely pinched brows, Kenna swept his gaze until it locked on Braska where he'd stepped out from behind his tree with drawn Colt held at waist level.

"Who the hell are you?"

"Among other things," Braska drawled, "I'm somebody who don't want to see his favorite swimmin' hole fouled by a pile of garbage like you."

Kenna frowned. "What's that supposed to mean?"

"I said it plain. I also said plain for you to back up." Braska waggled his Colt slightly. "Best step to it."

Kenna edged back, muttering, "You don't own the damn water."

"No. And you don't own what's in it."

"You still ain't makin' no sense. But what you are makin' is a big mistake, mister."

"You mean by not just goin' ahead and blastin' off

that little toothpick pecker of yours to make sure you don't bother no more gals with it ever again?"

Kenna winced in spite of himself. "Real funny. I mean, you're makin' a mistake, a damned serious one, not only by stickin' your nose in where it don't belong but doin' it against somebody you ought not be messin' with."

"Now you're scarin' me."

"You would be if you had brains enough to know what's good for you." Kenna paused, grinding his teeth in frustration. Then he added, "Look. I'm gonna raise my left hand—real slow—to show you something. Don't get trigger happy, you hear?"

"That'll depend on what you turn up," Brasca warned him.

Very slowly, very carefully, Kenna's left hand raised to chest level. There, it flipped back the lapel of the corduroy vest he had on and revealed a badge pinned to the front of his shirt. Braska could make out it was a deputy marshal's badge. Kenna was watching closely for his reaction, a trace of a smug smile tugging at his mouth. "That take some of the cockiness out of you, bub?" he wanted to know.

Braska gave it a beat before replying, "Not particularly."

Rosie, who up until then had been keeping silent as her head swiveled back and forth following the exchanges between the two men, now focused squarely on Braska and said in a dismayed tone, "Sad to say, that badge is the real thing, mister. He's chief deputy marshal for the nearby town of Piney Flats. I appreciate you trying to help, but you don't want to get yourself in worse trouble on account of me."

"I know all about the town of Piney Flats, ma'am. Matter of fact, I got kind of a history there," Braska told her. "I also know a thing or two about a little detail called jurisdiction. And the jurisdiction covered by the piece of tin your friend over yonder is wearin' don't stretch nowhere this far out."

"Don't be so sure about that," Kenna was quick to argue.

"Oh, but I am sure," Braska said. "And if you were any good at your job, you would be too. Which brings me to another point worth makin'—in my book, anybody who wears a badge and stands behind it to illegally bully and threaten vulnerable folks is a skunk even more low down than an owl hoot who's at least got the onions to be what he is straight up."

Kenna's right hand slapped down onto the butt of his Remington. "Goddamn you, I've heard about enough from outta that hole under your nose!"

Braska's Colt held level and rock steady. "Go ahead, you tub! If you think you can skin that smoke wagon quicker'n I can trigger this cutter already in my fist, go for it. I'll blow that chunk of tin plumb through and out between your shoulder blades."

"Good God!" shrieked Rosie. "This isn't worth you two killing each other over."

"I don't plan on gettin' killed, ma'am." Braska spoke calmly. "It's up to Deputy Marv whether he wants to be or not."

Tension crackled in the air over the creek for a long beat. Then, abruptly, Kenna's hand relaxed and dropped away from the grips of his gun. Hating Braska with his eyes, he licked his lips and then said, "Okay for this round, you lucky snake. But wherever you came from, wherever you're headed, you'd better keep on movin' steady. I see you in these parts ever again, I'll flat open up on you without hesitation."

"I'll be sure to keep that in mind."

Kenna's eyes cut to Rosie. "And don't think I'm done with you. Not by a long shot. I'll be seein' you again when you get back to town."

When the deputy started to turn, meaning to leave, Braska stopped him short. "Not so fast. With that last remark, you brayin' jackass, you just earned yourself some extra consideration. Shuck your gun belt—then we'll be happy to see you kick up dust outta here."

"No way in hell!" Kenna protested.

Braska extended his Colt meaningfully. "Leave it on and you can wear it to your grave. Peel it, and I'll see you get it back soon."

"How?"

"I'll deliver it to the marshal's office when I come to town later on."

At first, Kenna looked more than a little suspicious. Then, slowly, his mouth spread in a sly grin. As he began unbuckling the shell belt and holster rig, he said, "Okay. You just do that...and after it's returned, I'll use it to kill you."

Braska said nothing. Just stood watching and waiting.

When the gun belt was on the grass, Kenna turned once more to leave. This time, nobody stopped him. But, at the last minute, he added a little something to his departure. Moving with surprising speed, he suddenly swept one leg and kicked Rosie's discarded jeans out into the creek. Keeping on the move, he then leaned to snatch up her shirt and camisole and also flung them out onto the water. A second later, he was whooping and slapping at Rosie's ground-reined mare with his hat, causing her to bolt away in alarm as Kenna plunged out of sight into the bushes.

"Damn you, Marv Kenna!" Rosie shouted after him.

Braska held his fire for two reasons: One, there'd been the risk of hitting Rosie's horse. Two, it went against his grain to shoot at a man's back—especially for merely tossing some clothes in the drink.

As the rataplan of Rosie's fleeing mare started to fade, it was joined by the sound of another horse's pounding hooves heading away—obviously belonging to Kenna, retrieved from where he'd left it somewhere farther back in the bushes. Evidence of the deputy departing was welcome, though the same couldn't be said for the loss of Rosie's mount. Of more immediate concern, however, was the threatened loss of her clothes being carried away by the creek's current.

Luckily, Piney's current wasn't very strong and the garments hadn't been thrown that far out of reach. Rosie was able to make a quick lunge and reclaim her jeans fairly easily. But the shirt and camisole, which had been wadded together when tossed, had landed farther down current and presented more of a challenge. Braska was on hand to answer that, though. Positioned at an angle already a bit down from Rosie's, he was able to quickly step forward, plant one foot over the edge of the bank, reach out, and snag the wad before it sank or got away.

Stepping back up on the bank, he held the sopping mass out at arm's length and turned to Rosie, saying,

"Here's the rest of your duds. But I'm afraid they're a mite drenched to be steppin' back into."

"So are these jeans I managed to grab," Rosie replied. "But that's all right. Wet clothes are better than none—or having to wrap myself in an armful of scratchy bushes, which would've been the only other way to cover myself if everything had floated away."

She was keeping herself lowered in the water, just her head and shoulders above the surface, holding the soggy jeans clutched tight. Now that Kenna was gone and she found herself left in what could only be called delicate circumstances with a stranger who—in his own way, and in spite of so far being nothing but helpful to her—nevertheless appeared quite dangerous. Understandably, this gave her some trepidation.

In what was aimed to be an easy, relaxing drawl, Braska said, "Could be I got an option I think'd be better than wet clothes or scratchy bushes, either one."

Eyeing him, not wanting to reveal her reservations where he was concerned, Rosie remarked, "You seem to have a variety of options handy."

Braska shrugged. "Ain't a bad thing, is it?"

"No. No, I suppose not." Rosie shivered slightly, having been immersed in the cool water for quite a spell now. "What do you have in mind?"

"Happens just a few yards through the brush and trees behind me here," answered Braska, jabbing a thumb over his shoulder, "I got a little camp set up. I finished my noon meal a short while back and was relaxin' to let my eats settle some when I heard you splashin' about over this way. Then I heard that tub of a deputy startin' to give you a hard time."

"Well, I'm glad for that," Rosie allowed. "But I still don't see—"

"What I'm thinkin'," Braska said, explaining further, "is that I can stoke my campfire back up and hang your clothes on sticks, close-like. While you're waitin' for 'em to dry, I got coffee and a big, warm bedroll blanket you can keep yourself wrapped in."

Her gaze softened. "You'd do that for me? Sounds like it's bound to take some time. Don't you have anything else you need to attend to?"

"Nothing I'm especially in a hurry for." Braska cocked his head to one side and now he was the one eyeing her. "Listen, ma'am. If you think I saved you from that pesterin' slob Kenna just so I could take his place, you got the wrong idea. Reckon I can understand how, bein' a gal out here alone and havin' gone through that, you're a mite nervy and suspicious. But you're in a fix and I'm offerin' my help. Either you can choose to trust me and accept it...or you can take your wet clothes and go ahead on your own."

Rosie held his gaze for a long count. Finally, her shoulders sagged a little lower in the water and she said, "I'd be a fool not to accept your offer, wouldn't I? I no longer even have a horse."

"Unless she wanders back."

Rosie shook her head. "She won't. She's a rental from town. She'll almost certainly go back to the livery stable I got her from."

Braska said nothing, just waited.

Her mouth curving in a shy smile, Rosie said, "Very well. I most gratefully accept the kind offer of your option, Mr....what is your name, anyway?"

"Just call me Braska," came the answer.

6

THE FIRST THING BRASKA DID, ONCE HE HAD ROSIE out of the creek and into his camp, was to throw a saddle on Savvy and ride in a quick sweep of the surrounding area. He wanted to satisfy himself that Kenna was all the way gone and hadn't doubled back to try catching them by surprise in order to make good on his threats.

When he returned with a report that all was clear, Rosie regarded him and said, "You're a very cautious man, aren't you? I mean, we heard him ride off, and you had his gun—I would have thought those sufficient reasons not to have to worry about him anymore. At least not for a while."

"Yeah, reckon you could say I'm the cautious sort," Braska allowed, stripping off Savvy's saddle once again and setting it on the ground. "Places I've been, some hombres I've run into—ones like your friend Kenna— have made it kinda advisable if I wanted to keep my hide intact. As far as me havin' his handgun, yeah, that was a good start. But for all I knew, he still could've had one of these"—he leaned over to slap his Henry repeater in its saddle boot—"and I don't figure him for bein' above doin' some bushwhackin' if the mood struck him."

Rosie gasped. "My God. You really think he might —" she stopped short, frowning. Then the frown turned into a scowl of conviction. "No, you're right. He's a brute and a bully capable of extreme violence. That's been proven plenty of times. I once saw him pistol-whip a man who was so drunk he could barely stand up. Yet Kenna beat him mercilessly, to the point he almost died."

Braska's lips peeled back in a grimace. "And Elmer Coggins, the marshal, lets him get away with that kind of stuff?"

Rosie nodded meekly. "On a regular basis, from what I've seen."

While Braska was gone on his ride, Rosie had built up the campfire and hung her wet clothes on twigs and branches stuck in the ground up close, exactly as Braska had suggested, so they could start drying. She'd made a fresh pot of coffee, too, a cup of which she was now sipping from as she sat on the ground, also near the fire, wrapped in a blanket.

"You mentioned coffee, so I took the liberty of making some," she said, gesturing with the cup. "Hope you don't mind."

"Not at all. Matter of fact, I'll join you in havin' some." Braska dug a spare cup out of his gear and filled it. After taking a drink, he said, "You make good coffee, ma'am."

Rosie smiled wistfully. "It's pretty much the extent of my culinary skills. I suppose you're a good cook as well."

"I manage. Trail grub, that is. Bacon, beans, biscuits. Nothing much fancier than that."

Over the rim of his cup, as he tipped it up for another drink, he studied her more closely than he'd really had the chance to before. Middle twenties, he judged. Facial features formed with clean, bold strokes, the kind that would qualify as quite pretty for now, but as she matured would more likely be described as handsome. Cobalt eyes, slightly pinched nose, wide mouth with a particularly full bottom lip. Her hair was almost boyishly short, full in front and on top, tapered at the nape of her neck. It served to nicely set off her face. And the rest of her below the face, as Braska was keenly aware, was anything but boyish.

"You speak as if you've traveled some," Rosie said. "Yet earlier, you called this spot your favorite swimming hole, and you mentioned having a history with the town of Piney Flats. Are you from around here?"

"I mostly grew up on a ranch just a few miles north," Braska told her. "My pa moved us here from Illinois when I was just a toddler."

"Is the ranch still in your family?"

"'Fraid not. Hasn't been for a spell. Me, I've been... away, these past few years. Arrived back in the general area only yesterday."

"Coming home," Rosie said, again with a trace of wistfulness. "I never had a home I ever wanted to go back to. Just one to get away from."

Braska wasn't sure what to say to that. He gave it a beat, then asked, "So what's your tie to Piney Flats? I take it that's where you're planted these days?"

Rosie gave a little laugh. "Stuck is more like it. But not planted—at least I sure as hell hope not." She paused and took a sip of her coffee before continuing. "Long story short is that Piney Flats is as far as I got before my money ran out for stagecoach fare to go any farther. I'd fallen for a handsome, smooth-talking rogue who called himself an *entrepreneur*, a man with big ideas and big plans who was going to make a real splash someday. But in the meantime, he was basically just a gambler and a bit of a shyster who moved from town to town scouting opportunities. To me, though, that seemed terribly exciting and was enough for me to leave home from...well, never mind where, and run off with him. For nearly two years it remained exciting, to me at least. But I guess I knew all along how it would end. One evening in Cheyenne, I found out for sure. The rat went out to get some cigars and I never saw him again.

"That was eight months ago. I scraped together all the money I had and started off on a series of stagecoach hops, angling toward the Mississippi where I meant to gain passage on a riverboat queen and float down to New Orleans. The louse I ran away with promised to take me there, but we never made it. Never came close. So it happened there was a job available at the Palace Saloon & Dance Hall when I landed in Piney Flats, and that's been earning me enough to get by and put a little bit aside each week until I've got enough to move on the rest of the way on my own...there, that's the glamorous and exciting life of Lucille Devry in a nutshell."

"Lucille?" Braska echoed.

"It's certainly not Rosie. That's a name deemed to be more appropriate for my work at the Palace by Martha. Martha Buckner, that is. She and her husband Frank own and operate the Palace. Martha said the name Lucille wasn't floozy-ish enough for a dance hall gal. Said it might make male customers think too much about their mothers or aunts and not enough about buying me drinks."

Braska lifted his eyebrows. "Interesting way of lookin' at things."

"Just to be clear about something else," Lucille—not Rosie anymore, at least not in this setting—said with a sudden sharpness. "Dancing and hustling drinks are *all* I do at the Palace. Not like some of the other girls. If I'd've gone that route, I could have had a lot more money set aside and been a lot farther away from here by now."

"And holdin' that line, I take it, is part of what put you crossways of Kenna."

"That pig." Lucille's eyes narrowed. "He thinks he's God's gift to women in the first place. In the second place, what *that* doesn't get him he uses his badge to force cooperation out of girls and women who are afraid to resist. He's been trying to add me to his list for a long time, but I've always managed to never let him corner me. Until today—almost. I never would've thought in a hundred years the creep was watching me close enough to pick up on my habit of renting a horse and taking a ride out of town a couple times a week."

"You always come to this spot?" Braska asked.

"I have been lately. Ever since I discovered it. It's perfect for a swim and a bath. Night after night at the Palace leaves the stink of cigarette and cigar smoke in my hair that the fresh water here seems to get out better than any regular tub bath."

Braska lifted his brows. "Can't say I ever recognized that particular benefit before. But it's a good spot all the same."

Lucille frowned. "I hope so. I mean, I hope it still holds its appeal to me. But I'm afraid if I come back again it may be tainted by the memory of that pig Kenna showing up the way he did."

"What about reporting him to the marshal when you get back to town?"

"Fat lot of good that would do," Lucille scoffed. "I told you, Kenna's forced himself on other girls. Some tried going to Coggins, but nothing came of it. It's just one more thing the marshal lets him get away with."

Braska gritted his teeth. "That sure don't sound like the Elmer Coggins I used to know. When we get to town, me and him are gonna have us a talk about whatever the hell has got into him. I have a personal stake in findin' out why he's goin' along with the kind of things I'm hearin'."

"You're seriously going to brace him? And you mean to also return Kenna's gun like you said?"

"That's right. Just like I said."

"But you heard him say he'll kill you with it if you do."

Braska's eyes turned cold and flinty, making Lucille glad when he averted meeting her gaze and instead seemed to look off at something far away. "Sayin' and doin' are two different things, Miss Lucille. I full intend to do what I said I would. If Kenna has the stones to try backin' up his mouth...well, we'll have to see how that works out."

7

ELMER COGGINS JERKED BACK IN HIS CHAIR WHEN the gun belt thumped heavily onto the desktop in front of him. He stared wide-eyed at it for a moment, then shifted his gaze up and across to the man on the other side of the desk who had tossed it there. His eyes widened even more. "Holy shit. That was *you?*"

"Hello, Elmer," Braska drawled, standing in front of the marshal's desk with his saddlebags and possibles pack on one shoulder and a Henry rifle gripped in his fist.

The marshal sank back deeper in his chair. "Jesus, Virg—I mean, Braska. You're sure a sight for sore eyes."

"I imagine your eyes are sore a lot these days, lookin' out on the town you've let turn into such a sad version of what it used to be. Worse yet, they must ache like hell when you look in the mirror and see the face of a man who allows a piece of crud like the slob who was packin' that"—Braska jerked his chin to indicate the gun belt— "to represent the badge you used to treat so honorably."

"Now see here. You got no call to come barging in here and—"

"The hell I don't!" Braska cut him off. "I got plenty of call to come bargin' in here and every right to speak my piece while I'm at it. I earned that right by payin' my debt to society servin' six years in Hellstone prison —where you helped send me back when standin' up for that badge meant something to you."

"I didn't send you any damn where. Judge Sturnheim did, because your confession gave him no choice. Are you forgetting that part? All I was was the go-between when you shouldered the blame for that shooting right off the bat and never would back down an inch, no matter what anybody else tried to say."

"I ain't forgettin' none of that," Braska said, easing up some. "The way it turned out, I wish I could."

Coggins shifted in his chair, beginning to look somewhat less intimidated. "Then I take it you've heard about Link?"

"Enough to make me want to puke. That, and then runnin' into the jackass I took that off of"—another chin jerk toward Kenna's gun belt—"damn near make me wish I'd've stayed away."

The marshal regarded him for a beat, then made a gesture with his hand, indicating one of the straight-backed wooden chairs hitched up in front of the desk. "How about you sit down for a minute? Give me a chance to clear the air about a few things. I'm not aiming to try and whitewash myself, I'm well aware I've slipped too far to try and sell that. But if you get an understanding of how things have changed around here, maybe you can pull in your horns just a little bit before being so quick to use 'em for tearing into fresh trouble."

Outside the windows of the marshal's office, dusk was settling over the town. Long, thickening shadows were filling the street. Lantern light was starting to glow in more and more windows. Some of the shops down through the business section were pulling their shades, going dark, and closing for the day.

When Braska and Lucille first reached town, her riding double behind him on Savvy, at her request, they'd stopped at the livery to check and make sure her rental horse had returned okay. It had. She fed the livery operator a line about the horse spooking unexpectedly and taking off on her. She also made arrangements about the saddle they'd had to leave behind, promising to go fetch it and return it the next day. Braska assured the man he would assist her. From there, he'd taken her and left her off at the rear of a little bakery where she explained she shared an apartment up above the business with another girl who worked with her at the Palace.

Lucille said she was going to claim being sick and not go to work that night so as to avoid the risk of running into Kenna. Before they parted, she thanked Braska profusely and elicited from him a promise to be careful as well as one not to forget coming around again in the morning so they could go get that saddle.

Leaving Lucille, he had come straight to the marshal's office.

Acting now on the request to take a seat, Braska put his gear on one of the wooden chairs. Then, pulling the other one over to the side so his back wouldn't be to the front door, he lowered himself astraddle it with his arms folded across the top of the back rest.

Studying him, Coggins said, "You've changed. You're prison-hardened. I'd've spotted it right off, even if I didn't know your story."

"You *don't* know my story," Braska was quick to correct him. "Nobody who's never been on the inside ever could. And if that's your idea of talk that'll convince me to pull in my horns, then you're off to a mighty poor start."

During this exchange, Braska also did some closer studying of the marshal. Jesus, he'd changed too. Yeah, the years were piling up on him—Braska had expected that. But there was something more. His skin was hanging loose around his mouth and on his throat, like he was shrinking within it. And it had an odd, grayish cast to it, not hardly skin-colored at all. Damn, it almost looked like he was aging and rotting from the inside as well as the out.

"Tell me," Coggins said, starting over. "When you rode into town just now, what did you see? Piney Flats has grown. Right?"

"Quite a bit, yeah."

"Uh-huh. And did you notice where almost all the growth is? It's off the west end of the business district, that's where. The *old* business district. That part hasn't changed much at all, but the newer part is made up almost entirely of saloons, poker parlors where the biggest game of chance is who's gonna be the first one to get gut shot under the table, cheap hotels, and even cheaper flop houses where customers are stacked like cordwood, pool halls, slop-chute cafés, and whore cribs. Hell, we even got an indoor bowling alley, if you can believe it—but there are almost as many brawls using the pins as clubs as there are completed games."

Braska took out the makings and started to roll a smoke. "You paint a real colorful picture. But I don't see where any of it is skin off my nose."

"Bigger cattle ranches to the west and south is what started it," Coggins said moodily. "Bigger ranches mean bigger crews coming to town looking for a good time. The old Buffalo Wallow didn't offer near enough to satisfy 'em. So word spread, and before you could spit, more places offering more entertainment started popping up. And with 'em came a steady stream of drifters, gamblers, whores, connivers, and conmen of every stripe."

"I still don't see your point," Braska prodded. "Some folks would consider business growth like that to be progress."

"Some folks, yeah. The kind who see nothing but more money pouring in as progress. And, trust me, we've got plenty of current *city fathers* who look at it that way. As long, of course, as none of the rowdiness or trouble that comes with that kind of money flow spills over into the backyards of the more *genteel* parts of town."

"Ain't that where you and your badge are supposed to come in?"

"Exactly." Coggins's face sagged even more. "But I'm too old to be a town tamer, Braska. Hell, I was too old ten years ago...if I *ever* had the makings for such."

"Get out then. Let the businessmen and city fathers who enjoy the added money so much worry about keepin' the overflow grief outta their own backyards. Let 'em hire somebody else." Braska scowled through an exhaled cloud of smoke. "Jesus, Elmer, you've served Piney Flats long enough you must've earned some kind of decent pension. Claim it and go away somewhere, take it easy."

"That's the trouble. I can't do that," said the marshal, his mouth twisting bitterly. "I got a sick wife, Braska. Bad sick. Has been for a long time. Nowadays she's under constant care at a place over in Imperial. I've used up most of our savings and had to sell our house. I don't know how much longer she can last, but for however long it is, I want her as comfortable and free of pain as possible. That takes doctors and medicine, and those things take money. I'm stretched about as thin as I can stretch, even on full marshal's pay. No way in hell I can come close to making it on the measly pension I got coming."

Braska saw the rest of the picture taking shape. "So you got the city fathers to hire Kenna for handlin' the rough stuff on the rowdy end of town, leaving you to coast once again as a go-between bufferin' the old from the new."

"That's about the size of it. I ain't saying I'm proud of it, but all things considered, I can't say I'd do any different." Coggins's expression took on a touch of mournfulness. "You can believe or not that I regret much of how he handles things. I know the sonofabitch is too rough and is probably taking kickbacks on the side, sometimes in the form of forced sexual favors. But I'm stuck with him now, we've got a contract. And I don't have the strength or will to try and break it. As long as he keeps his tactics on the rowdy end of town, I can stand putting up with 'em...until my Sara is gone. When that day comes, I'll be pulling foot and never bothering to look back or giving a damn what I leave in my dust."

"You could do that? After all the years you put into looking out for things around here—you could just ride off and no longer care?"

"I could and would. What difference would it make?"

"Only to yourself, I'd've expected," Braska said quietly. "Because of things like self-respect. Honor. Things I saw in you that used to matter."

Coggins chuffed. "I learned real fast and real clear how far respect and honor get you when it comes to things like paying medical bills. Nowhere, that's how far. So then, what the hell are they worth?"

"More than finishin' out your time leanin' on the likes of Marv Kenna."

"What do you know about it? You or any of the others looking down their noses at me and feeling the same way." Coggins leaned forward and balled his fists atop the desk. "You speak of finishing out my time. What about all the time I *lost* to this job, time I left Sara waiting home alone, wondering when I'd be back or *if* I'd make it back at all. But it was time we always figured we'd someday make up, together, once I retired...only now that making up time ain't ever going to happen."

Braska took a final drag off his cigarette, then reached out and dropped the butt into the spittoon in front of the marshal's desk. "You and Sara have my deepest sympathy for her illness and what it's puttin' the two of you through. I truly mean that, Elmer," he said. "But this other business, you turnin' to Kenna and lettin' him run roughshod the way you are...I can't cut you no slack on that. It boils down to bein' bad for the town and for the reputation you spent so many years buildin'. It's damn wrong and you know it."

"I did what I did, and I stand by my reasons why," was all the marshal had to say in response.

Braska heaved a ragged sigh. "All right, let's cut to the gun belt I plopped there in front of you. You obviously recognized it right off and you almost seemed to be expectin' it to show up. What kind of yarn did your pet ape spin for how he came to be separated from it?"

Coggins recited an answer without emotion or inflection. "Kenna took a notion to go fishing out on Piney Creek earlier this morning. After he'd been sitting on the bank for a while, his gun belt started digging into his hip so he took it off and put it on the grass beside him. The fish weren't biting, so he ended up dozing some. He woke up to the sound of a horse riding away, and when he reached out, he found his gun belt had been stolen. He arrived back in town spitting fire and cuss words and telling everybody he could lay tongue to about it—warning 'em to be on the lookout in case the thief was loco enough to come around wearing the rig or maybe trying to sell it."

"With imagination like that," said Braska, chuckling dryly, "your boy oughta be scribblin' for one of those eastern newspapers or magazines that love to run stories about our so-called Wild West."

The marshal shrugged. "I dunno. Other than I've never known Kenna to be inclined toward fishing before, I didn't think it sounded too far-fetched."

"Are you ready to hear the real story behind how I ended up with his gun rig?" Braska asked.

"You seem busting to tell it, whether I'm ready or not."

"The only truth in his version is that it did happen on Piney Creek, out east a ways. At a swimmin' hole, not a fishin' spot. A young lady from here in town rode out there to have herself a private dip. But Kenna followed, figurin' to get himself a free show and then a lot more." Braska made a sour face. "Luckily for her, I happened along to help him change his mind. Part of it was convincin' him to shuck his gun belt so's he'd ride off and not have no foolish notions about comin' back around for another try."

"Damned few men'd be capable of getting the bulge on Kenna like that," Coggins remarked.

"All the same, that's how it went. I told him I'd return his gear here to you. If I did that, he said, he'd reclaim the gun and use it to kill me."

The marshal closed his eyes for a moment and expelled a sigh of his own. "Yeah, that sounds like something he'd say...and then do."

"Try," Braska corrected quietly.

"And I suppose you mean to stick around and find out which."

"I mean to stick around long enough to do what I came for. And that's talk to a few people. After that, I'll be movin' on. But I ain't gonna hurry my business or give the impression I'm runnin' just because your bully-boy deputy might come lookin' for me."

Sounding almost desperate, Coggins said, "Nothing I can say or do to change your mind?"

"Is there anything you can say or do to change *his* mind? How about callin' him to account for botherin' that girl the way he did?"

"Is she willing to come forth and file charges?"

"I doubt it. She has to live in this town."

Coggins spread his hands. "So there's nothing I can do. You know how it works. Whatever happened out there would come down to your word against Kenna's. That gives me nothing I can act on."

"Real convenient, eh?"

"Damn it! That's the way it is, and that's all there is to it."

Braska rose from his chair. "Let's hope that's all there is to it. I didn't come back lookin' for trouble, Elmer. But if your hired thug is bound and determined to force some on me, I'll drop him permanent-like. And if you all of a sudden decide *then* that there's something you oughta do, I'm warnin' you against it. I won't go behind bars again—not for you, not for nobody."

Picking up his rifle and hoisting his other gear up on one shoulder, Braska made it as far as the door. Before opening it, he stopped and turned part way back around. "Answer me one thing as whatever's left of a straight-up lawman in you...have you heard any talk about a hombre who fits mighty close to Link's description bein' spotted as part of a gang raisin' hell down in the Four Corners area?"

"Matter of fact," Coggins answered, his tone and expression impassive. "Yeah, I have. But a few scattered reports, dribs and drabs of loose talk is all it's been. None of it close to a for-certain thing. That's why I didn't bother mentioning it. If there's any truth to the matter, though, the gang in question is a mighty rough crowd run by the Mallet brothers."

"Hec and Merl Mallet?"

"You know 'em?"

"Know *of* 'em," Braska allowed. "They used to ride with Three Rivers Bascomb and his bunch all across the middle of Kansas and even up close this way. I was behind the walls at Hellstone with Bascomb for a while —up until somebody slit his gizzard in the breakfast lineup one morning. While he was still alive, Bascomb liked to gather a crowd around him out in the prison yard and brag about some of the jobs him and his boys had pulled. Way he told it, the Mallet brothers were about the wildest on his crew."

Coggins nodded. "That sounds about right. After Bascomb got captured and put away, the brothers took over the gang, and *wild* would be a mild description for some of their bloody doings. They didn't just rob and kill to fight their way clear, they killed without any reason other than just for the pure hell of it."

Braska grimaced at that, at the thought of Link possibly being part of such an outfit.

"Way I recall," the marshal continued, "things got so hot for 'em up around this way that they pulled foot a couple years back and skedaddled south of the border to raise hell down that way for quite a spell. Wasn't 'til six or so months ago that reports of 'em being spotted in the Four Corners area started drifting in. But if there's any truth to Link being associated with 'em, it might have been a short run."

"Why do you say that?"

"Because the most recent reports on the Mallet gang—going back five, six weeks now—tell how they were spotted and shot to shit robbing a bank in a Utah mining town called Fergus Hills. They got away with the money but paid a hard toll for it. One of 'em, a hombre named Epps, got left dead in the street. Day later, Merl Mallet himself was found dead out on the trail. You can bet the local marshal and his good citizens made quite a spectacle of his corpse after they brought it back to town. A picture of him propped up in a pine box for public display showed in plenty of newspapers. I'm surprised you didn't hear anything about it."

"After six years in cramped, noisy, smelly Hellstone, I made it a point for these past months, up until now, to keep myself mostly to the tall and uncut wide open, where the air's clean and quiet and empty of people and things like newspapers."

"Guess that explains you not hearing anything then. But it happened, all the same. And ain't been nothing else seen or heard of the gang since. Way the Fergus Hills marshal claims, at least one or two more rode off with some serious wounds."

The grimace returned to Braska's face.

Coggins heaved a sigh. "Look. For what it's worth, I hope to hell there's no truth to Link being part of that Mallet bunch. And if there is...well, I hope he wasn't one of the ones chewed up in that shoot-out."

Braska stood for a beat, considering everything. Then, giving a faint nod, he turned back to the door. He was opening it to leave when the marshal stopped him once more, saying in a low voice, "Regarding this more immediate situation. Right about now, Kenna will be starting his evening rounds through the saloons and such in the new part of town. He don't usually come to this part, I take care of that. But if he catches wind you've shown up, he may start looking wherever it takes him. And, no matter what he said, I wouldn't count on him going to any special bother to come 'round for this particular gun. He's got plenty of others.

"He's also got a partner of sorts, another deputy I hired name of McNally. Cut from similar cloth, not quite as coarse. But plenty mean and sticks to Kenna like a shadow. If Kenna comes looking for you, bet that McNally will be with him...keep your head on a swivel."

Before going on through the doorway, Braska said over his shoulder, "Thanks for that, and for the rest, Elmer."

8

"STEVE AND I ARE SO GLAD YOU STOPPED BY, VIRGIL. We weren't sure whether or not you'd come back to the area at all after—" Betty Clemons stopped short, both in what she was saying and in the act of pouring some more coffee into Braska's cup. Her wide eyes lifted to meet his. "Darn it all, there I go again. I'm sorry, I just can't get used to calling you by that other name."

Braska smiled. "Don't worry about it. After all, Virgil *is* my name. And I haven't been around very much for you to get used to the other."

"Still. You're a guest in my house," Betty insisted, "and I ought to have the presence of mind and common courtesy to—"

This time, it was her husband who cut her short, saying, "Careful, dear. You're going to have something even more serious to apologize for if you end up pouring hot coffee in Braska's lap."

The three of them were seated in the parlor of the Clemons home. Braska had arrived about half an hour earlier, just as the family was finishing supper. He declined an offer by Betty to fix him something, assuring her he'd already eaten. He did, however, accept the offer of some coffee while they visited. So he and Steve had repaired to the parlor, leaving Betty to start a fresh pot brewing and also see that their two pre-teen daughters got busy clearing the table and doing dishes. The homeyness and cheerful family activity surrounding him gave Braska a good feeling, but at the same time, he retained an awareness of how out of place he was in such a setting.

Steve Clemons was just the opposite—the perfect picture of a family man. Big, open-faced, friendly galoot who ran a modestly successful leather goods shop. Anything leather—boots, shoes, saddles, holsters, saddlebags or purses, anything you could name—he could repair or fabricate from scratch with a skilled hand. And here in his house, with an after-supper pipe clenched between his teeth and his wife and daughters chattering and fussing about him, he appeared just as skillfully adapted. As for rail-thin, delicately pretty Betty, she lent her services to various charities and community events, but it was clear nothing came before her devotion to her husband and daughters.

It was actually another family member of Betty's— her younger sister Linda, Braska's sister-in-law via her marriage to his brother Link—who was the main reason for Braska's visit this evening. Fossie had led him to believe that Linda and daughter Alicia were staying here with the Clemonses. But it turned out that information was a little outdated. Some three weeks earlier, Linda had gone to stay with a third sister down in New Mexico.

"The name of the town is Tulamoro. I'm sure Linda

would love to see you if you went for a visit," Betty said as they continued to talk over coffee. "After Link abandoned the Bar S, she went out and gathered some of your mother's personal things, including the medals and commendations won by you and your father during the war. She took it all with her when she decided to go stay with Trisha for a while, wanting to console her after learning in a recent letter about the breakup of Trisha's engagement to the fella she'd been seeing for some time. Plus she—Linda, that is—felt like she was imposing too much on our family here. That part about imposing on us was nonsense, of course, but it's hard to change Linda's mind once she has it made up. At any rate, she took your mother's things with her and is keeping them for you, for when you return."

A warm feeling passed through Braska upon hearing this unexpected piece of information. He'd never been a particularly sentimental man, and whatever capacity he did have for such was largely worn away by the experiences of war and Hellstone. Yet he'd always had a fondness for Linda, maybe even harbored a twinge of jealousy where she was concerned, thinking that Link was fortunate to find someone like her while Braska's heart remained as unfocused as his ultimate path forward. Inasmuch as Linda had been the only other person besides his mother to write him while he was in prison—initially to inform him of Ma's passing and then a few more letters afterward—but never a single line from Link—it shouldn't have come as a surprise that she'd also be thoughtful enough to think of retaining some items meaningful to the family.

Before Braska could respond in any way to what he'd just been told or try to express the thoughts they'd stirred in him, Betty continued to chat on, saying, "But if you're looking for information about your brother, I think you'll be disappointed. Linda hasn't heard a peep out of Link for nearly two years. Not since she moved herself and Alicia out of the Bar S."

"Back when it still was the Bar S—though just barely," Steve added somewhat glumly.

"It's true I was hopin' Linda would have some idea where I might be able to find my brother," admitted Braska. "I mean to run him down, one way or another. Based on what I've learned since gettin' back, it shouldn't be hard to understand why. Link owes answers for plenty. Things he did, as well as things he failed to do. Bein' snake-belly-low enough to totally turn his back on his wife and daughter ranks among the worst of it."

Betty looked uneasy. "You're not...not looking to kill him, are you?"

Braska flushed a little, realizing how grim his tone and words must have sounded. He tried to smooth it over with a disarming smile. "No, ma'am. That ain't in my plans. I don't know exactly what shape rattlin' his sorry hide is gonna take if and when I catch up with him...but he's still my kid brother. I ain't settin' out to kill him."

"After the sacrifice you made and the future you practically guaranteed Link—all of which he tossed in the garbage heap," said Steve, with an uncharacteristic surliness, "there are plenty of folks who wouldn't blame you, no matter how hard you rattled him."

"Steve!" Betty was quick to admonish.

Braska was getting weary of hearing about his *sacrifice*, so he simply let it ride this time and instead said,

"Gettin' back to Linda. That town where she's at now—Tulamoro, you said was the name? Whereabouts in New Mexico is it located?"

Both Betty and Steve frowned in thought. Until Steve replied, "We don't really have a good map of New Mexico, so I can't say for certain. But somewhere I got the impression it's not too far in, over toward the northeast corner."

Betty's head bobbed agreeably. "Yes, I think that's right. It was in one of Trisha's letters, I believe, when she first moved down there. She's a school teacher, you know."

"So," said Braska, musing aloud, "that would put it on the opposite side from the Four Corners area, where New Mexico bumps up against Colorado, Utah, and Arizona."

The Clemonses exchanged looks before Steve asked, "Does that matter for some reason?"

"Maybe, maybe not. Though nobody around these parts seems to have heard from or seen Link since he turned his back on the Bar S, that unfortunately may not be true for everywhere. Either of you caught wind of recent rumors that a fella matchin' close to Link's description has been spotted ridin' with a gang of no-goods down in the Four Corners area?"

"Goodness no!" exclaimed Betty.

But her husband wasn't so quick to protest. He didn't say anything right away, just clamped the stem of his pipe a little tighter in a downward-turned mouth. Then, puffing a tight cloud of smoke, he said, "Yeah, I'll admit to having heard some loose talk along those lines. But that's all I took it for—loose talk. Unless or until it amounted to more, I didn't figure it worth fretting over."

"This is the first I'm hearing about it," declared Betty, aiming a disapproving look at her husband.

"For reasons I just stated," Steve told her. "I didn't mention it because I didn't want you to get all worked up about a bunch of unfounded blabber."

"Nevertheless, I would like to know about such things. Not to mention having the right. Especially when it might affect my sister," Betty insisted.

"What's it got to do with Linda, even if there is any truth to those rumors?" Steve wanted to know. "Link never gave a damn about her or his child when they were up here, why would it be any different down there?"

"Look," interjected Braska, "I sure didn't mean to rile anybody. The only reason I brought it up was the New Mexico connection—Linda movin' down there fitted with the talk about Link maybe runnin' with those Four Corner owlhoots, makin' New Mexico part of their stompin' ground."

"But that's a mighty big stomping ground," Steve pointed out. "And if she's over in the northeast corner, like we decided a minute ago, then that puts her clear on the other side from the Four Corners. Not that Link would have any way of knowing she'd moved down that way anyhow. And, even if he did, I repeat—he never gave a damn about her up here, what would be any different down there?"

Again musing aloud, Braska said, "Link had a lot of reasons for wantin' to stay away from these parts. If he somehow *did* find out Linda had moved elsewhere, though, maybe there's still enough decency left in him to want to look in on her and his daughter."

Steve jerked the pipe from his mouth. "Doggone it,

man, stop tossing out nonsense notions like that. You're upsetting Betty for no good reason."

"You're right. Please excuse my rude thoughtlessness," Braska said earnestly. He put down his coffee cup and stood up. "Reckon I'm hankerin' so hard to get a line on my brother that I'm willin' to grasp at straws and let my words and thoughts tumble too freely." He set his gaze on Betty. "Please accept my apology, ma'am, and don't pay no attention to my speculatin'. Like Steve said, there's no logical reason to think that Link would even know about Linda's move. And no matter if he did —despite my hope it might be otherwise—I'm afraid he's done a pretty thorough job of provin' he's just plain too much of a skunk to care. Which, in the long run, is probably best for her and the little girl anyway."

9

It was full dark when Braska left the hospitality of the Clemonses. The residential district where they lived, small and tidily laid out though rather cramped, was in the older part of Piney Flats. This gave him less than two blocks to walk before once again reaching Center Street, the main east–west artery running through town, and coming out at a very familiar spot along the row of businesses. On the opposite side of Center, at a slight angle from the side street mouth he was exiting, stood the weather-bruised front facade of the Buffalo Wallow Saloon, looking neither particularly worse nor better than the last time he'd last seen it six and a half years before.

Braska slowed his stride and came to a halt. Resting one elbow on the rim of a tall wooden rain barrel positioned under an eaves spout of the corner apothecary shop, he took out his makings and leisurely started building a smoke. From the time he'd decided he would go ahead and make a swing into Piney Flats, there hadn't been much doubt a visit to the Wallow would be part of it. Nevertheless, leaning there looking across at the place now he felt a curious ripple of reservation run through him. After all, events on the other side of those batwings were what had led to his stay in Hellstone. Was returning to *the scene of the crime*, as the saying went, really a good idea?

Braska exhaled a plume of smoke and then bared his teeth in a wolfish grin. Damn right it was. What was to stop him—the ghosts of Duffy and Meade? He had a thirst for some cold beer and, despite what he'd told Betty Clemons because he didn't want to put her to extra trouble, he hadn't eaten since his creekside lunch, so he was also hungry. Unless things had changed, a bowl of stew or at least some cuts of cold meat and cheese ought to be available through those batwings too.

Not in any big hurry, though, Braska remained leaning against the barrel and took a thoughtful drag on his quirley. He was still contemplating some of what he'd learned at the Clemonses. He continued to be touched by his sister-in-law Linda's thoughtfulness at gathering up and saving some of his mother's personal items. Ma had been a very practical woman of simple tastes, so there couldn't have been very much and it likely had little value beyond the sentimental kind. A family Bible that had been handed down for three or four generations would be in the mix, Braska had little doubt, the music box Pa had got her one time in Omaha at the completion of a cattle drive, her bundle of family recipes, the little collection of hand-painted sewing thimbles she'd gathered over the years...and whatever else there might be. Likely not much more—except for the medals and commendations Betty had mentioned, the ones he and Pa had earned in the war.

As for himself, Braska didn't put any particularly special stock in those and he was pretty sure Pa would have felt the same. They hadn't fought for medals, they'd fought to survive. The thing every man who sees combat wants out of it the most is for their side to over-come and for themselves and those fighting beside them to come out alive and whole. Well, Pa hadn't made it, and Braska would have traded a boxcar full of medals for that to have turned out different. He was sure Ma must have felt the same. But, with such being impossi-ble, possessing the trinkets he died earning no doubt gave her some measure of comfort.

At any rate, just as stopping by the Buffalo Wallow had been pretty much a foregone conclusion, so it was with a visit to go see Linda and the little niece Braska never before had the chance to meet. Though it wasn't like he meant to take possession of the items Linda had secured, at least not right away. What would he do with them—being on the move the way he figured to be for the foreseeable future? Still, he wanted to thank her in person for thinking to gather them in the first place, and then ask her to continue hanging on to them until he eventually got settled somewhere.

Plus, Braska was forced to admit somewhat sourly to himself, he had another reason for wanting to visit Linda in New Mexico. Her decision to go stay with her younger sister down there—allegedly to console her in a time of despair—shortly after rumors started to float about sightings of Link riding with an outlaw gang not *that* far away from Tulamoro, and then even closer-timed to the gang getting badly shot-up during a robbery...accepting all of that as being strictly coinci-dental, that did not swallow down very easy.

Braska hated having that kind of suspicion, especially where Linda was concerned, but there it was. And he knew himself well enough to know that once something like that was stuck in his craw, he wouldn't be able to rest until he got it coughed out one way or another. If it turned out to truly be just a coincidence, he still had good reason for going down to see Linda anyway. There'd be no harm done and he'd be that much closer to the Four Corners, where he would proceed in his search for Link. If, on the other hand, he discovered Linda had covertly re-established contact with Link and he was somewhere near to where she'd relocated, then Braska's hunt would conclude that much sooner and easier.

Why a reunion of the pair might have occurred after all this time—and why Linda would keep it from her older sister—Braska could only guess. If that proved to be the case, he'd find out her reasoning when he determined the rest. In the meantime, half of him was hoping he was wrong—that he was being overly suspicious and grasping at straws in his eagerness to get a lead on Link—while the other half wanted it to work out so he could go ahead and get the inevitable confrontation with his brother over with. The only thing for certain was that tomorrow he'd be heading for New Mexico.

Braska finished his smoke and dropped the butt in the rain barrel. Stepping away from the barrel and starting across the street toward the Buffalo Wallow, he amended his thoughts: One other certain thing was that he was fixing to drink himself some cold beer and have something to eat.

Pushing through the Wallow's batwings was like stepping six-plus years into the past. Braska paused for a minute just inside the doorway, letting his eyes adjust to the smoky dimness. A slow scan over the simple layout revealed hardly any change. Still just a wide, square room, low-ceilinged, with a sawdust-strewn wood plank floor and a big pot-bellied stove toward the rear, cold now but known to glow cherry red when called upon to provide heat in the winter months. Long, scarred but durable old bar running along the wall to one side, a scattering of tables and mismatched chairs through the middle and along the opposite wall. No piano providing an annoying racket that passed for music, no pool table, no bare-shouldered barmaids drifting around hustling drinks. Merely a drinking man's saloon—nothing more, nothing less. A place to meet, chew the fat, play a little cards if so inclined, or brood off in a lonely corner if that's what suited you.

About a dozen customers were on hand this evening. Two loners, spaced well apart, stood holding up the bar. Five men had a poker game going at a table near the back. The rest sat in groups of two or three at the middle tables, smoking and jawboning, nursing their drinks.

Braska proceeded on in and went to the near end of the bar, where he leaned his Henry against the front and piled his other gear on an empty bar stool beside where he remained standing. A few eyes followed him but didn't appear to take any undue interest. Behind the bar, a sawed-off stub of a man was wrestling a freshly tapped keg of beer into place. Even before he straightened up, Braska had no trouble recognizing him. Mickey Gunnert, another unchanged relic from the past. Five-feet-nothing in height, damn near as wide, a bald dome of a head with a few long wisps of white hair that he stubbornly refused to shave clean. He had a round face whose features looked like the imprint of a fist shoved into wet sand, but when he smiled, it somehow took on an undeniable charm. And when he straightened up now and his eyes fell on Braska, that smile immediately spread wide.

"Well, Glory be and leapin' leprechauns! There's a face too long absent from these parts!" A diminutive paw was shoved across the bar top in the midst of the greeting. "How ya be, Braska lad?"

"Not as good as I'll be in a minute, after you pour me a tall, foamy one from that keg you just put up," answered a grinning Braska as he reached to shake the offered hand. "Otherwise, I'm gettin' by okay, Mick."

Grabbing a tall mug and starting to fill it, Mickey's expression turned sheepish. "That was a pretty stupid thing for me to ask, wasn't it? I mean, considerin'..."

Braska waved him off. "Forget it. I know what you meant."

Thumping the full, foamy mug down on the bar, Mickey said, "In that case, at the risk of stickin' my other foot in my mouth, mind if I ask whereabouts you been? We heard near six months ago how you'd got early release and so have been on the lookout for you to show up ever since. What took so long?"

Braska tipped up the mug and drained nearly half of it. It was crisp and tangy and not quite cold but still refreshingly cool. Everything he'd been hoping for. Lowering it, a smear of foam clinging to his top lip, he issued a loud, satisfied sigh. Then, lowering his tone considerably, he addressed the question put to him. "First, I needed to go off somewhere by myself for a while, Mick, where I could suck in deep gulps of fresh, clean air that hadn't already been breathed in and exhaled out by five hundred other men. I wanted to sleep under the stars at night, to fade out listening to the lonely wind and the even lonelier howl of coyotes instead of the snoring and tormented groans of penned-up men, then wake in the morning with the bite of left-over cold night air stingin' my cheeks and frost crystals formed on my eyebrows. And when sunrise came, I wanted to see that big ol' fiery ball lift up above a lumpy, uneven horizon rather than the hard, straight line of a prison wall decorated with barbed wire...in short, old friend, before coming back around folks I cared anything for and who might still have some favorable thoughts about me, I needed to purge myself of the stink and bitterness left by six years in prison."

Mickey regarded him somewhat skeptically. "You don't mind my sayin', the tone behind those words and that fire burnin' way deep in your eyes kinda suggests to me you might still have some purgin' left to do."

Braska took another drink of beer before replying, "No, I don't mind you speakin' your piece. Long as you say it straight-up to my face and don't make a habit of it. But even still...What you're readin' as more prison purge left unfinished inside of me, I'd argue, is unfinished business on another matter. Namely, my brother Link."

"Aye. Another matter, and a sorry piece of business indeed," muttered Mickey.

Braska drained the rest of his beer and thumped

down the empty mug. "We can talk more about that bit of sorriness," he said. "But first, how about refillin' my mug? And have you got any grub in the back for a thirsty, hungry wanderer who had the misfortune of stumblin' in here?"

"I'm thinkin' I could probably find some antelope stew and cornbread," came the answer. Then: "And I suppose, judgin' by the pile of gear I see piled on the stool next to you, one of my upstairs sleepin' rooms is also something you'll be wantin' after a while? If so, I won't knock a hole in the ceiling so you can sleep under the stars. But, considerin' how it's gonna turn nice and brisk outside tonight, you're welcome to open the shutters as wide as you like so's you can wake in the morning with frost on your eyebrows and maybe, if you're lucky, since you seem to enjoy such things so much"—here an impish grin split the little man's face— "on your onions as well!"

Without missing a beat, Braska replied dryly, "In that case, you ought to try openin' the shutters wherever you keep your kegs of beer. A little bit of frost would do them some good, and your customers would surely appreciate a cold drink for a change, instead of this piss-warm stuff you usually plop on the bar in front of 'em."

A grinning Mickey turned to go through the beaded curtains hanging over a doorway behind the bar, reaching back to make a rude gesture with one hand before he disappeared.

10

Braska's mouth curved slightly as he watched the hanging beads settle into place behind the barkeep. How long had it been, he wondered, since he'd traded friendly banter with anybody like he'd just done with Mickey. Pretty damn long, that was for sure. Wasn't a lot of humor to be found behind the walls of Hellstone, where a remark said in jest carried an almost greater chance to be taken wrong by some embittered wretch and result in a violent reaction than it did to earn a rare smile.

Braska's six months of drifting and keeping mostly to himself after getting released from prison had been aimed at shedding as much of that experience, that *feeling* as he reasonably could before trying to blend back in with old friends and family—until, that was, he discovered how broken things had become in regard to the latter. Now, since Link represented all the family he had left, it seemed to have turned into a question of whether or not he *wanted* to blend back in with the ungrateful young pup. But deciding that for certain boiled down to first finding him and finding out why he'd swerved so far off course.

Taking a pull of his beer, Braska tried to dismiss further pondering on the matter of his brother, at least for the time being. It felt good being here in the Buffalo Wallow once more and falling comfortably back into trading barbs with Mickey. He wanted to relax and enjoy just this for a little while.

Killing time while waiting for Mickey to return with his grub, Braska turned around and leaned his elbows on the ledge of the bar top. Peering over the rim of his mug as he tipped it up for another drink, he swept his gaze once more over the room, this time more leisurely and more thorough. He recognized about a third of the faces he scanned, though couldn't remember all of their names. Some of them took notice of him looking them over, and three or four of the ones he recognized acknowledged him with a tip of their heads. Braska grinned and hoisted his beer mug in response.

Before any of this built into more, Braska heard the rattle of the doorway beads behind him and swung back around to see Mickey emerging through them. He was carrying a varnished wood serving tray upon which sat a steaming bowl, a spoon, and several slices of rich golden cornbread.

"Plenty of stew left if you want more, but this is all the cornbread I got made up," Mickey said, placing the tray before him.

Braska inhaled the delicious aroma wafting out if the bowl and wasted no time scooping up a spoonful. "I think this is gonna suit me just fine," he declared.

While Braska dug in, Mickey leaned on the bar

from his side—an act accomplished by stepping up onto the narrow strip of platform that ran behind the bar expressly for such a purpose. "You remember Billy Three Moccasins, don't you?" he said, making conversation. "Well, he's the one bagged that 'lope and sold me part of the meat. Claimed the critter was near big as a Montana elk."

"If I recall proper," Braska replied around a mouthful of stew, "Billy wasn't ever above stretchin' the truth some. But no matter how big the critter whose meat is in this was or wasn't, it ain't no stretch to say it turned out some mighty good eatin'."

Mickey grunted. "Glad you think so. Too bad you ain't got nothing better than my lousy beer to wash it down with."

Before Braska had a chance to come back with anything, a third party joined the conversation. Announced by the heavy clump of bootheels approaching across the wood plank floor, one of the card players from the table near the back bellied up to the bar and plopped two empty beer pitchers onto it. "Speakin' of your lousy beer, Gunnert," he said, "we're needin' a couple refills to keep our game going."

"You came to the right place," Mickey told him, taking one of the pitchers and swinging it down under the spout behind the bar. "You're in luck, too—I just tapped this keg."

The card player snorted. "If that's the case, it'll be about the only luck this evening has brought me so far." He was a big, beefy hombre about Braska's height though a good twenty pounds heavier. He had a round, ruddy face with a heavy brow, eyes set a shade too close, and a thick-lipped mouth that stretched to reveal big, horsey teeth with a wide gap between the front two.

"Cards not fallin' in your favor, eh, Buford?" said Mickey, setting up the first refilled pitcher and then swinging down the second one.

Buford snorted again. "Not in my favor and not in hardly nobody else's either—nobody, that is, except for that stranger who showed up and asked to sit in with us. He must've brought along Lady Luck to lean steady-like on his shoulder, the way he keeps pullin' in pots."

Mickey's eyes lifted quickly and sharply from his refilling task. "Now hold on, Buford. If you think there's something fishy goin' on and you're figurin' to call the stranger on it and maybe start—"

"Whoa. Take it easy, you prickly old goat," Buford cut him short. "I ain't suggestin' nothing of the kind. I might be a little suspicious about the way he keeps winnin', but dogged if I can spot any shenanigans to it. So unless or until I do..."

"If it comes to that, don't forget there's a right and a wrong way to handle it. You come here often enough, you know my rules." Mickey brought up the second refilled pitcher. "And in case any of the others at your table need remindin', maybe you should be sure to mention when you go back."

"I got a better idea. How about you take these pitchers to the table and do your own reminding," said Buford. "You see, I already told 'em I was gonna be sittin' out a few hands. Happens I got some other business to look after...with your friend Smith here."

Up until then, Braska had been paying only peripheral attention to the exchange between Mickey and the card player. But when he heard his name brought into it, he naturally took an increased interest. Pausing with a piece of cornbread raised part way to his mouth, he cut his eyes to Buford and said, "Afraid you got me holdin' the short end of the stick, mister. You seem to know me, but I don't recollect us havin' ever met."

"No, we never have," agreed Buford. "But you was pointed out to me as bein' Link Smith's brother. That's how come me to know you. And Link is the connection that brings into play us needin' to have a talk."

Mickey's eyes flicked back and forth between the two men. Scowling somewhat suspiciously, he said, "This ain't got the makin's of some kind of beef, does it?"

Buford heaved a sigh. "Will you, for Chrissakes, relax and quit bein' such a cluckin' old hen, Gunnert? Didn't you hear me say I just wanted to talk? So give us a chance to do that. And, if you want to get paid for that beer, best get those pitchers on over to the table. Meadows is the one payin' for the round."

Mickey hesitated, continuing to scowl and not looking fully convinced there wasn't something brewing behind Buford's placating words. He gave in after a minute, though. Hoisted up the full pitchers and marched dutifully off around the far end of the bar and toward the men still at the card table.

Buford's eyes followed him part way, then swung back to Braska. "Damned old worry wart," he said, grinning.

"His place, his right to look out for it," Braska responded with a shrug. He'd put the piece of cornbread back down, resigned to the fact that his meal was interrupted for the moment and not being particularly pleased about it. Plus, like Mickey, he sensed something about this character that was vaguely unsettling.

Continuing to play it nice and friendly, the man said, "By way of full introduction, my name is Buford Gaines. I understand your proper handle is Virgil Smith, but most folks call you just Braska. That to your likin'?"

"Let's just say I don't mind not answerin' to Virgil."

Buford's grin widened. "Hey, I hear that. I ain't ever been crazy about carryin' around *Buford* neither, 'specially as a kid. Had to bloody more than a few noses to keep from gettin' teased about it. My luck, me or nobody else ever came up with anything different."

"You said something about my brother bein' cause for us needin' to talk," Braska reminded him.

"Yeah, that's so." The grin faded. "I originally got to know Link when I hired on as a wrangler for the Bar S, see. Gotta admit that didn't last long, though, on account of me not carin' for his way of treatin' his help."

"For what it's worth, he wasn't always like that," Braska said. "But I'll allow as to how I've heard the same as what you're sayin' elsewhere since I got back."

"Water under the bridge, that part. I had no trouble findin' work on other spreads, so there was no hard feelin's," Buford explained. "Later on, when Link and me ran into each other here in town—usually at a poker table—we hit it off like nothing happened."

"But then, if I'm readin' you right," Braska prodded, "something else *did* happen. How about we cut to it?"

Buford's lips pressed tight and his already ruddy face darkened more with a flush of annoyance. "Okay, if you want it flat out, you're damned right something else happened." He reached back abruptly and dug into the hip pocket of his pants—the suddenness of the act causing Braska's right hand to drop down to the grips of his Colt, thumb sweeping the keeper thong off its hammer. Seeming not to notice this, however, Buford produced a battered old wallet that he slapped on the bar top. From this, he withdrew a smudged, folded piece of paper that he opened up and pushed in front of Braska. "See for yourself. It's a couple years old and faded some, but it's still readable. What does it tell you?"

Braska gave the paper a quick glance. "It's a marker signed by my brother. An IOU for two hundred dollars."

"You read real good."

"Okay. I can read—but that don't mean I understand why you're showin' this to me."

"I'm showin' it to you because your no-good chiseler of a brother ain't nowhere around so I can call it in on *him*! Is that plain enough?" Buford snatched up the paper, re-folded it, and stuffed it back in his wallet. "Like I told you, there came a point where me and Link took to sittin' on the same poker games regular-like whenever we was in town at the same time. One night, when I happened to be on a hot streak and his luck was runnin' lousy, I felt generous enough to take that marker so's he could keep playin' and have a chance to gain back some of his losses. Well, it didn't work out for him. Link left the table cleaned out."

"Any time you take a marker, you take a risk," said Braska.

"Maybe so. But I didn't see no risk in this case," Buford argued. "Next time he came to town, Link promised to bring the cash to square up. Hell, he had a whole stinkin' ranch—where was the risk, I figured."

Braska waited, saying nothing. He had a pretty good idea of what was coming next.

It didn't take long to find out he was right when Buford's face twisted angrily and he spat, "But, boy, did I figure wrong! Next thing you know, the whole territory is buzzin' with talk of how Link pulled foot on the Bar S and rattled his hocks to parts unknown. Leavin' me and a whole bunch of other folks—includin' his own wife and kid—holdin' the bag and hangin' fire."

"I don't like hearin' it, not worth a damn," Braska allowed. "But ever since I got back, it's been nothing but one earful after another of the same tune. I got no excuse, no way to try and explain it...all I can say is that I'm sorry for the things Link did and the hurt it caused."

"Sorry?" Buford echoed in a loud, disdainful tone. "What the hell good is a mealy-mouthed sorry out of you gonna do to fill the two-hundred-dollar hole in this wallet of mine!" He banged a fist down on the folded leather still lying on the bar top.

Braska felt himself starting to bristle. He could muster a certain amount of sympathy for Buford, but he still didn't like his loud mouth or care much for the way he was using it to publicly rehash another of Link's wrongdoings. "Whatever your grievances are, mister," he responded in a low, tight voice, "I suggest you take 'em out of my face and find somewhere else to air 'em."

"To hell with that!" Buford bellowed louder than ever. "I been waitin' too goddamn long for a Smith to show back up and square things with me. You ain't the one I was hopin' for, but you're close enough to make do!"

Braska suddenly realized that much of Buford's belligerence was being fueled by a level of drunkenness greater than had at first been evident. The eyes of everybody in the place were now locked on the two them and an awareness of this seemed to be egging Buford on all the more.

At the table where he'd just delivered the pitchers of beer, Mickey's attention was quickly drawn by the loud voices, and the scowl that had never really left his face deepened as a result. He turned away from the table and started back toward the bar, saying, "Now see here, Buford. Damn it, I warned you about—"

His words were cut short by two of the card players thrusting suddenly to their feet and crowding close on either side of him. One of them reached out and clutched Mickey's arm, blunt fingers digging deep, halting him before he could take another step. "No need to get any closer to that scattergun behind the bar, Mick," he advised in a harsh growl. "Just stay here with us and keep out of it."

"That's right," agreed the second hombre who'd left his chair. "Buford's been waitin' a long time for this chance. Let him play it out."

The room had gone quiet enough for Braska to easily overhear all of this. So that was how it stacked up, he told himself. Buford had a couple of backers, making it three-to-one odds if things went far enough. Like the loud mouth himself, the pair didn't have the look of full-bore hardcases—just unshaven, saddle- and weather-toughened wrangler types who likely rode for the same brand Buford hired out to these days. But that didn't mean they lacked a tough layer of bark, and men unified by a brand tended to side with one another, for better or worse.

The two men who remained at the table sat very still with their hands resting in plain sight, signaling they wanted no part of what was taking place. One of them was a stocky number wearing a rumpled, faded blue work shirt, suspenders, and a slouch hat. A freighter of some kind, Braska judged him to be, and the way his eyes darted from side to side, it was clear he'd rather be working the reins on a string of stubborn mules right about then. The other gent was a lean specimen clad in a long-waisted, cream-colored suit jacket, crisp white shirt, and scarlet string tie. He had a narrow blade of a face, adorned by a precisely trimmed pencil mustache and, at the moment, set in a calm, almost bored expression. He looked like an out-of-place riverboat gambler, undoubtedly the big winner Buford had lamented about earlier, and evidently a veteran of enough gaming table distur-bances to know when to get involved and when to stay out of the way.

Braska settled his gaze on Buford. "Let me see if I got this straight," he grated. "You're operatin' on the notion that *I* am somehow obligated to make good on my brother's marker you're holdin'. Is that it?"

"You catch on real quick," Buford sneered.

Braska's mouth curved in a pitying smile. "Well, that makes one of us. When I got pointed out to you as bein' Link's brother, wasn't there any mention made of the little detail about where I've been for the past six years?"

"In prison, you mean?"

"That'd be it, yeah."

"Makes no never mind to me. That's your problem, not mine."

"It is if you expect I'm packin' around two hundred dollars—which I wouldn't feel inclined to hand over even if I had it," Braska told him. "You think they pay wages behind the walls of Hellstone?"

"Don't try to be cute," Buford said, his mouth twisting menacingly. "A-course I don't figure you walked out of Hellstone with any money. But you came here, didn't you? And here is where your family had a decent ranch operation goin' before your brother pissed it away. So even though he pulled foot and left a pile of debt behind, there must've still been *some* Bar S value carried over. With Link in the wind, that leaves you as the only remainin' family member with any right, even though you're a jailbird, to claim it. And when you do, I aim to be standin' right beside you, ready to claim what's owed me—with interest."

Braska had heard enough. His stew was growing cold and his temper was heating up. Fast. In a low, tight voice, his flinty gaze clashing with Buford's beer-murky glare, he said, "Okay, buster, the show's over. You've huffed and puffed and brayed like a jackass for everybody to hear. Now it's time to listen to what I have to say. It's real simple...you got every right to have sour feelin's toward my brother. I got a few of my own. But that don't make me responsible for any of his wrongs—not to you, not to nobody. So my advice is to back off, pronto-like, and take your bellyachin' somewhere else."

But Buford had too many others watching for him to let up now. "I've waited long enough and took my beef as far as I mean to go with it," he replied stubbornly. "That's right here and now to you, jailbird."

"That's a nice lookin' Henry rifle he's got leanin' against the bar, Buford," called the puncher across the way who still had hold of Mickey's arm. "And those saddlebags on the stool next to him must go with a saddle and horse somewhere. If he's another chiselin' Smith who won't hand over the cash owed you, maybe there are other ways to collect."

A sly glint shone in Buford's eyes. "Say. You might be onto something, Boyd."

"Sure he is," Braska said encouragingly. "You're lucky to have friends like Boyd there...to put even stupider ideas in your head than the ones you manage to come up with on your own. He's right, though, about my horse and gear probably addin' up to near the amount you're lookin' for. But he forgot to mention the Colt ridin' on my hip. It's a nice one, a newer model Peacemaker chambered to share the same .44 cartridges as the Henry. You toss that into the mix, it ought to tally up to more than two hundred. The bonus would be that interest you was lookin' for." Braska paused a beat and then added, in an even lower, flatter tone, "All you gotta do is take it."

"Be careful, Braska! You can't afford to get drawn into gunplay again!" wailed Mickey.

This brought a loud guffaw out of Boyd, still gripping the little barkeep's arm. "Haw. You hear that, Buford? For all his bluster, the jailbird knows he'd damn well better crawfish in order to keep from endin' back on the Hellstone rock pile. Haw!"

"There's some more sterling advice from your pal," Braska said to Buford. "But before you think about takin' it, I suggest you look deep into my eyes and then tell me—and him—if you see any sign of crawfishin' there."

The silence gripping the room squeezed tighter.

Buford's jaw sagged slack and his tongue passed slowly across his bottom lip.

And then the second wrangler who'd stood up to crowd Mickey abruptly blurted, "For Crissakes, Buford, make your play or don't! Any time you're ready, I got an angle on the sonofabitch to back you!"

There it was. The clincher. It was going to happen now, there was no getting around it. Braska saw the flare of a decision in Buford's eyes—his own big mouth and the encouragement of his backers leaving him no choice. Even as his own fingers flexed wide over the grips of his untethered Colt, Braska watched for the slight drop of Buford's shoulder that would signal him starting to grab for the hogleg holstered on his hip.

The tense silence was suddenly broken by a shout of, "Hey!" Accompanying this, the gambler in the cream jacket gave the table he was sitting at a hard shove forward. This drove the edge of said table into the backs of the legs of Mickey and the two punchers hemming him in place. All three were caught by surprise and sent staggering and stumbling into a neighboring unoccupied table. Empty chairs were knocked aside and upended, making a loud clatter that mixed with the sputtered curses of the stricken men.

Buford's head snapped around to see what was going on. Realizing a split second too late that he never should have allowed himself to be distracted, his face did a reverse swivel only to be met with the muzzle of Braska's Colt jammed up into the soft pad of flesh directly under the jut of his chin. Leaning in close, Braska said through clenched teeth, "One wrong twitch, I paint the ceiling with whatever comes outta the inside of your skull."

Buford's shoulders sagged and all his anger and aggression seemed to roll off them. His gun hand fell limply at his side, the fierce expression clutching his face turned mournful, his bugged eyes stared fearfully down past the tip of his nose to lock on the barrel of the Colt extending up from Braska's fist.

Across the room, however, things weren't so quick to settle down. Mickey and Boyd got their feet tangled together and ended up toppling to the floor in a flailing heap. But the puncher who'd seemed especially eager for Buford to make his play by claiming to have a backup angle on Braska, proved not only more adroit but also more determined to do some harm. He hopped agilely over a fallen chair, caught his balance on the neighboring table, then spun away from it with his gun unleathered and extended at arm's length, sweeping it in search of a target.

Before the persistent hombre could set his sights, though—presumably on Braska—the table-shoving gambler demonstrated he wasn't done playing another card in this unexpected game that had broken out. In a blur of speed, his hand reached behind the lapel of his jacket and, snagged from a breakaway shoulder holster nestled there, came out gripping a short-barreled, nickel-plated revolver. The snubby barked almost instantly and spat a .45 caliber slug that smashed into the gun hand of the puncher as his arm was still making its sweep. The gun was knocked from the puncher's hand and sent flying, discharging a round that gouged harmlessly into the floor. The puncher dropped to his knees, clutching his damaged hand and howling in pain.

11

FOR ALL THE TALK ABOUT WHAT AN INEFFECTIVE lawmen he'd become these days, Elmer Coggins's response to the shooting inside the Buffalo Wallow was quite prompt. He barged through the batwings, wielding a double-barreled shotgun and wearing an all-business expression on his face, before the final curls of powder smoke had dissipated from the air.

Those present who hadn't participated in any of the action were all bunched off to one side of the room, jabbering excitedly. Buford and his two backers were lined up at the bar, palms placed flat on top, their gun belts shucked and lying on the floor behind them. The one with the bullet-shattered hand—Meadows, his name was—continued mewling in pain and shifting his weight back and forth from one foot to the other as Mickey, who'd returned to his platform behind the bar, was wrapping the injured paw with a wet bar towel.

Braska stood at the near end of the lineup, looking poised and ready even though his Colt was back in its holster. At the other end of the line, the gambler stood with his feet planted wide and his shiny revolver still aimed casually from waist level.

The marshal took all of this in, then demanded, "All right. Somebody tell me the story. What've we got here?"

Mickey was quick to answer. "These three Slash K riders, with Buford takin' the lead and the other two chowderheads eggin' him on, are the whole of it. Buford was stupidly and stubbornly tryin' to get a money pay-out from Braska, and like I said, Boyd and Meadows were backin' his play."

Coggins frowned. "A money pay-out? What the hell do you mean—he was tryin' to rob him?"

"It wasn't like that all, Marshal!" Buford protested. "I was just tryin' to get what's been owed me for way too long!" He said this over his shoulder but made sure to keep his hands planted down on the bar.

Braska took a step closer to him, snapping, "Shut up!" Buford's face quickly turned back to look straight ahead.

Reaching out, Braska snatched up the wallet that had been left lying on the bar earlier and, from it, removed the worn, folded marker. Handing this to Coggins, he explained, "There's the crux of the whole thing."

"So?" the marshal said after reading it. "This is a marker from your brother Link."

"Exactly. But Buford the Brain here—and his two pals—seemed to reckon anybody named Smith oughta be willin' to honor it."

"Oh, for Christ's sake," Coggins groaned. Glaring at the back of Buford's head, he added. "And you thought that gave you some kind of right to go after it with a gun?"

"I never drew my hogleg. That was Meadows!" Buford responded.

At the other end of the line, Meadows stopped his groaning long enough to holler, "Damn you, Buford, you spineless wretch! You was just too stinkin' slow to clear leather!"

"So who fired the shots I heard?" Even as he said it, Coggins's eyes were coming to rest on the gambler with his still-drawn pistol, making at least part of the answer seem obvious.

The man didn't balk in the least. "I'll take responsibility for part of that, Marshal," he replied in an easy drawl. "I shot the gun out of the hand of that fellow Meadows, and his weapon discharged inadvertently from the impact."

"I don't know what the hell invertentally means, but my hand's busted to hell!" wailed Meadows. "I need a doctor!"

"The doc's been sent for, he'll get here as quick as he can," Mickey told him. "Now hold still and quit jerkin' around. You're just makin' your hand bleed worse and I ain't gonna waste more bar towels on you!"

Marshal Coggins stayed focused on the gambler. "You've been in town a few days, haven't you? Go by the name of Stark?"

With his free hand, the gambler pinched his hat. "That's right. Myles Stark, at your service, sir."

"Up until now, you've been plyin' your trade in the faster, higher stakes games to be found in the fancier saloons up on the newer end of town. Sorta surprised to see you drifted down this way."

Stark smiled. "My interests are wide and varied. Sometimes I like to sample things at a slower, more peaceful pace. Although this evening didn't entirely turn out that way."

"But it *has* tamed back down now." Coggins tapped the shotgun cradled in one arm. "So I think it's safe to go ahead and put your gun away."

"To be sure." The revolver disappeared behind the lapel of Stark's jacket.

Braska edged up alongside the marshal and addressed the gambler, saying, "Never really got a chance before now, but I need to extend my thanks for steppin' in on my behalf the way you did. That was some mighty slick gunwork, not to mention the table shove that broke it open to start with. You probably saved me from havin' to kill one or more of those jack-asses and maybe takin' some lead myself."

"Think nothing of it. I don't like lopsided odds," Stark replied lightly. "Besides, those three were already getting on my nerves with their clumsy card play and even clumsier attempts at cheating."

"We ain't no cheaters!" Boyd protested.

"You're abysmally *bad* cheaters, but certainly not for lack of trying," Stark corrected him. Then, bringing his gaze back to Braska and the marshal, he explained, "They were so bad it was actually amusing, that's why I let it ride for a while. Plus, it wasn't doing anything to prevent me from still winning most of the pots." He shrugged. "Nevertheless, it was growing a bit tiresome and bringing me close to calling them on it. So when the other bit of nonsense with that marker started up, it presented the opportunity to address two annoyances at once."

A corner of Braska's mouth quirked up faintly. He'd always been guarded about taking a liking to somebody, and prison had certainly reinforced that trait. Nevertheless, there was something in the cool, rake-hell manner of Stark—apart from his timely intervention in a dicey situation—that made it easy to lean toward liking him right on the spot.

Further discussion was interrupted by the arrival of Doc Worthington, accompanied by the freighter type—the fifth man from the card game—who'd been sent to fetch him. The doctor hadn't changed much since Braska had last seen him. A little more gray in his unruly mop of hair maybe, but otherwise just as rumpled and grumpy-looking, with bristly white whiskers in need of a shave running along his jawline, wrinkled suit and crooked tie, and vigorously swinging a battered old medical bag that looked like it had been trampled in a cattle stampede, maybe more than one.

He proceeded directly to the patient, so identified by the bloody towel-wrapped hand resting on the bar top in front of him. As he brushed past Braska, he muttered, "Heard you were headed back to these parts, Smith. Appears it didn't take long for you to leave your calling card."

Braska grinned wryly. "Good to see you again too, Doc. But you'd better stick to healin' and steer clear of speculatin'. What you're about to tie into there ain't my handiwork at all...well, not directly anyway."

Worthington had no immediate response, instead depositing his bag on a bar stool beside Meadows and then focusing his full attention on the injured hand. As he began unwrapping it, Mickey moved away down the bar and took up a position across from where Braska, Coggins, and Stark were standing.

"So how do you want to handle this?" the marshal asked. "It's your establishment, Mickey, and you were the intended victim, Braska. Either of you want to bring charges against these three idiots?"

Mickey made a face. "All I suffered was a bullet gouge in the floor. Ain't worth it to me to make no big deal out of that. Barrin' those ugly mutts from showin' back up here for, say, six weeks'd be enough to satisfy me."

When Coggins's gaze shifted to him, Braska considered a minute before saying, "I don't plan on stickin' around long enough to press charges. But I do want to settle something."

"What's that supposed to mean?"

Braska held out his hand. "Give me that marker back, I'll show you."

The marshal handed the slip of paper over, looking puzzled. Braska took the marker and turned to where Buford was still standing with his hands pressed flat on the bar. "Go ahead and relax for a minute," Braska said, stepping up beside him and shoving his abandoned wallet over in front of him. He placed the unfolded marker next to it. Then, with slow, deliberate movements, he drew his Colt, broke open the cylinder, and extracted a single cartridge. This he placed next to the marker.

Buford's eyes followed each move closely, the look on his face anxious, somewhat uncertain—matching the expression of Mickey, watching from the other side of the bar, as well as those of Coggins and Stark, also looking on.

"There's your payment for that marker," Braska told him. "Sign it off as received in full and we can consider the matter closed."

Buford frowned. "I don't follow."

"That bullet," Braska grated, "is the one I was fixin' to blow your head off with. But didn't. Therefore, I figure in its unfired condition, it ought to be looked at as something of value to you...unless you don't figure what's restin' on your shoulders is worth at least a couple hundred bucks."

Once again, the saloon turned very quiet. Even Doc Worthington paused in probing at Meadows's hand and looked over to see what Buford's reaction was going to be.

He was unable to meet Braska's stare. Instead, he looked down at what was spread on the bar top before him. First at the wallet and marker. Then at the bullet. Until, in a barely audible voice, he said, "You got a pencil I can use, Mick? I got a receipt to sign."

12

His homecoming, Braska reflected, had turned into quite an eventful day. Starting with the discovery that *home*, as represented by the Bar S ranch, no longer even existed—and from there spiraling quickly downward with the dismaying revelations about his brother and the role he'd played in allowing/facilitating its demise. Not to mention the disturbing personal side of Link that, according to all reports, had been revealed in the process.

And, if that wasn't enough, Braska had then managed to get crossways of a bully-boy town deputy, discover an old friend in the form of the town marshal was a meek shell of his former self, and from there come skin close to being drawn into the same kind of saloon shoot-out he'd just finished serving prison time for.

The only bright spots had been discovering Fossie still present at what *used* to be the Bar S, the pleasant encounter with Lucille at the swimming hole—minus the Deputy Kenna part—and the banter with barkeep Mickey. In its own way, the interaction with gambler

Myles Stark had been a positive thing too, Braska reminded himself.

He was mentally reviewing all of this as he sat smoking the day's last cigarette while perched on the edge of a cot in one of the sleeping rooms over the Buffalo Wallow saloon. It wasn't particularly late, but he'd decided to turn in anyway, partly because he simply wanted to have some time alone with his thoughts, and also because he wanted to be well-rested for the plans on tap for tomorrow. First, he'd promised to take Lucille back to fetch the livery saddle they'd left behind at the swimming hole. Then he'd need to stock up on trail supplies ahead of striking out for New Mexico to begin his tracking down of Link. He intended to put in long days of travel over terrain he was only marginally familiar with but knew would be rugged going in places. It wasn't a task he was especially looking forward to, but it was one he felt obligated to do and one he'd pursue doggedly until done.

The ties he'd only ever tenuously felt toward Piney Flats and its vicinity, to begin with, were now severed for good. Leaving nothing to hold him but a remote graveyard, a handful of old acquaintances he'd already been absent from for nearly seven years, a dalliance with a pretty girl whose presence was even more transient than his, and a simmering grudge harbored by a badge-packing bully that didn't warrant *not* avoiding if possible.

Nothing to hold him, nothing to bring him back... except the promise he'd made at the graves of his mother and sister to try and swing by to pay his respects to them again when and if he could.

Braska took a hard drag on his quirley and squinted

through the curl of smoke that rose up from the glowing tip.

Following the fracas downstairs, when they learned no charges were going to be brought against them, the Slash K riders Buford and Boyd were plenty eager to take their leave. They accepted without comment being told by Mickey they wouldn't be welcome back in his establishment any time soon. Nor did they protest Coggins giving them back their gun belts with the proviso they stuff them in their saddlebags and not strap them around their waists again until they were beyond the city limits. Meadows did not ride out with the other two, instead needing to remain behind for a while under the care of Doc Worthington, who delivered the good news/bad news diagnosis that, with attentive care, he could save the injured hand though it would never regain full function again.

Once all of them had cleared out, Braska had been talked into remaining in the saloon for a while, visiting with Mickey and Stark and some of the other customers who stayed and gathered around. In the course of this, he finally got to finish his stew—actually, a new bowl of it, fresh and hot, to replace the original one that had grown cold. The talk was loose and relaxing, with more of the kind of friendly banter Braska realized he had missed and, naturally, a healthy sprinkling of bawdy jokes. Surprisingly, none of the talk was in any way probing of Braska, like he kept expecting. The session was actually quite enjoyable and two hours passed quickly. When Stark bowed out, explaining the night was still young enough for him to go try for some winnings at the other end of town, Braska took that as a cue to excuse himself also. He said his good-nights and

asked Mick for the number of an upstairs room that was
made up and ready for an occupant.

Finishing his smoke now in said room, Braska
reached to stab out the butt in a nightstand ashtray.
Then, after kicking off his boots and slipping his .44
under the pillow, he lay back and stretched out full on
the cot. The mattress was thin and lumpy, but the
blanket was clean and fresh-smelling and the pillow
nicely plump. All in all, a favorable change from a
bedroll spread on a slice of trailside ground with his
head resting on an upturned saddle, the way he'd been
spending most nights of late. Although, if given the
ability to make an ideal blend, he would have traded the
murmur of voices seeping up from the saloon downstairs for a soft wind sighing in the open air, maybe even
a distant coyote yowl now and then. Still, with his head
sunk deep in the pillow and his churning thoughts
somewhat settled for a while, it didn't take long at all for
him to fall asleep.

Unfortunately, neither did that last for very long.
Re-awaking came in a series of jolts timed to match the
rap-rap-rap of somebody's fist knocking on the room's
door.

Braska jackknifed to a sitting position, dragging the
.44 out from under the pillow as he did so, then slid
smooth and cat-quick off the mattress and into the
deeper shadows at the foot of the bed where he
crouched low with eyes and gun trained tight on the
door.

"Mr. Smith...Braska Smith?" came a tentative voice
—a tentative *female* voice—from out in the hall.

Braska relaxed. But only a little. His first inclination
was to think that an unexpected visit from a woman

ought not be considered particularly threatening. On
the other hand, he knew damn well there were women
who could be plenty dangerous in their own right. And
just because it was a female who'd spoken, it didn't
mean she was alone on the other side of that door.

He was still weighing how to respond when the
voice spoke again. "I'm a friend of Lucille's. There's
trouble brewing, and she wanted me to warn you."

Lucille—not *Rosie*. The fact the speaker knew to
call her that and also knew that Braska would recognize
the difference was telling.

Braska straightened slowly out of his crouch but
kept his Colt trained on the door. Two faint light
sources—a weak wash pouring in through the window
from a lonely pole lamp on the street out front and a
wall lantern in the hall throwing a sliver of pale gold
visible under the bottom edge of the door—cast the
room in murky illumination. Keeping off-center of it,
Braska padded silently to the door. He removed the
chair he had earlier wedged under the knob, swept it
away, and set it to one side. Then, pressing his left
shoulder to the wall two feet back from the door frame
and holding the Colt at waist level, he said, "The door's
not locked, come on in. Move slow, keep your hands
where I can see 'em."

After a moment's hesitation, the door opened and
the slender, curvy form of a girl entered as instructed.
Light from the hall followed her, shining on a thick
mane of golden hair. She wore a light shawl over her
shoulders, open at the front to reveal the thrust of high,
proud breasts barely contained in a low-cut dress that
hugged her waist and hips and, through a long slit up
one side, displayed a shapely leg encased in a black

mesh stocking. Braska's mind jumped back to his earlier thought about how some women could be plenty dangerous—and here was one proving that in spades.

Somewhat gruffly, he told her, "Go stand beside the bed and hold there until I say otherwise."

Once again, the girl did as instructed.

Braska kept to one side of the doorway for a long beat. Then, bending at the waist and moving quickly, smoothly, he leaned out the doorway and scanned the hallway first to the left and then to the right. The Colt in his fist moved in concert with the turns of his head and the sweep of his gaze.

When he was satisfied the hallway was empty and therefore the girl was alone, he straightened up and stepped back into the room. Before closing the door, he gestured to the girl. "There are some matches there on the nightstand by the lantern. Use one of them to provide us some light."

As soon as the lantern was burning, Braska closed the door and hooked the chair under the knob again. Watching him, the girl said, "Lucille told me you were a very cautious man. I see what she meant."

"Not a habit I'll apologize for," Braska replied tersely. Then: "Now what's this about Lucille being in trouble? Have to do with that Kenna slob again?"

The girl's head bobbed. "Has everything to do with him."

"So where do you fit in?" Braska asked.

"I told you, I'm a friend of Lucille's. We work together at the Palace and we also share an apartment, the little place over the bakery where you dropped her off earlier. My name is Dolly, by the way."

"Okay then, Dolly...if Lucille felt I needed to be

warned about some trouble gettin' stirred up by Kenna, why didn't she come 'round herself?" Braska wanted to know.

"Because that's exactly what Kenna wants her to do —set you up for him," Dolly explained. "You see, he heard about you showing up in town and getting into a scrape here at the Wallow. As soon as he got wind of that, he came to the apartment demanding to know when and where Lucille would be meeting with you again. When she denied there was any such arrangement between the two of you, he called her a liar and threatened to beat the truth out of her. Lucille grabbed a carving knife from the kitchen and made him back down."

Braska swore under his breath.

"But Kenna wasn't done," Dolly continued. "He swore he wasn't finished with Lucille, but there'd be plenty of time for that after he settled with you. He said he was willing to be patient and allow her to be his bait —that sooner or later you'd be drawn to her and, when you were, he'd be waiting and ready."

"Like a lowdown yellow bushwhacker," Braska spat. "Yeah, that'd fit him right enough."

"That's why Lucille sent me to warn you. She didn't want to risk being followed and lead him straight to you. Besides, I'm way more familiar with this part of town than her. I grew up here. I've known Mickey since I was a little girl, and since your scrape was here at his place, I figured there was a good chance you'd be taking one of his upstairs rooms for the night."

"Mighty obligin'—not to mention mighty *un-*cautious, to my way of lookin' at things—for Mickey to send somebody up without advisin' me in any way. I'll be needin' to speak to the little runt about that."

"Don't be too hard on him. I told you, I've known him since I was a little girl."

"Which you no longer are," Braska pointed out.

Dolly emitted a mischievous little giggle. "I know. The way the randy old goat was eyeing me, he definitely took notice of that. Which probably gave him some naughty notions and made one more reason for him to be so obliging, as you put it, about sending me unannounced."

"And also one more reason to twist the damn leprechaun's nose," Braska grunted. "But I'll deal with him later. Where is Lucille now—still at the apartment?"

"No." Dolly shook her head. "All things considered, she figured she'd be better off going to the Palace, where there'd be a crowd around. Trouble is, part of that crowd is Kenna. He showed up there too. He's parked at one of the tables, waiting patiently like he said. Waiting and watching for you to make an appearance."

"Well then. Let's not disappoint him...move aside." Braska brushed past Dolly, took a seat on the edge of the bed, and began pulling on his boots.

"No!" Dolly protested. "That's exactly what Lucille *don't* want you to do. That's why she sent me to warn you. She said for you to forget about her saddle—whatever that means—and to just ride on and take care of your own business, not get caught up in new trouble here. She says she'll be able to handle Kenna okay on her own."

"Like I'm gonna leave it at that," Braska scoffed. He stood up and reached for his gun belt.

"I thought you were Mr. Cautious?"

"Bein' cautious and runnin' away are two different things," Braska snapped. "I was willin' to avoid Kenna to a reasonable degree. He just pushed it past reasonable."

"I told you I'm from around here. I recognize your name, know about your past trouble and where you just came home from." Dolly pinned him with a challenging look. "Do you really think it's smart to lock horns on your first day back with the town's chief deputy?"

Braska met her eyes as he returned the Colt to its holster now riding on his hip. "Ain't a matter of bein' smart, or even right or wrong. I see it as a matter of havin' stepped into the middle of something and not bein' willin' to ride off and leave it for somebody else to finish. Sounds to me like folks around here have been doin' too much of that where Marv Kenna is concerned...now you go back and tell that to Lucille. And tell her, too, that we'll still be takin' care of fetchin' her saddle come mornin'."

Dolly's mouth pressed into a tight, straight line and she turned to leave. Then she stopped suddenly and spun back around. "Okay. I need to get back for the next show anyway. I'll tell Lucille just like you said and I won't waste any more breath trying to talk you out of it. But are you too mule-headed stubborn not to at least listen to a suggestion that might help you keep from walking into a trap and maybe getting your head blown off in the first ten or fifteen seconds?"

Braska cocked an eyebrow. "I'm listenin'. Make it quick, and make it worth my while."

13

"OKAY. YOU'VE GOT A GOOD VIEW OF THE WHOLE main room from here," Dolly was saying. "Surely you don't need me to point out your pal Kenna plopped there at that table near the end of the dancers' runway, right? Normally, his sidekick—another deputy, name of McNally, who sticks to Kenna like stink on horse droppings—would be sitting with him. That's their special table, the one they always take whenever they come in and stick around to enjoy a show or two. Tonight, though, McNally has a different post, down on the other side of the runway, just below where the band is set up. He's the fella in the red shirt and black vest. See him?"

"I do," Braska confirmed. "That gives each of 'em a front-row seat for the show and also a clear line of sight on the front entrance."

"Uh-huh. And then there are those two human water buffaloes perched on elevated chairs to either side of the front door. They're our bouncers—Henry on the left, Marco on the right. They're technically in the employ of the owners, Martha and Frank, but any past time there's been trouble in here they're always mighty quick and willing to follow the lead of Kenna."

"Meaning," said Braska, "if he clued them in tonight that I was a troublemaker expected to be showin' up, then the pair of bouncers, along with Kenna and McNally, would've had me in a four-pronged pincer the minute I walked through the front door."

Dolly smiled somewhat smugly. "Which we circumvented by you accompanying me in through the much safer back entrance."

"Safer temporarily maybe," Lucille was quick to point out. "But not as safe as doing like I said and staying away entirely."

The three of them were peering out between the folds of a wide, thick, floor-to-ceiling curtain that ran across the back side of a narrow stage built at the rear of the Palace Saloon & Dance Hall's large, rectangular main room. They were huddled behind the curtain at the top of a short flight of steps that led from the back-stage area up to the stage level. The equipment for a three-piece band occupied a corner of the stage down from where Braska and the two girls were having their look-see. Jutting from the center point of the stage and extending twenty-five feet out into the middle of the room was a raised runway with a hard, polished wood surface. This was where, it had been explained to Braska, a six-girl chorus line—which would include both Lucille and Dolly—strutted out at regular intervals to perform their dance routines.

Rows of round-topped tables lined the runway on either side. More of the same were neatly arranged throughout the rest of the room. Off to the left of the front entrance was a long, ornate mahogany bar backed by a wide mirror and glass shelves displaying a colorful variety of bottled liquor. Two bartenders decked out in bowties and silk top hats were busily pushing drinks. On the other side of the room was a roulette wheel and, tucked into a semi-private alcove of sorts, four gaming tables with a cone-shaded lamp hanging low over each one. Out in the main room, everything was bathed in a brighter, silvery glow cast by concentric rings of gleaming chandeliers suspended high from the ceiling. Reveling under these was a crowd of forty or so customers ranging—as judged by attire—from cowboys and freighters to store clerks and businessmen and a few shifty-looking characters it was hard to put a stamp on.

All in all, Braska couldn't help thinking, it made for quite an impressive display and one hell of a contrast to the Buffalo Wallow. When he said as much, Lucille replied, "This is a relatively slow night. You ought to see it when things are really jumping." She was dressed very much like Dolly, in a snug costume cut revealingly low in front with a slit skirt exposing shapely, mesh stocking-encased legs. It wasn't that long ago that Braska had gotten a memorable view of her minus *any* attire, but somehow, seeing her gussied up in this manner was stirring in a whole new way.

Trying to keep his mind from straying too far off course, he stated, "It's clear all this showiness has a lot of appeal, but I reckon the Wallow suits my taste good enough. I prefer doin' my drinkin' where it's peaceful and quiet."

"Don't that kinda contradict you coming here then?" asked Dolly. "You didn't look like somebody setting out for peace and quiet the way you were so quick to strap on that gun belt."

"No contradiction," Braska countered. "Drinkin' ain't what I'm here for."

"And neither is showing good sense," Lucille interjected. "Damn it, you don't need to get involved any deeper in this. I've been holding Marv Kenna at bay this long, I can continue doing so 'til I'm ready to pull foot out of here myself. Dolly told me your history, how you've just returned from a prison hitch that had its own questionable back story. Kenna isn't worth the risk of you getting caught up in something like that all over again. Plus you heard what else Dolly said about him having the added edge of being backed up by McNally and our two bouncers. And don't forget, no matter how much of a loathsome, bullying pig he might be, he's still plenty mean and vicious all by himself!"

Braska grinned a wolf's grin. "Sounds like the makin's for something I'm plumb in the mood for."

"Then you're a stubborn fool! Maybe locked up is where you belong."

"Could be," Braska allowed in an easy drawl. "Then again, thanks to Miss Dolly here, maybe I've got an edge of my own to back up that mood I mentioned."

Dolly's brows pinched together. "I'm almost afraid to ask...but what did I say or do to rate that?"

"For starters," Braska replied, "you kept me from bargin' in through the front door straight into four sets of waiting fangs. Ten or fifteen seconds without gettin' my head bit off—remember? Instead, you introduced me to this back stage area and, along with it, provided me a handy little tool called the element of surprise."

Dolly and Lucille exchanged looks. Lucille

remarked, "You brought him, you'll have to do the interpreting."

"It's simple. Now I have the chance to—" Braska started to say.

But, before he could finish, he was cut short by the appearance of a stout, elderly woman with orange hair piled high atop her head and bright red lipstick rimming an oddly tiny mouth set in a wide, fleshy face caked thickly with makeup. She came marching into the backstage area and announced in a loud voice, "Okay, everybody, time to get ready for the next show. Five minutes. You band members, get out on the stage and start warming up. You girls, powder your noses and make sure everything is tucked securely in place. Remember, we tease a little but only show some legs and twitching fannies. The rest is left to the imagination—I don't want anything popping free that ain't supposed to be, like seems to keep happening from time to time."

She was dressed in a flowing, sequined blue gown with outrageously padded shoulders and a scoop neckline that barely restrained two massive, conical breasts, which—it appeared to Braska—tested to the limit her concerns about the potential for things *popping free*.

"That's Martha Buckner, our boss, and we just received our usual show prep orders," whispered Dolly. "We'd better go get powdered and tucked, like she said."

Right about then, Martha's gaze cut to the three of them up by the curtain. "What are you doing up there, Rosie and Dolly? And who's that man with you?" she demanded.

"He's, er, my cousin. My cousin Virgil," Dolly

answered. "He just got into town and I was showing him around where I work."

"Well let him have his look from the other side of the curtain—where he can pay for a couple drinks and earn his right to see the sights," snapped Martha. "Back stage is for employees, you know that."

Without waiting for a response, the orange-haired woman wheeled around and hollered, "Where's Maizie? I don't see her anywhere...she damn well better not be late again and delay the chorus line from going out. Somebody find her!"

While Martha and some of the other girls scurried in search of Maizie, Lucille said to Braska, "She's not really as bad as that might have seemed. She's like a mother hen to us girls."

"Mother hen?" he echoed. "A different critter is what came to my mind. I was thinkin' I might have met her sister once—a she-grizz I tangled with up in the Colorado Rockies."

The two girls laughed, but Braska didn't see it as too much of an exaggeration. Then they were off to powder their noses and otherwise prepare for their show set, leaving him on his own without him ever having gotten the chance to finish telling them about the element of surprise he had in mind. Oh well, they'd find out soon enough when he set it in motion. Between now and then, however, his main concern was staying out of Martha's way.

He found a good spot for that by standing quietly in a pool of shadows beside and partly behind a large clump of tall, outdated stage scenery leaning against the wall a few feet off to one side of the steps that led up to the stage. In addition to providing a place to go unno-

ticed for a while, it was in close proximity to a side door
that not only led out to the main room of the saloon but
—if Braska's distance estimations were correct—opened
just a few feet down from the table where Marv Kenna
sat alone. Given this, the way Braska had it figured was
that as soon as the chorus line pranced out onto the
runway, in those initial moments when all eyes in the
place would be automatically drawn to the appearance
of the gals, he would slip out that side door then glide
over and take a seat right beside Kenna in a move so
unexpected and bold it would surprise him and his
gawking cohorts clean out of their boots.

14

EVEN THE MOST CAREFULLY LAID PLANS SELDOM GO without a hitch. But this hastily formulated one of Braska's was that rarity where everything went right like it was supposed to.

"Evenin', Marv," Braska drawled, just loud enough to be heard over the rhythmic tap and click of the dancers' high heels on the hardwood runway surface just a few feet away. He spoke as he was settling onto a chair at Kenna's left elbow.

The deputy's first reactions were looks of surprise and then brief puzzlement flooding over his face before his expression locked into a fierce, angry scowl. "What the hell you think you're up to?" he growled.

"Just keep your hands on top of the table where I can see 'em, and we'll have ourselves a real nice discussion about that," Braska told him. "Mainly, I'm here to be accommodatin' and to spare you wear and tear on your bad knee."

"Why would I need any accommodation from the

likes of you?" Kenna snapped. "And what bad knee are you talkin' about—I got no such thing."

"Maybe not yet," Braska said with a smile as thin as a razor slash. "But you feel that pressure point suddenly against the side of your leg? In case you don't recognize it, it's the muzzle of my Colt, held under the table where nobody can see. What it's tellin' you is that if any noise I don't like comes outta the hole under your nose, or if you try signalin' any of the compadres you got posted around the room, then a .44 slug is gonna leave that muzzle and blow your kneecap into pieces of bone and gristle no bigger than kernels of corn. Now wouldn't you call it pretty damn accommodatin' of me to provide that warning?"

The band continued to play and the girls up on the runway continued to dance. So far, nobody seemed to be paying any particular attention to Braska having joined Kenna at his private table. Lucille and Dolly no doubt took notice from up on the runway, but they were disciplined enough not to show any outward reaction or let it disrupt keeping in time with their dance routine.

"You're a dead man," Kenna hissed, eyes blazing.

"Then unless you believe in ghosts, you got no worry," Braska replied dryly.

"What is it you want!"

"Right at the moment," Braska said, noting through the swinging, kicking legs of the chorus dancers that McNally had suddenly spotted his presence, "I want you to motion off your red-shirted deputy across the way and make him plant his ass back on a chair before he gets himself—and you—hurt."

Kenna hesitated only a second before he began frantically waving his arms in mannerisms signaling

Stay away! Keep out of this! A befuddled-looking McNally wasn't very quick on the uptake, but he finally got the message and, reluctantly, sat back down. His retreat, however, did nothing to erase the suspicious frown from his face or take the iciness out of the glare he now fixed on Braska.

"You just made a dangerous new enemy," said Kenna.

"He can take his place at the end of a long line."

"Don't count on it. He ain't exactly a patient man— Nor am I, especially not the way you keep stickin' your nose in my business!"

Braska regarded him with a flinty gaze. "Seems to me you've been mighty patient about goin' and re- claimin' your property that I left off at the marshal's office for you. The gun you swore you was gonna use to kill me with. Remember? Instead, you hid out on this end of town countin' on Rosie to be your bait for lurin' me to where you had plenty of backup."

"I don't need backup for the likes of you!" Kenna protested.

"Don't you now? Then why have you got 'em lined up three deep behind you?"

"I can't help it if I got friends and there are law- abidin' citizens of Piney Flats who just naturally have rightful concerns when a known troublemaker and ex- con shows up in town."

"Pig shit. I doubt you ever had a genuine friend in your life." Braska's lips peeled back disdainfully. "And the *real* law-abidin' citizens of this town are ashamed to have a slob like you representing 'em with that badge Elmer Coggins was stupid enough to pin on you."

"Maybe that's something you oughta be takin' up with ol' Elmer hisself," Kenna sneered.

"I did. Leastways the shell of what *used* to be Elmer Coggins."

This response seemed to embolden Kenna, rekindle his anger. "Then it sounds to me like you're kinda shit outta luck, bub. And my patience with you stickin' your nose in my business and shovin' your face up in mine is growin' damn thin!" His voice grew in volume to where it was starting to draw increased attention, even as the band and the dancers shifted un-affected into a new number.

Braska gouged harder with the Colt's muzzle. "I warned you about bein' careful what comes outta that mouth of yours. You figure you're still gonna talk so tough while hoppin' around on one leg?"

Kenna ground his teeth. "Then say what the hell you want from me. What's your aim with all of this?"

"My aim is to remind this town what every school boy should be taught before he's dry behind the ears—how to deal with a bully. Because that's all you are, you tub," Braska snarled. "A big blowhard of a bully who nobody ever took the time to deflate with a good, solid belt in the mouth!"

"And you figure you're man enough for the job?" Kenna challenged, a dangerous glint flaring in his slitted eyes.

"One way to find out," Braska responded. "You up for it? Plain old ground and pound, rough and tumble, just the two of us outside somewhere. No guns, no knives, nobody else mixin' in. Otherwise—fists, teeth, bootheels—anything goes."

"Sounds like my kind of game. What're the rules for who's left standin'?"

"If it's me—"

"It won't be."

"If it's me," Braska continued, "then I'll drift on like I intended all along. What becomes of you in that case, I reckon will be up to the town."

"And *when* it's me still standin'?"

"Reckon that'll be up to you and Elmer. Don't expect you can muster up grounds to slap a hangrope on me, but short of that, I guess I'll have to take my chances."

Kenna bared his teeth in a cold smile. "I'll be sure to make it something real entertaining."

"So it's on, then?"

"Just name the time and—"

Braska didn't wait for him to say any more. He thrust suddenly to his feet, pointed his Colt straight up, and triggered three rapid-fire rounds into the ceiling. Cries of alarm rippled through the crowd, pieces of plaster and wood slivers spilled down from the punctured ceiling, and the band and dancers abruptly halted their performance.

Into the tense quiet thus created, Braska said, "Pardon the noisy interruption, folks, but me and Deputy Kenna have a big announcement we want you all to hear. First off, take careful note of this hogleg I'm now wavin' close to his head. That's to make sure nobody gets over anxious"—here he cut a meaningful glance over at McNally—"and takes a potshot at me before you find out what this is about."

"For Chrissakes, just listen!" implored Kenna, his eyes nervously following the bore at the end of the

Colt's muzzle that seemed to be staring menacingly back at him.

"Some of you know me, some of you don't," Braska continued. "But the thing is, see, me and Kenna plumb don't like each other. It's a private beef, not a legal one. So we've decided to settle our differences in an old-fashioned knuckle and skull dust-up. No weapons, nobody else hornin' in. Just the two of us, out in the middle of the street until only one of us is still on his feet...tell 'em, Kenna."

The big deputy stood up slowly. A low buzz of excitement was building around the room. He swept a glare to all sides, and when it came back to Braska, there was fresh outrage simmering in it. Braska recognized plainly what it was. Kenna hadn't expected this. When he'd so readily agreed to fight Braska, he'd been envisioning a side alley or back lot somewhere. An out-of-the-way spot where—if need be, no matter what he'd outwardly agreed to—he could call on an assist from McNally or one of the bouncers. Now, with this public announcement and calling for it to take place right out front and right away, he'd been snookered into having no recourse but to see it through without delay.

Biting out the words through clenched teeth, he said, "Ain't much I can add. Smith said it all. We're gonna hammer out our differences, just the two of us, and everybody else stay out of it!"

With the excited buzz building, a well-groomed, middle-aged man wearing a bowtie and a swallow-tail suit coat strode rather officiously to the center of the room. Making sweeping gestures with both arms, he said, "Okay, everybody. You heard 'em. I don't want to have anything more busted up in here"—this with a disapproving glance up at the bullet-pocked ceiling— "so let's take it outside. I'm closing up until after the fight, then we'll open the doors again. You can take your drinks out with you, but make sure the glasses and pitchers get brought back where they belong!"

Braska concluded this dapper gent must be Frank Buckner, husband to orange-haired Martha and thereby co-owner of the Palace. In any case, his instructions and accompanying gestures got prompt results. Looking anxious and even downright eager in many cases, customers began leaving their tables and bar stools and flowing toward and out through the front door. Braska allowed himself to be carried along with the tide but made sure to stay behind Kenna so he could keep both him and McNally within his range of vision. Somehow, which was hard to believe considering their hulking size, he lost sight of the two bouncers, Henry and Marco. Not so surprising was also losing track of Lucille and Dolly. He'd heard and seen a couple of the chorus girls squeal in alarm and go darting backstage to escape any fighting that might break out—but he knew darn well that such timid behavior didn't fit either of his gals. They'd show up, they were just temporarily lost in the crowd.

Outside, the evening air was crisp and refreshingly clear of the cigar and cigarette smoke just exited. As the Palace throng poured out onto the street, those comprising it seemed to almost instinctively spread out to form a wide, loose circle. Fortuitously, there were two street lamps—one on either side—in close proximity, making the center of the circle relatively well-lighted. Also, half a dozen or so patrons had carried out lanterns, which, when held high, added a bit more illumination.

As if magically transported, Frank Buckner suddenly appeared in the middle of the street circle and began officiating much as he had on the inside. "As previously stated and as defined by the combatants themselves," he began, "the rules for this contest are simple. No guns, no knives, no weapons of any kind nor involvement by any other party. Other than that, anything goes—until one man yields or can no longer rise to his feet. Is that understood and agreed to by each of you?" He looked first to Braska then Kenna and received nods and affirmative grunts in response.

"Very well. Then all that remains is for you both to shuck your gun belts and rid your persons of any additional weapons. Once you've done that...you may proceed."

Braska unbuckled and stripped off his gun belt. He took the jackknife from his pocket and removed the bone-handled hunting knife from its sheath. These he wrapped within the coiled cartridge belt, then looked around for some place to put the bundle.

Suddenly Lucille was before him, holding out her hands. "I'll hang on to that for you, if you want."

"Might mean takin' hold of more trouble," Braska warned her.

"That seems to be what we do for each other."

Braska gazed into her eyes for a long beat before putting the gun belt in her upturned palms. She clutched it tight, then abruptly stretched up and gave him a quick kiss. "For luck," she whispered huskily.

Braska felt his ears burn while at the same time mentally kicking himself for not being quicker to lean *into* that kiss.

"Reckon I'll pass on the smoochin' part. But I'll still toss in a wish for good luck."

Braska and Lucille turned to find the gambler Myles Stark standing there, wearing a wry smile.

On the other side of the circle, Kenna had handed off his gear to McNally and was now rolling up his shirt sleeves, revealing corded forearms and fists the size of wagon wheel hubs.

Noting this, Braska said dryly, "I'll take all the good luck wishes you care to toss my way."

"All I ask," Stark added, "is that next time you give me some advance warning so I can get a decent bet laid down."

15

Braska had Kenna pegged as likely employing a bull-rush style of fighting. And it turned out he wasn't wrong.

They advanced on one another, circled warily for a handful of seconds, and then the big deputy charged! At the last instant, however, he threw in an unexpected wrinkle. As he hurtled forward, he swung his right leg up with blinding speed and thrust it out ahead, the toe of his boot digging hard into Braska's left thigh. This not only hurt like hell, but it tipped Braska slightly to one side and put him immediately off balance—so that when the bulk of Kenna came ramming into him, he was driven back and knocked to the ground.

The crowd of onlookers reacted with a loud groan of dismay, taking this as an indication the fight might turn into a quick, lopsided victory.

Braska spat out a curse. If the crowd was dismayed, how did they think he felt getting so promptly dumped on his ass? He had a bigger worry than wounded pride, however, when a second feature of Kenna's fighting style became quickly evident. That rushing kick was just one example of how he liked to use his feet. When he had a man down, he became hell-bent on keeping him that way by trying to stomp him plumb into the dirt!

Having landed flat on his back, Braska looked up in time to see this attempt coming. He twisted his shoulder and hip and rolled to one side, barely ahead of Kenna's downward slamming size twelve. The deputy issued a loud grunt of effort and spurts of dust shot out all around the edges of his foot as it hammered the rutted street.

Braska rolled again. While he was still in motion, Kenna didn't hesitate to kick at him with his other foot and came within a hair's breadth of battering the side of Braska's head. Then, windmilling his arms and cussing in frustration, the lawman *leaped* after Braska and came down in a double stomp that produced an impressive cloud of dust but accomplished nothing else. If the intent of the act hadn't been so brutal, it might have been almost comical to witness.

From Braska's perspective, still on the ground and having barely escaped getting his head kicked off or his ribs crushed, there damn sure was nothing comical about the attack he was enduring. And Kenna clearly wasn't done yet. He was re-setting his balance and advancing for more.

Braska went into another roll. But this time, he turned over only as far as onto his stomach, where he stopped and scrambled to get his hands and knees under him. Kenna loomed in close and started to draw his foot back for a head kick. Braska clambered desperately from knees to feet, balling into a low, tight crouch. When Kenna's foot was pulled all the way back and ready to slash viciously forward, Braska came out of his crouch like a compressed spring suddenly released.

He rammed the top of his head hard and deep into the pit of Kenna's stomach. A great gush of air whooshed out of the big deputy, along with an exclamation of surprise and pain that sounded something like *"gawp!"* as he doubled forward over Braska's back. Braska kept driving into him, feet digging and churning. He was unable to straighten all the way up, however, with Kenna's weight sagging down on him. He lurched and staggered to one side, then the two of them toppled down in a tangle.

Determined not to get caught on the ground again, Braska flailed free and shoved quickly back to his feet. With balled fists held at the ready, he spun around to face the also rising Kenna. Kenna seemed to lurch slightly and was sucking loudly to try and regain some breath, but he too had his fists up and ready The faces and shirts of both men were already smudged and heavily streaked with dust. The voices of the onlookers were a low, steady background drone.

The two men circled briefly, then lunged at each other to trade a flurry of blows, most of them blocked or partially ducked, none doing any serious damage. Although Braska did get in a couple more solid punches to Kenna's gut. The deputy had him by twenty pounds or so, but too much of it was fatty softness around the middle from excesses of greasy food and beer. Braska, on the other hand, was all whang leather and barbed wire. Nobody got fat on Hellstone gruel and burned coffee, and day-to-day survival in the prison yard hardened body and mind in other ways.

Kenna suddenly came in another rush, leading once more with a thrust kick. This time, Braska was ready. He leaned in and swatted the pistoning leg away to one side with a sweep of his right hand. Straightening up and twisting his upper body, he then swung that same right—a fist now—in a chopping backhand blow to the hinge of Kenna's jaw. Continuing to twist his torso, he followed instantly with a left hook to the same spot. The crunch of gristle and bone and splitting teeth could be heard clearly.

Kenna spat blood and staggered on rubbery legs. Braska went after him.

But he got reckless, a little too cocky, and waded into a jarring roundhouse that Kenna had waiting for him. This halted him, rocked him back on his heels. When Kenna tried to follow up with a jab that was too slow and pawing, though, Braska managed to slip in under it. He hammered more punches to Kenna's middle, and then, when the deputy started to double forward, Braska timed a beauty of an uppercut that sent his opponent backpedaling wildly.

Kenna fought valiantly to maintain his balance and, for a moment, seemed like he was going to get an assist when he staggered up against the nearest of four horses who stood tied to a hitch rail out front of the Palace. Unfortunately, grasping desperately at the animal's saddle in an attempt to steady himself caused the horse to suddenly shy away in alarm, not only spilling Kenna to the ground but actually pitching him in under the critter's belly. This put the deputy in the precarious situation of squirming amid the shifting, skittering hooves of the first horse as well as the one next in line!

An outburst of combined gasps sounded from the encircling crowd.

This was heightened all the more by the murky shadows underneath the horses and the dust haze being stirred up by their feet, making Kenna virtually disappear from sight. One of the onlookers holding a lantern hurried in closer, extending his light to better provide some illumination. Suddenly, Kenna's head popped into view as he came to his feet between the first and second animal.

Now Braska moved closer, calling, "You might be a horse's ass, Kenna, but that ain't enough to keep you hidden in there very long. Come on out and take the rest of what you got comin'!"

The reaction that got from the crowd contained a good deal of whooping and taunting laughter.

Menacing anger gripped Kenna's face and he snarled in response, "You damn betcha I'm comin' out, convict! And you're gonna be mighty sorry when I do!"

Then, cursing and swatting savagely to scatter the animals apart in order to give him a clear path, he came barging out. But he wasn't empty-handed. In his right fist, he gripped a coiled lasso that he'd stripped from one of the horses. Heading straight for Braska, he swung this back and forth in front of himself in hard, slashing motions that chewed the air with a throaty buzz not unlike the sound of a crosscut saw ripping apart wood.

Braska checked his advance and dropped into a slight, guarded crouch, balancing on the balls of his feet. Kenna snorted. "Come on, tough nut. This may not be the hangrope you deserve, but one way or 'nother, you're gonna get a taste of hemp this night."

Braska braced himself, waiting. He could taste blood in his mouth and feel grainy bits of sand crunching between his teeth. The thigh that had received Kenna's initial kick was throbbing, threatening to cramp.

Kenna bulled forward once more, swinging the coil of coarse rope from side to side as if brandishing a sword. Braska held his position, eyes locked intently on the movement of the lasso. He was counting on his speed being a shade faster than Kenna's and thereby giving him a chance to time it so he could slip inside one of those swings, nullifying its effect, and then instead do some damage of his own. Two problems got in his way. One, he underestimated Kenna's speed. Two, he misjudged how much-added reach the coiled rope provided.

When Kenna lunged, Braska juked to one side and darted inward. But the lasso whipped up and across faster than he was ready for and a thick bunch of the braided strands whacked a hard blow high to his left shoulder and against the side of his head. By design, a lasso is a thick, stiffened length of rope that—especially in coiled form before being shaken out to cast its loop— has considerable heft. Enough, in this case, to knock Braska sideways and send him staggering.

As Braska fought to get stopped and re-balanced and was turning back around, Kenna swarmed all over him. He swung the coiled rope forehand and backhand, using it like a club, landing punishing wallops that raked Braska's face and kept him reeling.

But then the big deputy got too carried away, too

eager, and—by crowding in closer than he should have —gave Braska the opening he'd failed to gain on his own. When Kenna swung the lasso in a wide, wild roundhouse, Braska threw himself forward, slamming tight against Kenna's chest. This caused the fist gripping the coil to overshoot, missing another telling strike to Braska's head and face and instead only slapping down with little consequence onto his broad back. Simultaneously, with their noses only inches apart, Braska took the opportunity to draw his head back and then ram it forward in a mouth-smashing blow of his own.

The two men broke apart, each staggering. From his mangled lips, Kenna spewed blood and a string of curses. Braska dragged a hand down over his face, wiping the stinging sweat and blood—from the numerous scrapes left by the lasso strikes—out of his eyes.

The excited rumbling of the crowd was steadily increasing in volume.

As if urged on and fueled by this, the combatants again clashed together. This time, Braska got his own grip on the lasso, and there ensued a twisting, turning, in-close tug of war. Part of this included much kicking and kneeing of one another and additional head-butting attempted by both men, though none of it landing with as much impact as Braska's first strike.

In the course of all this, the lasso became uncoiled and each man found himself holding several feet of loosened rope. These were then doubled into shorter lengths that they began using as shirt- and flesh-tearing whips. The crowd, working itself into a near-blood frenzy now, howled for more.

Kenna's extra belly weight, on top of Braska's

relentless attack, was taking a serious toll. He was dripping sweat and blood and sucking wind hard. But the bullying bastard was stubborn and tough, nobody could deny him that. Even though Braska had begun forcing him steadily backward, he was still dangerous and determined. This paid off in a sudden and unexpected way when he made a desperate slash with his rope-whip that slipped through Braska's defenses to lay open a short but deep cut just above his left eye.

With blood gushing down, essentially blinding him in that eye—plus delivering the instinctive jolt of panic that any person experiences when their sight is put at risk—now it was Braska who began backing up. Kenna, naturally, was re-energized by this and leaped at the opportunity to gain even more advantage. He did so by temporarily abandoning the whip-rope attack and resorting to a barrage of kicks and punches that a half-blind Braska had limited chance to ward off. He absorbed impacts until his knees sagged and he could barely lift his fists.

Reacting to this, Kenna picked that moment to bring the lasso back into play. Skirting around behind Braska, he created a foot-and-a-half of slack in the rope that he gripped tight between his fists before jerking it down over Braska's face and back against his windpipe. Raising a knee and planting it square between Braska's shoulder blades to establish a pressure counter-point, Kenna threw his full weight back and yanked the strangle cord deep into Braska's throat.

This drew another loud reaction from the onlookers, this time including a strain of sharper concern for what they were seeing.

Already battered and weakened, Braska knew he

couldn't last very long with his breathing choked off. Desperation can create an adrenaline surge to both body and mind. Propelled by such a surge, Braska fought and clawed frantically to break free from the fix he was in. After gouging bloody furrows in his neck trying to get his fingers in behind the strangle cord, he gave that up as hopeless and changed tactics. Reaching with both hands up and back above his head, he clawed and pounded at Kenna's face. But he had no proper leverage to be effective, and the combination of exhaustion, blood loss, and lack of air was badly draining him. He had to come up with some way to break Kenna's grip and come up with it fast, Braska told himself, or he was going to be done for.

What he came up with was ears. At almost the exact same instant, each of his blindly reaching, grasping hands closed around one of Kenna's ears. Closed around and clamped on tight. With all the strength he had left, Braska realized what he had to do, what he had to execute immediately as the only chance he had left.

Since his knees were already buckling and Kenna was already dragging him down, it was easy enough for Braska to simply relax his full weight and drop his rump to the ground. Refusing to release his grip on the strangle cord and essentially standing on only one foot due to having a knee raised and planted in Braska's back, this sudden shift tugged Kenna forward and down, overbalancing him. Adding to this momentum, Braska jackknifed forward at the waist and simultaneously yanked as hard as he could on Kenna's ears. Where the ears go, the head must follow. As a result, Kenna was pulled the rest of the way off balance and into a front somersault over Braska's shoulder that left him sprawled on his back.

With the strangle cord gone from his throat, Braska's first instinct was to gulp big mouthfuls of breath. But at the same time he was keenly aware that he had shed himself of Kenna for only a matter of moments. The fight was far from over and he remained decidedly the worst for wear. But then he got a badly needed break. Momentarily disoriented as he scrambled to stand back up, Kenna first rolled over onto his hands and knees. This inadvertently placed him facing Braska with his head no more than six inches from Braska's feet. Without a second's hesitation, Braska cocked back his leg and drove a boot heel full force to the middle of Kenna's forehead.

The big deputy's head got driven back and he was sent rolling away with a yelp of pain and surprise. Partly from the force of the blow and partly from purposely wanting to get clearer of Braska, Kenna added an extra turn or two to his roll—carrying him all the way to one of the lantern holders who'd ventured close in order to cast some better illumination on the two men when they were locked in their stationary struggle. To his misfortune, the lantern holder proved too slow to jump back out of the way before Kenna plowed into him and knocked him off balance, spilling him to the ground. From there, misfortune made a leap and transferred itself to Kenna when the dropped lantern landed on him, shattered, and coal oil spilling from the reservoir and soaking Kenna's shirt sleeve was ignited by the still burning wick.

Shrieking in terror, Kenna flung the former lantern holder off him, leaped to his feet, and ran, waving his flaming arm, for a nearby water trough. Seeing this, Braska was lifted to his own feet by a fresh surge of adrenaline and immediately raced after Kenna. He caught up with him right after he had plunged his arm into the contents of the trough, quenching the flames, and was pulling it back out. Despite the initial terrifying moment, it was quickly evident Kenna had suffered no serious burn damage. Based on that, though it may have seemed mighty cold reasoning to some, Braska felt no compunction to give quarter nor discontinue the fight. After all, if the circumstances were reversed, he didn't have a whisker of doubt that's how Kenna would have looked at it—just like he'd shown no sign of letting up on the choke rope.

Having made his decision, Braska spun Kenna around and laid into him with a barrage of rights and lefts. When that had him sufficiently stunned, he twisted him back around and locked an arm over the back of his neck in a reverse headlock. Cinching this tight, he bent him down and shoved his head into the water. The old saying *hold 'em under 'til the bubbles stop coming* ran through his mind as he kept him there. He also reflected once again on how far Kenna would go if it was the other way around.

But killing had never been part of tonight's plan. Not Braska's, anyway.

He leaned back and lifted Kenna's head. "Say you yield!" he demanded.

Spitting and sputtering, Kenna responded, "Go to hell!"

Back under his head went. After he'd held it there a little longer this time, Braska lifted it again. "Say it."

"Never!"

When Braska shoved Kenna's head down for a third time, he held it there so long the crowd of onlookers began rumbling and squirming nervously, fearing they might be witnessing a murder.

But the third time proved to be the charm. Gasping, choking, half-sobbing when his head was at last lifted, Kenna managed to rasp, "Enough...I-I yield."

The crowd heaved a collective sigh of relief.

Braska released his hold and let Kenna collapse to the sodden ground beside the trough. Standing over him, chest heaving, Braska raked a glare from his good eye across the circle of faces staring back. "There. It's done," he said. "I just beat somebody you all had a hand in allowin' to ride roughshod over you for too stinkin' long. He didn't go down easy, I'll give him that. But steppin' aside for his like only ever reaps more abuse... you do the same again, you'll get what you damn well deserve."

With that, he pulled a wilted hanky from his hip pocket and started turning back to the trough with the intent of wetting it so he could use it to clean the caked blood from around his cut eye.

In mid-turn, he was halted by these words: "Freeze right there, mister, and keep those hands up where I can see 'em. I'm placin' you under arrest." This came from Reese McNally, stepping forward with a six-gun held at waist level and trained on Braska.

The crowd was quick to grumble in protest and Frank Buckner didn't hesitate to give their noise a singular voice. "Hold on a minute, McNally! That was a fair fight in accordance with the arrangements agreed to up front. Including by Kenna. Knuckle and skull, no weapons and no interference by—"

"Did you see anybody interferin' with the fight?" McNally cut him short. "I'm talkin' about after all the fight was out of Marv and this damn ex-con, this proven killer, tried to drown him! I'm callin' that attempted murder, and I don't intend to let it stand!"

"That's a dirty lie, you gutless weasel, and everybody here knows it! Now stop this nonsense and drop that gun, else I swear I will drop you!"

This declaration came from a new voice—that of Lucille Devry, also stepping forward and also holding a gun. The gun was Braska's .44, pulled from the holster of his gun belt and extended at arm's length, aimed dead center on McNally.

McNally took note of this with a sidelong glance. His initial look of concern vanished quickly and he issued a disdainful snort. "Put down that gun, you crazy bitch. Before you hurt somebody and get your own self tossed in a jail cell."

He barely got that out before Myles Stark, standing not far to one side of Lucille, took his own step forward. One moment he'd been standing motionless, the next his nickel-plated .45 was in his fist and also trained on McNally. "I suggest," he drawled calmly, "you take heed to what the young lady said, and do so very quickly. What's more, an equally hasty apology for your coarse language is in order as well."

McNally looked incredulous. "Are both of you plumb loco? Do neither of you see this badge pinned to my shirt?"

A response to that came from yet another added voice. Shouldering his way through a knot of onlookers, Marshal Elmer Coggins appeared with a sour look on his face and a double-barreled shotgun in the crook of his arm. "I see that badge," he said to McNally, "and I'm damned sorry for it. Sorry I'm the one responsible for puttin' it there and, most of all, sorry for allowin' it to stay for so long. Goes double for the one on Kenna."

McNally's expression gave way to a scowl. "What're you sayin', Marshal?"

"For starters, I'm telling you—and you other two as well—to put away those goddamn guns before me and this gut shredder show you some real firepower."

The pistols were promptly re-holstered.

From where he lay, Kenna pushed up on one elbow and managed a battered scowl of his own. "Now what? What else are you sayin', Elmer? And shouldn't you be back down on your nice, quiet end of town?"

Coggins gave him a flinty-eyed look. "No, that's where I've kept hunkered too much of the time for too long. Like Braska said, doing my part in allowing you two to run roughshod. Keeping my head in the sand, you might say." For the first time in a long time, Coggins's mouth showed a wolf's smile. "Well, my head's up now, and the sand is out of my eyes. And I don't want to use 'em seeing the pair of you shaming those badges—and me—any longer. In other words, you're both fired."

Silently looking on and listening to all of this, Braska's mouth gradually curved into a pleased, somewhat bemused smile.

Spitting and sputtering indignantly, Kenna argued, "You can't fire us, we got contracts!"

"Which each of you has violated seven ways from Sunday, right from the start," the marshal countered. "If you really want to go down that road, I figure I can present examples that'll convince the city attorney in about five minutes. That should effectively wipe out any back pay owed you and maybe make you subject to some fines...otherwise, you can turn in your badges now and in the morning, on your way out of town, stop by the office to collect any wages you got coming."

PART TWO
TRAILS TO
TULAMORO

16

When Braska rode away from Piney Flats the next day, he was not alone. Lucille Devry rode alongside him, mounted on the same sleek black mare he'd first seen her on the previous day at the swimming hole. She had purchased the animal—along with the saddle she and Braska made a swing to retrieve—from the livery stable where she'd previously been renting it for her periodic rides out into the countryside.

After his brawl with Marv Kenna, following a local doctor providing some cursory treatment and closing the cut over his eye with a handful of stitches, Braska had given in to the insistence by both Lucille and Dolly that he spend the night at their place where they could further comfort and care for him. He'd put up some token resistance, but, after all, it wasn't like Kenna had hit hard enough to knock the good sense out of him. There was a limit to how much pretending a fella could do *not* to want such care offered by two pretty gals.

In the morning, over a hearty breakfast of ham and eggs, was when Lucille sprang her notion of riding off with him. It was trotted out half as a question and half as a statement of intent. "Your little speech last night about how everybody played a part in letting things get out of hand set me to thinking," she said. "I kept saying I wanted to get away from Piney Flats, but at the same time, I kept finding excuses for not leaving. In other words, playing a hand in holding myself here even though I'd reached a point quite a while back where I *could* have pulled foot like I claimed I wanted to.

"But now, after last night, even with Kenna out of the picture, I figure I've burned my bridges here, making it time to move on. And since you're also fixing to move on, I figure I could travel with you for a ways until something turns up. We get along okay and we've even sorta stuck our necks out for each other...shouldn't be a problem. Right?"

Before Braska could begin to form any kind of answer, Dolly had chimed in, saying, "Lucille knows how much I hate the thought of her leaving. But, at the same time, I knew all along that this day would come. And now it has. The only good thing"—and here she pinned Braska with a very direct gaze—"is that, if she leaves with you, I know she'll be safe."

Braska flushed under that look and those words. "In case you ain't noticed, things don't exactly stay peaceful and quiet around me. And since I'm purposely settin' out after my lowdown skunk of a brother who's rumored to be runnin' with a bad bunch, a big change don't seem to be loomin' on my horizon any time soon."

"I didn't say there wouldn't be trouble. I said I counted on you to keep her safe," was Dolly's flat response.

Braska felt pinned down. His gaze cut back and

forth between the two women. Then, locking on Lucille, he said, "I got two questions for you. Would you really have shot McNally last night if neither Stark nor the marshal had stepped in? And have you ever even fired a gun before?"

She met his gaze with a steady one of her own. "Yes. And yes."

Braska gave it a beat, then said, "Okay. We can give it a try. But if we reach a place where circumstances become such that I say you need to ride off...will you listen?"

A corner of Lucille's mouth quirked up. "That makes three questions...but yes, I'll do as you say if it comes to that."

Given the preparations necessary before heading out—stocking up on supplies, making the deal on Lucille's horse, fetching the errant saddle, and so forth—it was nearly noon before they were actually on the trail south. Part of this included Lucille taking time to say goodbye to the Buckners and some of the chorus line girls she'd been working with. Martha Buckner and Dolly sobbed at these farewells, and even dapper Frank looked like he had a bit of a lump in his throat. It spoke well of a person, Braska thought, to be thought of so fondly by others.

He took time to say a farewell of his own, stopping in to see Elmer Coggins before pulling out. "Sorry if my kickin' over the apple barrel left you a mess to clean up," he told the old marshal. "But I stand by dumpin' out those rotten apples as not bein' a bad thing."

"I got no argument for that," Coggins replied. "Your kick to the barrel was also the kick in the pants I needed to quit feeling sorry for myself and remember who I am.

And—no matter what I said before—remind myself what this badge means and what I want to leave behind when I give it up."

"Just *keep* remindin' yourself."

Coggins cocked an eyebrow slyly. "Maybe you ought to stick around a while and make sure I don't forget again. Happens I've got a couple deputy positions open."

"Nice try, you old fox," Braska replied with a wry grin. "But you know I got obligations elsewhere."

"Could be that's something better left alone. If you don't, it might end up tearing a worse hole in you than what you're already carrying around now."

"Not sure that's possible," Braska allowed. "But what I *am* sure of is that I can't hold off makin' the attempt to find out."

As the sun reached its peak in a cloudless sky and then gradually began its downward slide, the afternoon heat climbed contrastingly higher. Braska set a reasonable pace, one he knew Savvy could maintain easily. What he needed was to test Lucille's mare, though, and get a feel for what she was made of. She had good lines and a sturdy look, but it was over four hundred miles to Tulamoro if Lucille stuck with him all the way. Braska was familiar with some of the terrain they'd be traversing, but not all of it. It wouldn't all be as easy-going as these rolling, grassy plains of southern Nebraska and the initial portion of Kansas they'd be angling through, he knew that much.

They pushed on steadily, eating lunch in the saddle —ham sandwiches packed for them by Dolly—and stopping only a couple times to water the horses and give them a breather. As they rode, Braska kept an eye on

Lucille's mare and was pleased to see that she showed every sign of holding up well. The same was true of her rider. Lucille sat her saddle with easy, natural grace and handled her mount expertly.

Having had no chance to wash the articles of clothing that had gotten dunked in the creek yesterday, Lucille was attired today in a split riding skirt, chocolate brown in color, and a lemon yellow blouse with a matching neckerchief. In other words, she made a damned fetching sight to look upon. Glancing her way from time to time, Braska couldn't help grinning a little when it crossed his mind what a vast visual improvement she made over any previous saddle mate he'd ever ridden with, while working cattle or during his soldiering years...not to mention—it also crossed his mind, somewhat guiltily—the breathtaking sight she made minus any attire at all.

By Braska's reckoning, they'd crossed over into Kansas when he signaled a stop for night camp. The spot he chose was a clearing atop a low, rounded hill with some pine growth and a few sparse trees surrounding it. The pines curled inward around the northwest edge, providing a good break in case a wind worked up during the night, and the trees provided fuel for a fire. There was plenty of good graze for the horses and even a twisty little ribbon of a stream down at the base of the hill.

While Braska tended the horses, Lucille got a fire going and set some coffee to brewing. Then she sliced and fried some potatoes to go with the last of the ham Dolly had sent along. After they'd eaten, they leaned back against their upturned saddles with cups of brown sugar-laced coffee and talked while the darkness thickened around them and the stars overhead grew brighter in contrast. Braska fashioned a cigarette and smoked. The purplish-black discoloration encircling his injured eye took on an especially ghastly appearance in the mix of shadow and throbbing firelight.

"If I'm not being too nosy or unless it's something too personal," Lucille eventually said, "I gotta ask about this *Braska* thing. How is it you call yourself that when everybody—at least a lot of folks around Piney Flats—know you as Virgil Smith?"

Braska smiled behind a cloud of exhaled smoke. "One of these days, I'm gonna have to come up with a real excitin' story to tell in answer to that question. In the meantime, the truth is pretty plain. It came about when I went off to join the Army and fight in the war, you see. When I reported for duty I got thrown in with a mixed bag of fellas from all over. As it turned out, there was four of us all with the last name of Smith, though none of us was related or knew each other from a hill of beans.

"Kelso, the crusty old sergeant assigned to whip us into a fightin' unit, was about as friendly and patient as a bear with a boil on its rump. Every time he went to holler *Smith!* at just one of us for messin' up and we all four came tangle-footin' in response, it just made him that much madder. So he quick decided to start callin' us something different, and you can bet it wasn't gonna be anything friendly-seemin' like our first names. So one who was tall and skinny became *Slim,* one who had red hair was naturally *Red,* and a third who was kinda stocky became *Fats.* That left me. Since I was just sorta ordinary lookin', Kelso was stuck for a minute on what to make of me. Then, when he asked me where I was from, and I said Nebraska, he declared that'd be it. I'd be *Nebraska*. That didn't last long, though, before he decided that was too much of a mouthful for cussin' out purposes so he shortened it to just *Braska*, and that's what stuck."

"Even after you came back from the war?"

Braska shrugged. "To tell the truth, I never was too crazy about *Virgil*. And I'd gotten pretty used to *Braska* by then. So you might say I, er, strongly encouraged others to start usin' one over the other."

"I can imagine how you did that," Lucille said, giving him a look.

Braska just shrugged again.

After a pause, she added, "I have to agree, though, that Virgil doesn't suit you. And you want to know something else?"

"What's that?"

"You really do need to come up with a more exciting story to explain why you made the change."

―――

AT A DIFFERENT NIGHT CAMP SOME MILES TO THE west of Piney Flats, two men sat cross-legged beside a crackling campfire. Each held a cup of steaming coffee, the already stout-brewed mud laced with something considerably stronger than brown sugar.

"New Mexico," Reese McNally chuffed. "Why the hell would anybody—less'n he had a posse chasin' him or some such—light out for that godforsaken sprawl of burned sand and cactus? And, if that was the case, he might as well cut all the way to the border and cross over into Mexico itself."

"It don't matter *why* Smith is doin' whatever he's up to," Marv Kenna grumbled in response. "All we needed to know was that he'd left town and which way he's headed. Our business with him will be concluded long before he gets very far, no matter what."

"Providin' we can cut his sign and catch up with him. Way Marco told it, he set out cross country—not by no stage route or main trail."

Kenna scowled. "So what? You always claimed you was an experienced tracker, didn't you?"

"Well, yeah. I scouted a fair amount for ol Square-head Brittles durin' the war," said McNally. "But scoutin' and readin' sign left by whole bodies of men is a heap different than trackin' just two riders in open country. I ain't sayin' I can't, mind you, I just might be a little rusty is all."

"It'll come back to you." Kenna took a sip of bitter coffee. "In my time, I've dogged a few trails myself. If, between the two of us, we can't run down that pair with only a half day's start, then we don't deserve to catch up and get our payback."

"And there's something else. The *pair* of 'em, like you just said. What do you suppose made Smith and that dance hall floozy—who, as far as anybody can tell, never laid eyes on each other before—all of a sudden take a notion to ride off together?"

"Who the hell knows. You ever see a woman yet who all the way made sense?" Over the rim of his cup, Kenna glared narrow-eyed into the fire. "In this case, though, their combined odd behavior serves to favor our cause in more ways than we'd've dared hope. For starters, if that snooty Rosie hadn't gone around sayin' goodbye to some of the other dancers and mentioned

New Mexico as where they were settin' out for, then Maizie wouldn't have known to pass it on to Marco so he could tell us. The second thing is that havin' 'em together gives us the sweet chance to settle two scores instead of just one."

"But the main score to settle," said McNally, "is still with Smith for that humiliatin' beat-down he gave you. Right?"

"It wasn't a beat-down, dammit!" Kenna snapped, one hand lifting involuntarily to a bruised and swollen cheekbone. "The sonofabitch got lucky, that's all. And even then, I'd've finished him if that idiot with the lantern hadn't set me on fire!"

"A-course, Marv. Everybody saw that. I didn't mean for it to sound otherwise," McNally was quick to respond.

"If you want to see a beat-down," Kenna said, his mouth pulling into a grimace, "wait 'til you see what I do to that bastard when we catch up with him. You might have a hard time bein' able to tell from what's left, but he'll be toes down by the time I'm done, I guarantee it."

"What about the girl?" McNally asked, his eyes turning glassy. "You gonna work her over too?"

Kenna gave him a look. "Not the way you mean— not how you like to work your women over. But that don't mean our gal Rosie ain't gonna provide us some sport. That little tease has been dodgin' me for too long —now she's gonna damn well give up what I been after. You can have a turn too, as long as you don't get carried away like you're inclined. With her looks and body, if we keep her in decent condition, I know some brothels in Denver or up in the mining camps where we can make a profit handin' her over when we're tired of her. But nobody'll pay if she's all busted up by one of your fits. Understood?"

"Okay, okay. You don't need to keep lecturin' me," McNally sulked. "I ain't done none of that in a long time."

"No, you haven't. And that's good," Kenna allowed. "But we both know you have trouble holdin' back sometimes. And we also know things go better when you keep it in check. That's all I'm sayin'."

"And I'm sayin' I got the message. You don't have to keep harpin' on it."

They sat and drank coffee in silence for a few minutes.

Until McNally asked, "What about Coggins? We get done settlin' with Smith and the girl, we gonna do any dealin' with that ungrateful old bastard for firin' us like he done?"

Kenna pressed his lips together, considering for a moment, before answering, "Tempting as such a notion is, I reckon it's best we leave him alone. Especially after a public firin' in front of so many people. Runnin' down these other two no-accounts out here in the middle of nowhere is one thing. Not hardly gonna be noticed by nobody. But anything was to happen to the marshal after tanglin' with us so recent-like, our names would be mighty quick on the mind and tongues of too many folks. Maybe even cause a US Marshal to get called in to do some huntin' for us." Kenna shook his head. "No, it ain't worth the risk of possibly callin' that much wrong attention to ourselves. Besides, without you and me there to handle the town's rowdy element, how long you wonder before that ol' mossyhorn Coggins waddles into the path of a knife blade or a bullet and somebody else will have took care of dealin' with him for us."

"Hey, I like the thought of that." McNally's mouth curled into a nasty smile. "I like the thought of it a lot."

Kenna drained his cup. "Good. Then you can go to sleep and dream about it. We better turn in now and grab some shuteye so we can get an early start in the mornin' for pickin' up the trail of those two. Might even be that by this time tomorrow night we'll have caught up to 'em."

"Hey. I like the sound of *that* even better yet!"

17

Next morning, after breakfast, Braska sat smoking and sipping a final cup of coffee near the dying embers of the campfire. He was studying a set of maps he'd gotten from the newspaper office in Piney Flats. The sky was once again clear and bright, the air cool at the moment but shaping up to turn into another hot day.

Lucille came walking over from where she'd just finished packing away their mess gear. Against the morning briskness, she'd added a light jacket to her attire.

"I kept out that salve the doctor sent for the cut above your eye," she announced. "You probably ought to let me apply some before we start out."

Braska made a face. "I'd as soon pass. When I start to sweat later on, that goop will run down in my eye and make it sting worse than the cut does."

"You could always dab it off then if you needed to. In the meantime it can help the cut to heal."

"The cut's doin' fine. I can tell. But I'll compromise

and put some of the goop on when we stop at the next camp. It's healin' powers can work overnight while I'm sleepin'. How's that?"

Lucille sighed. "I suppose it's the best I'm going to get out of your stubbornness. How do you feel otherwise?"

"What do you mean?"

"I mean it's only been a little over twenty-four hours since you and Marv Kenna whaled the tar out of each other so—"

"I whaled the tar outta *him*," Braska corrected. "I was the one left standin'. Remember?"

"Okay, Mr. Technical. But I also remember the bruises and welts all over you that Dolly and I helped Doc Powly patch up afterward. And then you were in the saddle for hours yesterday afternoon. So, even though your black eye is fading remarkably well, I was merely trying to be polite by inquiring about the other aches and pains I figured you must still have. From now on, I won't bother to give a damn."

Braska promptly adopted a sheepish look. "Okay. I deserved that—the scoldin', I mean, for snappin' at your courteous inquiry. Thank you for carin'. Though I hate to admit it, yeah, that doggone Kenna left me more than a little stiff and sore. But it'll fade, just like the black eye. In the meantime, though, come night camp this time around I can pretty much guarantee I'll be doctorin' my coffee with something stronger than brown sugar."

"Just as long as you aren't planning on being too stingy with it," Lucille said. "I may not have visible welts and bruises, but following just half a day of steady riding, I could surely feel it when I climbed out of my bedroll a little while ago. I can only imagine what it will be like after a full day."

Braska grinned. "Little bit different than a couple hours' ride out into the countryside, eh?"

"So I'm finding out."

"We can turn around and I can take you back."

"You trying to get rid of me?"

"Not at all. But after another day or so, accordin' to what it shows here"—Braska brandished the map he was holding—"we're gonna hit a stretch where there ain't gonna be no towns, leastways not none big enough to appear on this, where you can turn back *to*."

"Nobody's talking about turning back but you. I didn't start out expecting this to be no picnic," Lucille replied, displaying her own stubbornness. "Like I said, just don't be stingy with that coffee adder and excuse me a few moans and groans until I get the kinks worked out. Do that, and watch me keep up just fine."

Braska nodded. "In that case, let's quit burnin' daylight and get a move on."

———

THEY RODE STEADILY THROUGH THE MORNING, stopping only once to water the horses and walk them for a ways. Braska set a pace similar to yesterday's, maybe a tad more aggressive now that he had a feel for the capabilities of Lucille and her mare. Not knowing how rugged the terrain might turn once they got farther along, he wanted to take advantage of Kansas's and eastern Colorado's rolling, relatively flat landscape for as long as it lasted.

His planned route, based on his limited first-hand

knowledge and the maps he'd been studying, was to angle across the northwest tip of Kansas and then proceed down through eastern Colorado at a slightly lesser angle before dropping into New Mexico. All he knew for sure after that, since he would be in unfamiliar territory and the maps he'd been able to get hold of were somewhat outdated and lacking certain details, like not even showing Tulamoro, for example, was that the town lay off to the east of the Sangre de Cristo Mountains and somewhere north of a place he'd heard of, a notorious hellhole called Los Mecos. Once they got in closer—but not too close to Los Mecos, Braska hoped —he figured on being able to get the necessary final directions to Tulamoro.

The day grew hot, as expected. They stopped for a leisurely lunch in a patch of deep shade under a cluster of leafy trees. A faint, welcome breeze began stirring out of the west. Boding to be less welcome, however, was the smudge of dark clouds off on the western horizon that the breeze seemed to be pulling along with it.

"That breeze feels mighty good," said Lucille, tipping her head back to fully expose her long, graceful throat to the cooling currents of air. Then, tipping her head back down after a minute, she added, "Those storm clouds off in the distance don't look so appealing, though."

"Not to us maybe," allowed Braska. "But the land hereabouts sure could use some rain. All we've been travelin' over has been awful dry."

"Farmers and ranchers are always saying that."

"That's because the whims of Mother Nature carry a powerful lot of sway over their lot," Braska told her.

"Take those clouds off yonder, for instance—no matter how much a rancher seein' 'em hopes they might bring some much-needed rain, at the same time he knows dang well they might drain out before they ever get here."

"Well, not to wish any bad luck on anybody, but I'll admit that the selfish part of me hopes they *do* drain out before reaching us."

Braska shrugged. "Either way, we'll be okay. I outfitted you with a new rain slicker and a waterproof soogan like the one I carry. Plus I packed a roll of light canvas that'll make a serviceable tent if need be. We can weather anything short of a tornado."

"If you say so," replied Lucille, eyeing the distant dark clouds. "But I'll still hold out hope for no rain reaching us."

————

"YEAH, THEY NIGHTED HERE SURE ENOUGH," declared McNally, kicking at the ashes of a cold campfire. "Big, deep bootprints of the Smith hombre all around, and smaller, shallower ones left by the girl. It's for certain the two we're after."

Glancing upward at the sun nearing its noon zenith in the sky, Kenna muttered, "If they got an early start from here, though, that still puts 'em near a half day ahead. Damn. I'd hoped we would've closed more than that by now."

"We're still in pretty good shape," McNally argued. "It took us a while to pick up their trail to start with, remember. Now we're locked on. And I'm bettin' we can push harder and steadier than them."

"Yeah, there's that," Kenna allowed, his scowl lessening some. "They got no reason to suspect anybody's doggin' 'em, so they'll probably even stop for lunch and the like. We'll eat ours in the saddle. And Smith havin' Rosie with him is bound to slow him in general. Hell, she ain't cut out for trail life—not with her havin' done nothing for the past months but shake her ass in a dance hall. She'll soon find out that bouncin' it on the back of a nag for hours on end is something a whole lot different."

"Yeah," agreed McNally, wincing slightly. "Truth to tell, I'm experiencin' a piece of that myself. Patrollin' the streets of Piney Flats, mostly on foot the way we been doin', has sorta made my own tailbone forget any friendship it ever had with a saddle."

"Try gettin' used to it again just a few hours after you been punched and stomped and half set on fire," grumbled Kenna. "But that makes all the more reason to hurry and catch up with those two. Gettin' my hands on Smith again and doin' what I aim do to him this time is gonna feel so good it'll erase a whole heap of other miseries. And then how good Rosie's gonna feel when it comes her turn...that'll be like frosting on the cake!"

"Yeah...frosting," McNally murmured, his eyes once again taking on that glassy look.

"C'mon, let's ride!" Kenna urged.

Neither man seemed to notice the smudge of dark clouds creeping up above the western horizon.

18

DESPITE ALL OF LUCILLE'S HOPES TO THE
contrary, the rain did not dissipate before reaching her
and Braska. It came on slow but steady all afternoon,
preceded by a sooty gray cloud cover that first blotted
out the sun and then grew denser until it hastened the
early gloom of evening. Next came a light mist, eventually giving way to a cold, constant drizzle that showed
every sign of settling in for a while.

Well provisioned for bad weather though they
might be, when the rain started coming down heavier,
Braska was caught somewhat at a loss for the means to
fully brace against it. He broke out the rain slickers
immediately, of course, but beyond that, the empty,
wide open terrain offered nothing in the way of even
the most meager bit of natural shelter—a cliff face or
flat-sided hill, a rock outcrop, a scrubby lone tree—
anything he could use to set up against. He was beginning to think they'd have to settle for laying down their
horses and then spreading the soogans and the light tarp
in between the grounded animals.

But then, stubbornly plodding on a ways farther, scanning ahead and to all sides through the relentless drizzle, he came to the blunted crest of a shallow bowl and gazed down into it at one of the prettiest sights he'd ever laid eyes on. Below, weed-choked and with tilted walls and a partially collapsed roof, stood a battered old abandoned cabin.

Braska dragged a palmful of rain off his face and declared, "Welcome to the Hotel Paradise."

"Sure looks like it to me," agreed Lucille, reining up alongside him. "We going to opt for a whole suite, or just settle for a standard room?"

"Hell, I feel like celebratin' whole hog," Braska said. "We'll lay claim to the entire joint—leastways all that still has a roof over it."

Lucille laughed. "Complete with room service and a hot bath!"

Braska clapped his heels against Savvy's sides. "C'mon. Let's get down there."

It was only after they'd nearly reached the dilapidated old structure that Braska saw, through the blurring rain, a wisp of smoke trailing up from the chimney and the faint glow of light through a burlap-covered window. Checking down his buckskin, he held out a hand to signal the same from Lucille. Over his shoulder, he said, "Looks like we ain't the first guests who've shown up."

"I'm willing to share space with a yak if it gets me in out of this rain."

"Just stay in the back of me a bit until I get a feel for who's in there," he told her. Then, sweeping back his slicker to access the Colt on his hip and slipping the keeper thong off its hammer, he rode up and again halted Savvy, this time about a dozen feet from the crookedly hanging front door. Off to one side stood a high-wheeled, half-canopied wagon but with no sign of a pulling team. A corner of Braska's mouth lifted wryly as Lucille's remark about being willing to share space with a critter crossed his mind, she just might have to back that up.

"Hello the cabin!" he called in a strong voice. "We're a pair of friendlies out here—lookin' for a place to get in out of the rain."

There was no verbal response, but the glow behind the burlapped window quickly faded.

Braska called again. "I have a young woman with me. Like I said, we're friendly travelers unlucky enough to get caught in this storm."

After a pause, the door creaked open far enough to allow the barrel of a musket to be extended out. A male voice, young-sounding, a lad roughly in his early teens, spoke. "We be colored folks in here...young'uns and a granny woman...we let you in, you won't be after kickin' us out, will you?"

"No, of course not. We're meanin' no harm nor seekin' none in return." Braska's brows pinched together. "Makes no never mind to us whether you're black, white, or polka-dot."

There was another pause. A second voice, muffled and unintelligible, spoke from deeper inside. Then the musket barrel withdrew and the youth called, "All right. Come ahead on."

Braska motioned Lucille up beside him. The two of them dismounted and tied their mounts to an upright post that was the only remnant of an old hitch rack. After smoothing down his slicker but keeping his hand inside the fold, resting lightly on the grips of his Colt, Braska led the way inside.

They found themselves in a square, moderate-sized room. Off to one side, where it would have extended into a larger, more rectangular space but where the roof had caved in, some past occupant had hung up a heavy canvas sheet to section off the damaged portion.

Off to the opposite side, within the habitable part, there was a fireplace with a meager fire burning in it. Close beside it was a tiny, wizened old Negro woman perched in a sturdy-looking rocking chair that Braska judged was a proud possession she had brought in with her. Sitting on the floor at the feet of the old lady were two children—a boy and a girl of about five, maybe six, clearly twins. The children and granny were all draped in colorful quilts against the damp and cold. Across from the old woman, also situated up close to the fire, a grown man lay on a crude pallet with more quilts covering him. And though his ebony face shone with drops of sweat, his lips were trembling and he was shivering visibly, even with all the blankets piled on him.

In the middle of the room was a rickety table with a lone candle flickering atop it, providing weak illumination along with the flames in the fireplace. Standing beside the table, eyeing Braska and Lucille closely as they came through the door, was a tall, skinny, chocolate-skinned lad of fourteen or so dressed in baggy, many times-patched clothes and heavy work shoes at least one size too large for his feet. A pair of wire-rim spectacles with very thick lenses perched on his nub of a nose and he was still holding the musket, though down at waist level in a non-threatening manner.

"We be the Traverses," he announce once they

were inside and Lucille had pulled the door shut behind her. "I'm Ansel. Over yonder be my sister and brother—Reba and Ralston, they twins. In the rockin' chair is Grannymaw, my pap's mam. Layin' there in the blankets is my pap, Clevon Travers. We be headed for Greely, Colorado, where my pap's brother is holdin' a good job for him so's we can make a fresh start after the passin' of our ma."

Braska lifted his hand off his Colt and eased it out from the fold of the slicker. He and Lucille bobbed their heads to all, expressing *pleased to meet yous*. Braska introduced themselves in turn and then added, "We regret bargin' in on you folks, but at the same time are mighty grateful you opened your door to us."

"Only Christian thing to do," stated Grannymaw.

All during the introductions, Lucille had been studying Clevon Travers with obvious concern. Not one to hold back for very long, she leveled this worried expression on Ansel and said, "I'm sorry to pry, but your father is clearly in a bad way. Has he been injured in some manner—or is he ill?"

Ansel looked almost relieved at the interest and the inquiry. "He gots the malaria. He catched it as a young man workin' in the Loosyanna swamps," the boy explained. "Mostly it don't bother him much, but every once in a while, a spell of it comes back on him."

"He a Travers. He tough. He'll get through it okay, just like always," said Grannymaw.

Ansel gave her a sidelong glance, looking like he didn't want to contradict her but at the same time lacking her same level of blunt confidence.

"Don't you keep any medicine on hand for it? Quinine or some such?" asked Braska.

Ansel hung his head. "We runned out."

And then the little girl, Reba, suddenly chimed in with high-pitched, childlike indignity. "And the mean people in town wouldn't help Ansel neither!"

"No they wouldn't—the meanies!" added her brother with a fierce scowl.

"Hush up, children," admonished Grannymaw.

But Braska had heard enough to work up a pretty good scowl of his own. "What's that all about?" he wanted to know.

Ansel had trouble meeting Braska's gaze. "They's a town not far. We don't got much money, so I took what we had and also some stuff I hoped to trade. Pap's spare rifle, his good Sunday boots, three of Grannymaw's fine hand-sewn quilts—the kind folks back home is always eager to buy. I was hopin' to get some medicine for Pap and maybe some bread and tins of fruit for the little ones. We got plenty of hardtack and jerky to eat, see, but it's hard for their little teeth to chew, so they don't take enough to keep 'em strong and growin' like they oughta. When Pap ain't sick, he's a good shot and is able to bag fresh meat regular-like, so that makes the difference." He twisted his mouth ruefully. "But me, with my bad eyes, I can't hit nuthin'."

"So what happened when you went to that town?" Lucille prodded.

Ansel hung his head again and wagged it slowly back and forth. "They runned me off...on account of me bein' colored. Wouldn't even listen to what I wanted or had to trade. Said if they catched me comin' 'round again, they'd cut off my ears and feed 'em to they hounds 'fore they sicced 'em on me."

Lucille's eyes flashed. "Those dirty lowdown—"

"Take it easy, there are toddlers listenin'," Braska warned her.

She checked her words and pressed her lips into a tight, straight line. At the same time, her nostrils flared wide and Braska half expected steam to come out of them.

Determined to help Lucille finish what had gotten interrupted, little Reba said, "Those people be dirty lowdown meanies—ain't that right, missy-ma'am?"

Lucille smiled at her. "Yes, they are, honey. Dirty lowdown meanies who somebody"—here her eyes flashed anew as she cut a sharp gaze over at Braska— "needs to teach some manners."

"That might could be arranged," replied Braska in a low voice, his flinty gaze meeting Lucille's fiery one. "But first things first."

"Meaning?"

"Meanin' a more immediate need strikes me as bein' to work up some better heat in here and to get some food into the bellies of those kids." Braska turned to Ansel. "How come you got such a puny fire goin' in your fire-place, son? Even if the rain stops, it's gonna stay damp and get considerably colder before the night's over."

"I taken our axe and chopped up as much wood and brush as I could find on the outside," the boy answered. "I was workin' on a couple ol' fence posts when the rain came. Since then, I been tryin' to nurse along what fuel I'd got in ahead."

"What about all this clutter?" Braska asked, sweeping a hand to indicate the array of broken-down old furniture and cabinets scattered about. "You got all kinds of fuel to chop up and burn."

Ansel's eyes widened. "Lordy. They be the belongin's of whoever lived here past. White folks likely. I didn't figure I had no right to—"

"Whoever lived here before is long gone. Probably dead," Braska cut him off. "And most of this stuff is only fit for burnin' anyway. So you got my permission to go to work with that axe and stoke up a good, hot fire for the benefit of your family."

Turning next to the old woman, Braska said, "Out on our horses, Grannymaw, we've got a couple well-stocked grub sacks. Bacon, beans, biscuit fixin's, coffee, and several airtights of fruit along with some embalmed beef that'd make a good broth for your son. Was we to bring those sacks in, it sound like something you could make a feed out of?"

"'Deed so. 'Ceptin' us Traverses don't hold with charity," came the response.

"I understand. But Ansel has explained that you *do* barter. So tell me this—I bet you whip up some mighty fine pan biscuits, don't you?"

Grannymaw displayed a wide, toothless smile. "Child, I make biscuits so light an' tasty they pract'ly float right off the plate an' up to yo mouth."

Braska nodded. "There's our trade then. You get to make use of those provisions for a family feed, and I get a promise that I'll have a heap of fresh biscuits and a pot of coffee waitin' for me when I get back."

Ansel looked around, halting a swing of his axe. "Back from where?"

"From the town you spoke of," Braska answered flatly. "I'm headin' in to get your pap some medicine... among other things."

To which Lucille quickly added, "Just don't think you're going alone."

19

THE NAME OF THE PLACE, AS ANNOUNCED BY A signpost on its outskirts, was Blodgett's Crossing. It wasn't a town so much as what more accurately might be called a settlement—a handful of buildings clustered around intersecting trails. When first discernible through the murky rain, it was a clump of shadowy, angular shapes with smears of yellowish light that, upon drawing nearer, proved to be lantern glow showing through a scattering of windows.

Just beyond the signpost stood a sturdy-looking barnlike structure with a small corral out behind. Letters painted on the front of the barn proclaimed that blacksmithing and livery services could be found within. Next came five or six modest-sized houses sprinkled off to either side. It was still early enough in the evening so that light glowed in the windows of all but one.

The hub of the whole shebang, though, was a large, two-story wood frame building with a professionally painted sign high above its centermost door reading in big letters: *Blodgett's.* Down below, a smaller sign directly over the doorway said *Store.* Off on the right end of the main building, a one-story addition had a sign over its doorway identifying it as *Cafe.* A single-story addition on the left end was in the same manner labeled *Saloon.* The store windows were dim, signaling it closed to business for the day, but the lighted windows of both the café and the saloon indicated a different story.

As she and Braska drew rein before the layout, Lucille said, "So, do we flip a coin for which one to try first?"

"Not that I'm feelin' particularly friendly," Braska replied, "but I expect we'd find things more sociable and informative if we started in the café."

"Okay. Like you said, though, not because we're looking to make friends."

They dismounted and tied their horses to the hitch rail. Before going inside, Braska hesitated and regarded Lucille through the hissing rain. "You said you know how to handle a gun. Just in case things turn especially *un*-friendly in there, I got a spare six-shooter in my saddlebags. Think it might be a good idea for you to slip that in your pocket before enterin'?"

Lucille returned his look, her expression turning oddly uncomfortable for a moment. Then, smiling somewhat sheepishly, she said, "I think it would only be smart. It happens, however, I already have it covered." To demonstrate, she rummaged inside her slicker and produced a short-barreled pistol that she held out for Braska to see—a weapon he recognized as a Smith & Wesson model commonly called a *Baby Russian.*

"Where in blazes did you get that?" he wanted to know.

"Frank Buckner gave it to me before I left," Lucille answered. With an impish twinkle in her eye, she added, "I think he believed your intentions where I was concerned might not be entirely honorable."

Braska chuffed. "That fancified little turd. I ever run into him again, I might decide to give him a dishonorable cuff alongside the head."

"He was only thinking of my well-being."

Braska chuffed again. "If he really wanted to protect you, he should've gave you something with more firepower...though it *does* make a good hideaway popper for you, I guess."

"I wasn't trying to hide it from you or anything," Lucille insisted. "In fact, I was going to have you help me with some target practice when we stopped for camp last night. But I was too doggone tired to bring it up. Then tonight, this evening..."

"Well, just put it back under your slicker and hang on to it for now," Braska told her. "If things should happen to bust open on the inside, those'll be the kind of close quarters where it's well suited."

Once through the café door, steamy warmth and pleasant cooking aromas immediately washed over Braska and Lucille. It was a welcome transition from the cold and the damp outside, but not welcoming enough to offset their underlying moods fueled by knowing the kind of welcome Ansel Travers had received hereabouts.

There were five customers in the place. A man and a woman seated together at one of the tables, two men at another, and a lone man on a stool at the serving counter. Behind the counter was a hefty woman wearing her iron-gray hair in a severe bun except for a few stubborn strands having worked loose this late in the day. All present appeared middle-aged, clad in simple working-class attire, and wore the overall stamp of vague weariness to be found in many of their ilk. The flower pattern on the apron of the woman behind the counter made the brightest splash of color in the room.

Nevertheless, the greeting boomed out by the woman sounded sincere enough when she addressed the new arrivals as they stood just inside the door, taking a minute to shake off some rain. "Hello to you on this mean night, strangers. Take a seat when you're ready, and I'll fetch you steaming cups of coffee."

"Much obliged, ma'am. But we ain't stoppin' by for vittles or coffee," Braska countered.

The woman's eyebrows lifted. "Oh?"

"There happen to be a doctor of any kind in Blodgett's Crossing?"

"You're in luck. Indeed there is—Dr. Ross Pollard."

"That's good to hear."

"He's a very capable man who settled here right after the war and has been taking real good care of folks here and also on all the surrounding farms and ranches ever since." The woman studied Braska and Lucille. "You two appear sound. You have an ill or injured friend somewhere?"

"Matter of fact, we do," Braska answered. "Actually, he came to town himself earlier today. But he had trouble gettin' took care of by your real capable medicine man."

The hefty woman frowned. "That don't sound right —not unless Doc was away out of town at the time. But don't I remember him..." She let her words trail off and looked over at one of the men sharing a table. "Howard, you live right across from Doc Pollard. He go out on a call any time today?"

"Nope," came the answer. "His buggy never came out from under that lean-to beside his house. He didn't go nowhere until he came over here for supper a little while ago."

"See there?" the woman said, bringing her gaze back to Braska. "I can't figure how your friend could've missed the doc. How serious is he...what's his ailment?"

"Being colored," Lucille was quick to answer.

This left the woman looking quite befuddled. But the other man sitting at the table with Howard caught on right away. He was a tall, skinny number with long, dirty blond hair falling limply around a pock-marked face. The latter jerked up sharply at Lucille's remark and he said, "Wait a minute. Are you talkin' about that nigger boy who came around this fore noon?"

Braska cut the man a hard look. "Them ain't exactly the words I'd use. But yeah, I reckon we're talkin' the same."

"The same what?" the woman wanted to know. "What was it that happened?"

The man at the table waved a hand dismissively. "I don't know where you were, Malene. But, like I said, about mid-morning, this raggedy-assed nigger brat showed up beggin'—"

"He wasn't *begging*," Lucille broke in. "He didn't have a lot of money, it's true, but he was looking to back it up with other items he brought and was hoping to barter with. Also, just for the record, he wasn't in rags.

His clothes may have been heavily mended, but they were clean and not ragged."

The man at the counter turned his head and sneered, "Hate to think it of such a pretty gal as you, but bein' so quick with all those excuses makes you sound like nothing more'n a damn nigger-lover!"

Braska wheeled on him. "Mister, if you want to worry about bein' quick, then that's what you'd better be with a mighty sincere-soundin' apology."

"Damned if I'll apologize to any nig—"

That's all he got out before a whistling right hook from Braska lifted the loudmouth up off his stool and sent him crashing against the wall at the end of the counter.

The stool the man had been sitting on fell over with a clatter. The sound of frantically scraping chairs quickly joined in as the man and woman seated at the second table jumped to their feet and hurried toward the door. Over his shoulder, the man called, "I'll be by tomorrow to square up with you, Malene, but I won't keep Esther around the kind of trouble brewing here right now."

"That's all right. You do that, Jerome," Malene called after him as he and his wife scurried out the door.

From the kitchen area behind Malene, somebody else's exit—the unseen cook, most likely—was marked by the banging of a different door. It was further likely, Braska's instincts told him, that whoever it was was on the way to get some backup to help handle the *brewing* trouble here. Once he was sure the man he'd knocked down wasn't getting back up any time soon, Braska looked around and found Malane glaring at him with a smug glint in her eye that further convinced him help had been gone for.

Her lips curling back, she said, "In case you ain't figured it out yet, bub, you're about to learn how us in Blodgett's Crossing stick together—and none of us much cotton to coloreds."

"That's right, big man," crowed Pock Face, slouched back in his chair at the table. "And you're also gonna find out that sucker punchin' an un-suspectin' man off a stool is a lot easier than dealin' with the likes of Ike and Ferlin Blodgett!" Howard, the man at the table with Pock Face, hung his head and looked like he wished he would have skedaddled with Jerome and Esther.

In response to Pock Face's taunting, Braska smiled thinly and said, "In that case, maybe I oughta come over there and warm up some more on you."

"And maybe I'll grab a rollin' pin out of the kitchen and have a say in the matter!" threatened Malene.

This resulted in the Baby Russian suddenly appearing in Lucille's hand and her advising the hefty woman calmly, "Go ahead and try it, you cow. We'll see how many bullets it takes to knock loose that stupid bun you've got cranked so tight it must be squeezing off the blood to your brain."

Braska was as surprised as anybody by this move. His smile turning half bemused, he said, "Whoa, take it a little easy. I'd as soon do this without gunplay if we can. But as long as you got that popper out, keep it ready and make sure nobody tries comin' in through the back."

Moments later, the tromp of heavy boots outside the front door announced that the first wave of intervention was coming from there. Braska turned to face it, tugging back his slicker to access the Colt on his hip and thumbing off its keeper thong. The door burst open and two men crowded through. First was a stocky, somewhat paunchy individual with a bristly white mustache and a fierce scowl. Right behind was a younger version of him, only about three inches taller and minus the mustache and the paunch.

"What the devil's this I hear about strangers bargin' in and bustin' up the place?" demanded the older man in a booming voice that fairly rattled the windows.

Holding his tone in purposeful contrast, Braska said mildly, "Reckon you're talkin' about me. Only neither me or my friend did any bargin' in, nor did I bust up anything...except maybe the jaw of that fella layin' over there who didn't have the sense to not run his mouth and then not apologize when given the chance after he did."

"Who're you, and what was Jillson supposed to apologize for?"

Braska blinked lazily and maintained his mild tone. "If you don't mind my askin'...who are you to be makin' demands, and why should I feel obliged to answer 'em?"

"Who—who'm...*me*? Who am *I*?" The man's face swelled up and turned purple. He became so infuriated he couldn't sputter out words through his rage.

The younger man stepped around him, his own face red with anger. "This is Ike Blodgett, you idiot! He's the he-goose of this whole territory, and you damn well better show him the respect of answering anything he asks you."

"Who're you—Ike Jr.?"

"I'm his son, yeah. But Ferlin's the name, not Junior. Now enough of your damn questions—start coughin' up some answers. Who're you, and who's the cold-eyed floozy givin' me a look fixin' to earn her a backhand across the mouth?"

"Watch out for her, Ferlin," warned Pock Face. "She's a she-devil and she's got a gun!"

Ike had calmed down enough to get his voice back, at least a rasp that passed for same. He used it to say, "Any scum of the earth—man or woman, no matter— who pulls a gun on a Blodgett will dance on the end of a rope. I swear it!"

"Well, I'm your own sister, Ike," replied Malene through bared teeth, "and that bitch pulled a gun on me just minutes ago. On top of that, the two of 'em are nothing but nigger-loving white trash! I say you can't throw a rope around their necks quick enough!"

20

Malene's words and the sheer venom with which they were spoken froze everybody for a startled instant.

Until Braska broke into motion. In a lightning-fast lunge he closed the distance between him and Ike Blodgett, at the same time unleathering his Colt in a blinding flourish. As soon as he was close enough, he lashed out with his left foot—taking a page from Marv Kenna's book of fight tactics—and kicked Ike in the groin. When the recipient doubled forward with a yelp of pain, Braska grabbed a fistful of shirtfront with his left hand and used the man's momentum to yank him forward and around and then sling him staggering back toward the service counter.

Unwinding from this, Braska extended his right arm and whipped the Colt gripped at its end in a slashing backhand that laid the barrel hard along Ferlin's jawline. The younger Blodgett was knocked back into the knot of men—all coming from the saloon down at the other end of the building, Braska guessed—who had gathered just outside the doorway behind him. The knot parted under the hurtling bulk of Ferlin and he ended up toppling out into the rain and mud of the street.

Braska wheeled around and closed again on Ike, shouting to Lucille, "*Now* put your gun on the hag, and keep her pinned in place!"

Lucille responded by quickly, agilely vaulting over the service counter and ramming a shoulder against Malene before the hefty woman had a chance to brace herself. Next thing she knew, the muzzle of Lucille's revolver was shoved up under her chin and she was the one frozen into immobility. "Sorry I don't have a rope handy to return the favor of what you wanted to do to *my* neck," Lucille said, pushing her face close, "but I've got a little something else here that'll do the job on *yours*, if necessary."

Just as Braska was reaching to grab hold of Ike again, Pock Face made the bad choice to try and be a hero. Out the corner of his eye, Braska saw him thrust to his feet in order to get clear of the table and then claw for the gun he was packing. There was no time to hesitate or make any attempt at just winging the dumb bastard. Braska raised the Colt hanging loose at his side and fired, punching a bullet center mass and blowing a hole through the heart. Pock flew back and fell to the floor in a dead sprawl.

"God *damn* it, I didn't want to have to do that!" Braska swore. He finished his grab for Ike and hauled the groaning man violently to his feet. "You sorry old sonofabitch! It's the kind of poison spewed by you and your kind that twists the minds of others and keeps fannin' the flames of senseless hate—even at the cost of lives to help it continue burnin'!"

"You bet you're gonna know the cost of life soon enough—your own!" Ike spat back at him.

"If it comes to that," Braska growled, "an even safer bet is that you won't be around to see it!"

"Ike!" wailed Malene, feeling desperate enough to speak even with Lucille's gun at her throat. "Don't take any chances—these people are crazy!"

"Your sister's squawkin' good sense, Ike. You oughta listen," Braska told him. "We can finish this without any more killin'."

"You already crossed that line!"

"Only because he didn't give me any choice. You can make the choice to let that be the end of it."

"He's got friends who'll want to get even. I got no say over what they might do."

"The hell you don't! You're the he-goose around here, remember?" Braska jerked Ike around so they were both facing the front door. With his left fist clutching the back of Ike's shirt collar, he forced the man to stand full in front of him while his right hand lifted to press the Colt's muzzle to his ear. "If you can't stop those morons out there from turnin' trigger happy like their pal, then any lead they throw will have to go through you to get to me. Get the picture?"

"You *are* crazy!"

"Like I said, your sister was squawkin' good sense and truth all the way," Braska grated. Over his shoulder, he said to Lucille, "Stay behind the counter and keep Malene in front of you like I'm doin' with this one. If anybody tries the back, spin her that way."

"Got it," Lucille responded.

Now Braska locked his attention on the front door. "You men out there," he called. "Get Ferlin back on his feet and fetch him 'round to help negotiate this situation. Somebody fetch Doc Pollard, too. I said I don't want to do no more killin', but that don't mean I ain't willin' to do some persuadin' by shootin' off a couple pieces of your he-goose if I have to."

"He's bluffin', boys," snarled Ike. "He's already spent one round out of his six-shooter—he ain't gonna waste more just nippin' off pieces of me."

"You're startin' the negotiatin' with some bad thinkin' and bad advice, old man. Happens I got a fully-loaded backup cutter under this slicker," Braska lied, "and my lady friend has the same. That means I can nick you up plenty if I take the notion. And remember, if all else fails, it'd only take one bullet through this ear hole of yours to finish the job permanent-like."

There was some shuffling of activity in the doorway and then Ferlin staggered clumsily back into sight, hands reaching in from both sides to steady him. He was drenched and muddy, a bright red welt running the length of his jawline and a worm of blood crawling out that corner of his mouth. He fought to get his eyes focused on his father and Braska.

Dully, he said, "Pa...what do you want me to do?"

Braska pressed the Colt muzzle harder against Ike's ear.

Grudgingly, the stubborn settlement boss husked, "Tell everybody to hold easy for the time being. Let's hear what it is this...what these two scoundrels came here for."

"I ain't seen no doctor yet," Braska said impatiently.

There was another shuffling of bodies just outside the doorway as Ferlin edged aside to make way for a short, portly man wearing a rumpled frock coat and holding an umbrella. He handed off the umbrella to an unseen someone and took a tentative step inside. He took a second step and then halted to cast a concerned look over at the fallen form of Pock Face.

"You can't do him any good, Doc. He's dead. There's a still-breathin' one over here at the end of the counter"—this spoken along with a brief tilt of Braska's head to indicate who he meant—"sufferin' a jaw problem similar to Ferlin out front. You can worry about them later. But first, I need a quinine solution made up for an adult male sufferin' a relapse of malaria."

Pollard looked around. "Where is he?"

"His skin color don't allow him inside your city limits. You just fix up the quinine, I'll see he gets it."

The doc's eyes shifted and came to rest on Ike, looking uncertain.

"Go ahead if you got the makin's," said Ike.

"It'll take me a few minutes to prepare."

"Get to it then," Braska told him. "While you're doin' that, I got a list of some other stuff we'll need from the store. Listen tight to what I'm about to rattle off, then somebody go bag 'em up. And keep track of the cost. This ain't no robbery, I intend to pay. This whole thing could have been nothing more than some simple business transactions if all of you wasn't wallowin' in such a festerin' pocket of senseless hate..."

IN LESS THAN HALF AN HOUR, THE ITEMS BRASKA requested had been gathered and were ready. The clincher was a saddled horse to be ready out front in addition to the mounts Braska and Lucille had ridden in on.

"What do you need an extra horse for?" Ike had demanded in a surly, suspicious tone.

"Ain't the horse we're needin'," Braska answered. "It's the safe passage insurance it'll be carryin'...namely, Malene."

"No! No, damn you! You've put her through enough already with that stinkin' gun to her head. If you want a hostage, take me!"

Braska shook his head. "No dice. Takin' you would be too risky. You're salty enough to maybe try something on your own, or possibly Ferlin and the boys would even take a chance at tryin' to snatch you away. But with a woman, especially your own sister, I expect you'll make sure everybody stays real cautious and well-behaved and does exactly as I say."

Ike's face turned purple again, but this time, he managed to control himself enough to keep his sputtering mostly coherent. "You unspeakable cur...you harm one hair on her head, I swear I'll hunt you down and...and—"

"Save your breath, old man," Braska cut him off. "Save it to control yourself and the rabid pack you've gathered around you. Do that, and your sister *will* stay unharmed. Once my friend and me are in the clear, we'll turn her loose. But hear what *I* swear, every mother's son of you, and understand it loud and clear: You try to follow and make any trouble for us after this—for us, or for that colored family out on the plains—I'll come back here and burn this whole shit pile to the ground with your blackened bodies left layin' in the ashes!"

21

THE RAIN HAD LESSENED TO A LIGHT BUT STEADY drizzle by the time Braska and Lucille made it back to the cabin. Their departure from Blodgett's Crossing, with Ike's sister at all times under the gun of at least one of them, had gone without further incident. About a half mile out, with pinpricks of light still visible through the rain and dark to mark her way back to the settlement, they'd released Malene. They then rode a ways farther before Braska signaled a halt at a point where, from concealment atop a small knob behind a fringe of rock outcrop, they could look down on the trail from town without being seen by anyone approaching. They held there for half an hour before Braska was satisfied there'd be no immediate pursuit from the settlement, then they proceeded on to the cabin.

Upon entering, they were immediately assailed by the aromas of fresh coffee and biscuits—not to mention the welcome wash of warmth pouring from the crackling fireplace. After peeling off their wet outerwear, they wasted no time sitting down with cups of smoking coffee and a plate of still-warm biscuits sided by strips of crispy bacon. The anticipation and the promise of the aromas were met and exceeded.

While Braska and Lucille thus indulged themselves, Grannymaw administered a dose of the quinine to her son. She also announced that she'd earlier gotten him to take a good amount of broth and the warmth of the built-up fire had greatly diminished his shivering. The overall mood in the rundown little cabin was markedly brighter than it had been before. Grannymaw appeared much sprier than the first rocking chair-bound impression she'd made, the toddlers were beaming, and even the somber-beyond-his-years Ansel showed a couple of faint smiles. It made Braska feel good to see this, yet at the same time, it made the hate and bitterness he and Lucille had encountered back at the Crossing seem even uglier and sadder.

Not surprisingly, it didn't take long for questions to arise about what Braska and Lucille had encountered at said Crossing. Bold little Reba was the first to bring it up, asking Lucille, "Did you and Mr. Braska teach some manners to those meanies in town, missy-ma'am?"

"As a matter of fact, yes, we did, honey," Lucille assured her. "We scolded them very firmly and then Mr. Braska made sure that they, er, understood the error of their ways."

"What means *arrow of they ways*?" Ralston wanted to know.

"It means how they treated Ansel was bad and mean," Reba explained patiently, "and missy-ma'am and Mr. Braska told 'em not to treat nobody like that no more!"

"That's right," Lucille said. "And once they were

clear on that, then they were willing to provide the medicine your daddy needs as well as the other things Ansel went there to trade for in the first place."

Demonstrating this, she emptied out the bag of store goods Braska had demanded. Among these were tins of condensed milk for the children, some dried fruit, flour, salt, sugar, coffee and tea, a slab of bacon, and various other airtights of fruit and a couple more of embalmed beef.

The eyes of the children, and Ansel too, grew wide with delight at this display. But Grannymaw's reaction was considerably different. Looking at Braska, she said, "Not to sound ungrateful, but I 'splained before how us Traverses don't take no charity. We got nuthin' to trade that comes close to the value of all that."

"Well now, Grannymaw," Braska replied, choosing his words carefully, "maybe—with all due respect— you've got to stop and reconsider the worth of certain things."

Her eyes narrowed suspiciously. "Meanin'?"

"Well, for starters, you're allowin' me and Lucille to spend the night under this roof with you all instead of leavin' us out in the wet and cold. If we was to go back to the settlement or some town and rent a couple rooms, it'd surely cost us money. So there's worth in the hospitality you're allowin' instead. See? And Ansel choppin' a bunch of wood to make the heat we're soakin' up. There's worth in that. And if he was to put our horses away in that lean-to out back with your wagon mule and save us havin' to go back outside and do it ourselves, there'd surely be worth in that. And these biscuits of yours that are the best I ever ate...another batch of those again tomorrow, some for breakfast and also some we can take in our grub sack, there'd sure be worth in havin' them as part of our next couple trail meals."

"And your beautiful quilts," Lucille said, stepping forward and getting caught up in the pitch Braska was making. "It sure would be worth plenty having one of those in each of our bedrolls on these chill nights."

"We better hold off and weigh this out before we go much farther," Braska said with exaggerated seriousness. "We don't want to talk ourselves into bein' on the short end of the trade we're lookin' to make."

The skepticism earlier in Grannymaw's eyes had now turned into a bemused twinkle that she shifted back and forth between the pair before her. "You two," she said, lips pursed in her own display of exaggerated seriousness. "You a coupla scamps, ain't you? Thinkin' you can so easy outfox an ol' granny woman."

"Ain't a matter of anybody lookin' to outfox anybody. Not at all," Braska countered. "We just want to see you and your family get some of the things you need and not offend your pride in the process."

Grannymaw's mouth pursed tighter as she considered. She glanced over at the children, lingering on their hopeful faces over the tins of milk and the dried fruit spread before them. Returning her eyes back to Braska and Lucille, she said, "I take back callin' you scamps. You just plain good peoples, that's all. Sumpin' we ain't hardly runned 'cross since we set out from home. Which is why I had trouble reckanizin' it when it showed...makin' it all the more reason to let my stubborn, sometimes foolish pride bend a mite. For the sake of these chilluns, and in the face of simple goodness."

Braska and Lucille exchanged looks of relief. Wide

smiles spread across the faces of Reba, Ralston, and Ansel.

"But only," Grannymaw was quick to add, "if you two hold up your end when it comes to stowin' away a heap more of my biscuits come mornin' and then packin' off another heap in your grub sack. And pickin' out any two of my quilts that catches your fancy."

"Done and done," declared Braska.

"And that also means you hoppin' to tend their horses, Ansel. Don't forget that part."

"I surely won't, Grannymaw."

Braska got to his feet. "I'll go out with him for a minute. I'll fetch in our bedrolls and possibles before Ansel takes the animals 'round back."

———

AT THE HITCH POST OUT FRONT, AFTER shouldering the bedrolls and possibles pack, Braska had some specific instructions for Ansel. "In the left side of my saddlebags you'll find a grain pouch. Give each horse—and your mule too, if you want—a couple handfuls from that. Put some warmth in their bellies against this damp and cold. They got no worry for graze or water. Then unsaddle Miss Lucille's mare and give her a good rubdown. But my buckskin, I want you to leave saddled."

When Ansel looked puzzled by this, Braska explained, "Things didn't go totally smooth durin' our visit to the Crossing. I don't figure on trouble spillin' out from it anymore tonight, hopefully not at all. But there's a chance that, come morning, some of the hotter heads back there might still have enough steam built up to overcome their good sense. In case of that, I aim to ride out before daybreak and stand lookout over the trail from town. Any fool comes lookin' for more of a scrap, I'll be ready to discourage 'em once and for good."

When Ansel's eyes grew wide listening to this, Braska added, "Now I don't want you repeatin' any of this, you understand? Miss Lucille will know, but otherwise, there's no need to worry Grannymaw or the kids."

"I understand."

"Good. Now go ahead and tend these animals. Leave my buckskin on the near end so I can find him easy when I come back out."

Once more inside the cabin, Braska sat down to have a couple more biscuits and another piece of bacon. Grannymaw was settled in her rocking chair again, with the children gathered up close. Clevon Travers appeared to be resting comfortably, showing no signs of shivering or heavy sweating.

Lucille came over and handed Braska a cup of coffee. As he took it in one hand, he held up with the other a whiskey flask he'd snared from the possibles pack. "Remember that *adder* we talked about? Well, I'm thinkin' this coffee would make a fine home for a generous splash of some. How about you? You gonna join me—or did dancin' around with Malene limber you up enough so's you no longer need any?"

Lucille made a face. "Are you kidding? Wrestling that cow strained me to the point of needing even more. Let me get my cup."

Noting that Grannymaw was watching and listening, Braska held up the flask again in a show of full disclosure. "Hope you don't mind, Grannymaw. We ain't drunkards or no such like. But after a long day in the saddle, a body is left with its share of kinks and aches that a nighttime touch of, er, spirits can ease considerable."

Grannymaw's face remained expressionless for a long beat before her mouth slowly spread into a wide, tolerant smile like one might bestow on an innocently foolish question from a child. "Mister man," she drawled, "you think I gots to all these years I'm at 'thout ackumalatin' a heap of my own aches and kinks? And 'thout also seekin' out some tonic to help hold 'em at bay?" Reaching down beside her chair, from in behind the folds of the quilt draped over her lap, she raised a stoneware gallon jug with a finger loop and a cork stopper in its snout. Plopping this on her lap, she added, "Here what I be talkin' 'bout. Made fresh by myself 'fore we headed out on this trip."

Braska wagged his head in amazement. "Ma'am, you are a caution!"

"Maybe such thing," Grannymaw said, "as you'd want to save that other likker you got for the trail and tonight try some of my tonic instead. I speckalate it'll provide the soothin' you be lookin' for."

Braska had had a couple experiences with home-made 'shine and knew well how potent it could be. But at the same time, he also knew a challenge when one was laid down before him, and that's what this offer surely was, no matter how politely presented.

"I gots to say, though," Grannymaw added, "I don't know how good it'll go in your coffee. Me, when I has me some tonic, I has tonic. When I drink coffee or tea, I drink coffee or tea."

So there it was. The gauntlet thrown down even plainer.

"If your homebrew is anywhere near as good as your home cookin', I don't see how I can turn down such an offer," Braska said. Setting aside his cup of coffee, he went over and took the jug Grannymaw held out to him. She'd already removed the cork. Braska hooked a finger, cradled the jug on a bent elbow, and hoisted it. After a somewhat dubious glance in Lucille's direction, he tipped it up and took a pull.

It started with a fireball dancing across his tongue that turned into a lightning bolt shooting to the back of his throat before ricocheting down into his stomach to ignite a final grand explosion. All the breath was sucked out of him, and when he tried to inhale some back in, it felt like the tiny hairs inside his nostrils had been singed.

"Whooeee!" Braska exclaimed, squinting his eyes to try and hide how badly they wanted to water. "That is *not* for the tender-hearted!"

Grannymaw emitted a giggle of girlish delight and, in that fleeting moment, revealed how pretty she must have been in years gone by. "I reckon I should have warned you 'bout that batch comin' out a mite stouter than most."

"A *mite* stouter?" Braska echoed.

"But that just means it'll work that much quicker and better on your ailments. Give it a minute, you'll see."

"I don't need a minute. I feel numb most everywhere already." Braska turned to Lucille and, arching a brow, asked, "Care for a touch?"

"That's all right. I'm getting a pretty good dose just having you breathe my way. Don't exhale too close to the fire."

When Braska went to give the jug back to Granny-maw, she said, "Was you to take another pull, it'd go down a lot smoother the second time. And I can pract'ly guarantee that, after you did, crawlin' into your bedroll would feel better than ever before."

Another challenge. And one Braska was too damn proud to back down from. But he had to admit that stretching out on his bedroll a short time later did seem to feel especially good...

22

Despite his general weariness and the added depth of relaxation provided by Grannymaw's potent *tonic*, Braska still managed to roust himself before daybreak and ride out to the lookout knob he and Lucille had used previously in order to once again monitor the trail out of Blodgett's Crossing. He bush-tied Savvy low on the back side of the knob then took a position up top in the fringe of rock, with his Henry rifle braced close at hand and his Colt holstered on his hip. He built a cigarette, lit it, and settled in to wait.

The rain had stopped entirely by this point. The air remained chill, damp. A few faint stars could be seen through the dispersing clouds overhead, and far to the east, the horizon-hugging cloud mass that hadn't broken up yet was turning paler gray, tinged with a hint of pre-dawn pinkish gold.

Braska smoked and rolled things over in his mind. Hard to believe it was only three days ago, this being the morning of the fourth, that he'd gazed down on what used to be—and what damn well should still have been—his family's Bar S ranch. The fact it no longer was and the subsequent revelations of how that had come to be had rapidly set everything else in motion, everything that accounted for Braska being where he was now. Sitting in the cold and damp, waiting for potentially *more* trouble on top of that which had already filled much of those interim three days. All due, either directly or indirectly, to his ungrateful shit of a brother for failing to hold up his end by following through on what so many had counted on and expected from him—based largely on what he'd spent so many years indicating it was what he wanted for himself.

And the part about it that continued to stick in Braska's craw the most was that it wasn't a failure of noble struggle and defeat. No, that could grind down any man. But, by all reports, Link's failure had come from dismay and poor decisions compounded by mistrust, mistreatment, and downright foolishness until, most unforgivable of all, it ended in betrayal and abandonment.

That wasn't the brother Braska had grown up with. Wasn't somebody he wanted to *call* brother. As unclear as what he exactly sought to accomplish if and when he was able to catch up with Link, did it only come down to something as petty as that? To tell him to his face how disappointed and ashamed he was of him?

Jesus. If that's all there was, was it really worth it? After six years of being penned up, being told every minute of every day and night where he had to be and what he could or couldn't do when he got there...now he was out, free, with a whole country to drift across on his own whim. Did he really want to confine himself all over again to the singular pursuit of the same person already partly responsible for those lost six years? Where would be the meaningful gain—and what else might he be passing up if he allowed himself to become so narrow-focused?

Lucille.

Lord knew that, like every red-blooded male behind bars, he'd thought plenty about women during his time in Hellstone. No particular one, in Braska's case, as he'd never set out to rope any single filly due to his plans for going on the drift once his Bar S obligations were behind him. Which meant that his prison thoughts along those lines were mostly pretty basic and crude. Yet toward the end of his stretch, somewhat to his surprise, his musings had begun turning more to consideration of the empty years already gone by and wondering if the notion of more empty years on the drift alone still carried the allure it once had.

Seemed like even the most footloose fella ought to reach a point where he should start bending his mind in the direction of sinking roots and making some kind of lasting mark. And having a woman at his side, maybe a family sprouting out of the union, all seemed like a logical part of the picture. Though Braska had never envisioned sticking with cattle ranching and the Bar S, he'd always maintained a strong sense of family...that was until Link pulled his stunt.

None of which was to say the presence of Lucille had him picturing her as potential wife material. Good God, he barely knew her. When he paused to reflect on it in any depth, he didn't quite know *how* he felt about her. They'd pretty much been thrown together, and then things had propelled so fast, practically from the start, that time for thinking had been mighty scarce. Yet there was no denying he'd quickly felt at ease around her, and she'd just as quickly shown the same. As she said back at hers and Dolly's apartment: *"We get along okay, and we've even sorta stuck our necks out for each other."* The latter had been demonstrated even more since then, as recently as last night's fracas at the Crossing. And, in case of the crazy happenstance that their feelings toward one another actually took a romantic turn, she was certainly attractive enough—as Braska knew in great detail, albeit somewhat guiltily yet nonetheless admiringly.

Damn! He cursed himself. What kind of crap was that to be thinking about? Especially with all else hanging fire right now. That was the good part about action popping fast and things moving along in a hurry. Your brain didn't have time to wander off into stupid thoughts.

Before he turned in last night, he'd discreetly let Lucille know of his plan to slip out early and post this lookout. Displaying her usual spunk, she had at first insisted on wanting to come along. But he'd talked her into staying behind this time by pointing out the potential value in it. In case some riders from Blodgett's *did* appear, he explained, his shots to turn them back would give her warning to prepare the cabin defensively on the chance they got by him. She hadn't liked the sound of that but understood the importance of taking the precaution.

Now, watching the rosy gold tint grow brighter along the eastern horizon, Braska built another cigarette and hoped to hell this whole exercise proved to be nothing but an unnecessary precaution.

———

HE GAVE IT UNTIL THE SUN HAD BEEN UP FOR TWO hours before he called off his lookout. He was sufficiently satisfied that no retaliation by the Crossing's citizens was going to take place. Braska and Lucille had plucked the feathers of the he-goose and his gaggle too close for any of them to want to risk losing more.

The sky was clear overhead as he pointed Savvy back toward the cabin. The air was warming rapidly and the puddles of rainwater still standing in various depressions would be long gone by noon—victims of the combined forces of the thirsty ground and the steadily climbing sun.

"In just a few minutes, boy," Braska told his buckskin, leaning forward to pat the side of the animal's muscular neck, "I'll see that you're finally shed of this wet, heavy saddle for a while and you get a good rubdown and some grain. You put in a long night, you've earned it."

Only a couple minutes later, the cabin came into sight. Braska was particularly glad to see a thick twist of smoke rising up out of the chimney. He took that as a sure sign that Grannymaw was awake and up and had breakfast working. Even at a distance, he imagined he could smell the fresh coffee and biscuits and frying bacon. He'd also put in a fair chunk of long, uncomfortable night and liked to think he'd earned some taking care of, too, once he got inside.

After tying up at the hitching post out front, Braska proceeded eagerly through the door without knocking, figuring on asking Ansel to see to Savvy for him. That was when he discovered that the taking care of him he had waiting was nothing like what he'd been hoping for.

First came a Winchester barrel rammed hard into his stomach, just above the belt buckle. This doubled him up, driving out a great rush of breath and buckling his knees. Seconds later, the butt stock of that same rifle was slammed to the side of his head in a brutal, slashing motion that pitched him face-first onto the floor.

Bright lights popped and whirled inside Braska's head as he fought against them, fading into blackness. Through this, he heard a burst of noises and fragmented, excited voices that sounded at times far away, yet he knew they were in the same room with him... "Cowardly bastard!" "Shut up or you'll get some of the same!" The sharp *crack!* of a slap being delivered... "Hold that damn brat back!" Frightened wailing...more cursing...

Braska tried to suck some breath back in, but with his cheek mashed to the packed earth floor, he got some loosened grains of dirt along with it that only set him to coughing until he spat out a gob of muddy phlegm.

"Come on, tough nut—fer Chrissakes, where's your manners, spittin' all over the floor like that? Keep yer face down there and clean it up, you rude sonofabitch!" This last command, coming from a gruff voice that sounded vaguely familiar, was accompanied by the sole of a boot pressing Braska's head back down. But the sheer outrage of the attempt was too much. It triggered an unexpected reaction from Braska, tapping into a core of molten fury that drove him out of his near unconsciousness and lifted him suddenly, palms shoving down and thrusting his head and shoulders up. The man connected to the foot that had been trying to press him down—none other than Marv Kenna—was unbalanced and sent staggering back.

Braska snarled like a lobo, drawing his feet underneath him, his body coiling, getting ready to spring. But then the barrel of a Colt .45 crashed onto the back of his head. It raised quickly and crashed down again. After the second blow, Braska had an odd moment of clarity where he felt a worm of hot blood crawling down the back of his neck from the gash in his scalp. Then he pitched forward once more, and this time, a black pool of unconsciousness was there immediately and was very deep.

23

SOMEBODY HAD TURNED LOOSE A BUCKING BRONCO inside his head, and it was kicking and stomping furiously in an attempt to break free. Braska groaned, wishing to hell the nag would hurry up and either find a way to succeed or knock him back out again.

"Looks like he's startin' to come around." Another gruff, vaguely familiar voice. But vague for only a moment. The recollection of having caught a glimpse of Marv Kenna just before somebody cold-cocked him from behind jarred Braska into recognizing the voice as that of Reese McNally. Meaning he most likely was responsible for the cold-cocking, too.

Confirming this came Kenna's voice. "It's a good thing. The way you bashed him over the head, you might've killed him."

Braska could see neither men—primarily because he was keeping his eyes closed but also because he was still sprawled on the floor, turned partially onto one side, with the pair standing over him. Even if he'd opened his eyes, his line of sight would be limited.

Better to lie motionless and quiet and just keep listening for the time being. It helped, too, that knowing who they were and hearing them run their mouths was stirring his anger, and the madder he got, the less he noticed those bronco hooves pounding inside his head.

"Instead of bashing him over the head," McNally responded to Kenna's remark, "would you rather I'd've let him get his hands on you? Besides, so what if I *had* beefed him—that's what we're gonna do anyway, ain't it?"

"But in *my* sweet time and in *my* particular way. I'm the one who has the personal grudge, don't forget!"

"Hey, I got a piece of one too," McNally argued. "This sonofabitch cost me a nice, cushy job and caused me to end up freezin' and half-drowned in that stinkin' rainstorm last night. Might end up with pewmonia on account of him before this is all over!"

The toe of a boot dug into Braska's ribs. "Come on, tough nut. We heard you groan, saw you stir a little. Don't try to play possum. Drag your ass outta the fog and get those eyes open."

Braska complied. Slowly, grudgingly. It only worsened the pounding in his head, but at least he was able to get his bearings, establish where and how he was situated. He lay not too far inside the doorway, about where he'd fallen after being clobbered the second time. He was on his left side with his wrists as well as his ankles bound together. He was facing the fireplace, where he could see Ansel and the children huddled close around Grannymaw in her chair, all wearing looks of wide-eyed concern. Across from them, Clevon Travers still lay on his pallet but was propped on one elbow, appearing awake and alert for the first time—but also grim-faced.

Wherever Lucille was, she was outside Braska's field of vision.

Kenna chuckled nastily. "Don't look so hot, does it, tough nut?"

Braska rolled his eyes to glare up at the face hovering over him. "Where's Lucille?" he grated.

"You mean Rosie?" Kenna smirked mockingly, then emitted another chuckle. "You don't need to worry about her. We'll see she gets took care of real good. And you better believe we got plans for takin' care of your meddlin' ass too." To emphasize this, he brandished the six-shooter he gripped in one fist.

McNally, also holding a drawn gun, added a menacing chuckle of his own.

"What about that family over there you've obviously frightened the hell out of?" Braska wanted to know. "They're gentle people who are no part of this except for bein' willin' to share their shelter."

"They didn't share no damn shelter with us—not 'til we saw their chimney smoke at daybreak after the rain was all over!" snapped McNally. "Besides, niggers ain't *people* anyway. And we wouldn't've wanted to spend the night among 'em nohow."

"No, but we'd've gladly throwed *their* black asses out into the rain and kept the shelter for ourselves!" crowed Kenna.

"You're disgusting pigs in every way!"

This last remark came from someone Braska couldn't see, but the voice was unmistakably that of Lucille.

Kenna looked over and, still smirking, said, "Go ahead with your sassy talk for now. I like a gal with some spirit. Soon enough, I'll have you purrin' like a kitten."

"Ask me, she's more wildcat than kitten," remarked McNally. "Not that that don't still have its own appeal."

"Either way, we'll get to it in time. *After* we finish with her boyfriend. Speakin' of which, haul him up to a sittin' position—I'm gettin' a crick in my neck lookin' down at him."

Braska was roughly twisted around and lifted to a sitting position. This gave him a view of the whole room, and the first thing he did was sweep his gaze until it came to rest on Lucille. She was seated very rigidly on a straight-backed wooden chair, one of the few pieces of furniture still intact and not yet chopped up for fuel by Ansel. The reason for her stiff posture, it took Braska a second to realize, was the fact that her arms were wrenched behind her and tied to the chair's backrest. A bruise and some swelling were visible on the left side of her face.

Lucille met Braska's gaze with an anguished expression. "They barged in right after first light. They had us under their guns before I could do anything. They recognized my mare out in the lean-to and forced Ansel to tell them where you were and when you might be back."

"I's sorry, Mr. Braska," Ansel was quick to add in a mournful tone. "B-but they was threatenin' the chillun and I...I couldn't..."

"It's all right," Braska told him. "You had to look out for your family."

"Ah, stop with the nigger coddlin' before you make me puke," snarled McNally. "That brat would've spilled everything he knew for a lousy nickel."

"Would not!" Ansel was quick to protest.

McNally took a step toward him. "Don't you sass me, you little—"

"Knock it off!" barked Kenna, halting him. "Save your energy for takin' care of the tough nut and the girl. *That's* what we want to get to, not waste any more time than we have to on this black trash."

"Yeah, yeah. Okay," allowed McNally.

The anguished look on her face suddenly increasing, Lucille said in a strained voice, "Their plan is to give you a Dutch ride, Braska, and then take me away with them when they're done!"

Braska winced at these words, at both fates named. A *Dutch ride* was the term for a kind of harsh punishment sometimes practiced in cattle country. It involved tying a man behind a horse and then dragging him at a hard gallop across rugged country. Sometimes only to the point of a savage battering, other times all the way to death. Braska had a pretty good hunch what the intended goal was for him. And what this loathsome pair had in mind for Lucille could, in its own way, perhaps be considered even worse.

Reinforcing cause to expect the worst, Kenna boasted loudly, "Little Rosie laid it out pretty accurate, tough nut. The only little tidbit she forgot was how I'm first gonna knock you around some, just for personal satisfaction. *Then* we're gonna tie you behind your own horse and Dutch ride your meddlin' ass until you ain't nothing but a blob of shredded meat barely hangin' on your bones. That mess we'll leave in a gully somewhere for the coyotes and buzzards to finish off. A couple weeks from now, all that'll be left of you will be some picked-clean bones for the worms and bugs to play hide-and-seek among. And, at the same time, me and McNally will be playin' fun games with Rosie...how do you like the sound of that?"

"I should've kept your miserable head under when I had in that water trough," Braska said, glaring hatefully up at him.

"Yeah. Well, should-haves don't get the job done, mister. That's why I ain't makin' the same mistake." Kenna turned to McNally. "Go bring the horses around. The nigger stink in here is startin' to get to me. We need to clear out and commence with our business."

McNally holstered his Colt and went out the door.

Kenna moved to stand beside Lucille. "Now listen and get this straight," he said to her. "You can't do nothing to save your boyfriend and you *are* gonna come with Reese and me, even if I have to club you senseless and fetch you face down over a saddle. So you might as well play it smart and make it easy on yourself. And if you still insist on kickin' up a fuss when I untie you, then I'll plant a couple slugs in your nigger friends over yonder to prove I mean business. Got it?"

Lucille just regarded him with blazing eyes and said nothing.

Kenna began untying her, fumbling somewhat awkwardly because he kept his gun in one hand. When he had her freed from the chair, though with her wrists still bound behind her, he stood her up. Just as he started to say something, he was cut short by the clatter of falling boards from the lean-to out back.

Kenna frowned. "That clumsy damn..." Turning his face to the hanging canvas that sectioned off the collapsed part of the cabin, beyond which was the lean-to where the horses were, he hollered, "Everything okay back there, Reese?"

No answer.

Kenna paused for a minute, frown deepening. Then, jabbing his forefinger to within a hair's breadth of the tip of Lucille's nose, he growled, "You stand right there and don't move, you hear? No funny business, remember I got this gun and won't hesitate to use it."

He stepped away, circling wide around Braska, and moved to the front door. Without opening it, he called through, "You got those horses out there, Reese?"

Again no answer.

Kenna's frown turned impatient, angry. Thumbing his Colt to full cock and raising it to chest level, he pulled the door slowly open about ten inches and hollered again, "Goddammit, Reese, what's keepin'...?" He stopped short, obviously seeing something. "You!" He jerked his head back while at the same swinging up his arm and thrusting his gun through the opening.

Two shots roared in quick succession. First one on the outside, then Kenna's a second later. A bullet pounded into the ex-deputy, slamming him hard against the door frame. But he didn't go down. He kept his arm extended and fired again, almost simultaneously with another shot from without. Kenna jerked once more from impact. He still didn't go down, but he tilted slightly into the room, and a third bullet from outside tore away slivers of wood a fraction of an inch from his head.

Shouting "Everybody down!" to the others inside the cabin, Braska frantically twisted and kicked part way up out of his sitting position and managed to ram a shoulder against Kenna's hip, driving him back into the doorway. A fourth shot roared from outside, and the bullet it sent punched square to the center of Kenna's chest. He fell away, tripping over Braska, and toppled flat onto his back with arms flung wide. The gun flew from his dead grasp and went skidding across the floor.

A moment later, the door pushed open all the way, and standing there was Myles Stark with blood running down the side of his left leg and a smoking .45 in his right fist.

24

It was nearly noon by the time everybody was packed and ready to pull out, part of the time taken by burying the bodies of Kenna and McNally. The latter had also been dispatched by Stark—strangling him in the lean-to, silently except for the board he'd kicked loose during his death struggle. If left up to Braska and Stark, the pair wouldn't have rated the effort and the sweat to put them in the ground. But Grannymaw's strong Christian faith, in spite of the past deeds, bad treatment, and harsh threats the men were responsible for, caused her to insist they were still due proper treatment as children of God.

At first, since Clevon—though his bout with malaria was remarkably improved—still remained too weak, and Stark was hobbled due to the thigh wound he'd received as part of his lead exchange with Kenna, and Braska flat refused...it fell to Ansel to begin digging. But after a handful of minutes watching the skinny kid struggle, Braska grudgingly grabbed a second shovel and went to work beside him. When the job was done, they all stood around and allowed Grannymaw to say a brief, simple prayer.

Under different circumstances, with the day half gone and Clevon still ideally in need of additional rest and healing, it would have been more practical for the Travers family to remain at the cabin through another night. But given the events associated with the place and the locale in general, the desire to put the whole works behind them proved stronger than practicality. The weather showed every sign of remaining fair, they were now well supplied, and Clevon would be made suitably comfortable to ride out the afternoon in the wagon.

As for Braska and Lucille, it was an easy choice for them to seek making up as much time and distance as soon as possible.

That left Myles Stark. His reason for being present and for once again providing a most welcome intervention had been explained during the course of the morning. It boiled down to him having been told by Dolly back in Piney Flats that another of the Palace chorus girls who'd heard about Lucille heading for New Mexico with Braska had passed that information on to Marco, one of the Palace bouncers who'd always been tight with Marv Kenna. It was speculated by many that Kenna and McNally were still lurking somewhere close outside of town, licking their wounds and hungry for some payback.

Suspecting Marco wasn't above being somebody who'd help feed that hunger, Stark had followed him that night, and sure enough, he led to where Kenna and McNally were camped. Stark heard enough for it to be clear the two ousted deputies were planning to go after

Braska and Lucille, but he unfortunately hadn't come prepared to try and stop them right then and there. When he came back the next day, they had already pulled foot and all he could do then was set out to trail them—something he admittedly was not very skilled at. Hence, it had taken him until yesterday to finally close on them. Just in time for the storm to blow in and hold him at bay through the night. Come morning, he feared he'd lost their trail. But then, like them, he spotted the smoke from the cabin chimney.

Working his way in cautiously, he found their horses in the lean-to and recognized Lucille's mare there as well. Continuing to play it cautious, he'd crept in through the collapsed section of the cabin and, listening close behind the hanging canvas, heard enough to get a pretty good idea of how things stood and to start formulating a plan to turn the tables. It wasn't long before Braska showed up and his table-turning plan got propelled into motion...

"I think you held back until the last minute because you just plain like making big, dramatic entrances," Lucille teased him.

Stark replied, "Not admitting anything, but if that ever *was* the case, then I assure you this little memento from Kenna"—here he indicated the bullet gash to his thigh—"has cured me of such histrionics in the future."

"That's all well and good," said Braska, "just as long as it don't stop you from showin' up to save my hide in case I need it again in the future."

Stark arched a brow. "The way you seem to court trouble, there's not much doubt your hide *will* be at risk again sometime in the future. But I can't always be there. What's more, if you keep pulling reckless stunts like the one this morning when you purposely threw yourself *into* the line of fire, then it might be hopeless anyway."

"I threw myself against Kenna to make sure *he* stayed in your line of fire," Braska argued.

"It was still damned reckless of you."

"But it worked, didn't it? I set him up for your final, fatal shot."

"Enough, the both of you," interjected Lucille. "Let's leave it at being grateful that Stark showed up when he did. Maybe next time it will be Braska's turn to do the hide saving."

"Bein' three times obligated, I'd welcome the chance," said Braska.

"Fair enough," allowed Stark. "I don't know where or when our paths may cross again, but as long as you'll excuse me if I'm in no hurry to get in a fix where I *need* my hide saved, we can be in agreement."

Stark's current leg wound was serious enough, even though sufficiently shallow to have not broken bone or torn any major muscles, that immediately climbing back into a saddle would have been both painful and counterproductive to the start of proper healing. For this reason it had been decided he would travel for a ways with the Travers, riding in their wagon, until they reached a town that suited him for staying behind and finishing his recuperating.

In conjunction with this, there was a final piece of business to be settled.

"Kenna and McNally may have been lowdown skunks in most ways," Braska explained to the Travers, "but it turns out they had a pretty good eye for horse-flesh. Meanin', I figure the mounts and saddle gear they left behind could bring in the neighborhood of a hundred dollars if sold with the right touch of negotiatin'. Since Stark is gonna be travelin' with you until you get to a proper-sized town, he's willin' to handle that negotiatin' for you. I hate to say it—but we all know it's true—you bein' a colored man, Clevon, would have a harder time gettin' a good deal or maybe even explainin' how you came by the animals to begin with. But Stark will handle it and see you folks get a right nice start for when you reach Greely. How does that sound?"

Clevon's mouth sagged open. "A hunnert dollars? I ain't never seen no more than ten at any one time in my whole life."

"Then it's time you do. You have a fine family that's been through a lot with hardly ever catchin' any breaks. Lucille, Stark, and me are all already outfitted with good mounts. We don't need more. If you'll take these off our hands, then you deserve any benefit to be gained from 'em." Braska cut his gaze to Grannymaw. "And I surely hope you don't see that as crossin' the line of not acceptin' charity, ma'am."

The old woman held his gaze for a long beat before her mouth curved slowly into a smile. "Mister man, not even my stubbornness would ever turn down a true blessin' when one is bestowed."

———

BRASKA AND LUCILLE TOOK FULL ADVANTAGE OF the afternoon's pleasant weather and an empty, easily traversed countryside. They rode well into dusk before stopping to make night camp. Supper was a spread of Grannymaw's biscuits topped with embalmed beef and served with stewed tomatoes. Afterward, they stretched back against their upturned saddles, palming cups of coffee doctored with brown sugar and laced with generous splashes of redeye from Braska's flask.

"This is going to seem like an awfully tame nightcap compared to Grannymaw's special tonic, isn't it?" said Lucille.

Braska rolled his eyes. "Anything short of swallowin' a hot coal fresh outta that campfire would compare as tame."

"Mostly, I'm glad I resisted trying some. But a part of me will always wonder just how potent it really was."

"If you really want to find out, it's not too late," Braska said, lowering his cup after taking a drink. "Grannymaw insisted I bring some of her tonic with me, so she fixed up a little bottle that I've got in my saddlebags."

Lucille's eyes widened. "Really?"

Braska couldn't keep a straight face. "No, I'm kidding. I just wanted to see your reaction. Hell, I'd be afraid to carry any of that stuff in my saddlebags—if I put Savvy to a gallop and the tonic got jiggled too much, it might explode!"

"That was a dirty trick, saying you had some. You just wanted to see me crawfish again, didn't you?"

"I wouldn't call it crawfishin'. I'd call it bein' smart, just like when you turned it down the first time." Braska wagged his head. "Beats me how Grannymaw can drink that stuff regular-like and still stay upright. She must pack the constitution of an ox in that scrawny little body of hers."

"I think she's just plain an amazing woman," Lucille said with conviction. "Sassy and stubborn and tough, yet loving and devoted to her family. Not to mention her devotion to God and her Christian faith— the way she insisted Kenna and McNally rated a decent burial."

Braska made a sour face. "Stretchin' the teachings of the Good Book for a lowdown pair like them two was a far reach to my way of thinkin'."

"That's my whole point. At her age and coming from Louisiana, she surely must have spent time as a slave. Clevon too, most likely. Yet having endured that, not to mention the way some people talk about and treat coloreds still today—those in Blodgett's Crossing, for example, as well as the Kennas and McNallys to be found elsewhere—Grannymaw's faith remains so strong and pure it can embrace even their like. I can't help but admire that."

"Maybe so." Braska set his jaw firmly. "But I hold the belief there comes a time when that turnin' the other cheek business flat don't cut it."

Lucille smiled. "Yes, you don't exactly hide it. You think Grannymaw missed that about you? Yet it was something more she accepted and embraced...even to the point of calling what you did to help her and her family a blessing."

"I didn't ask for that and wasn't comfortable hearin' it. I ain't hardly in the business of dishin' out blessings." Braska scowled and took a gulp of his redeye-laced coffee. "What's more, you and Stark had hands in helpin' those poor folks back there, right along with me."

"Speaking for myself, I'd like to think so. I appreciate hearing it. And Stark no doubt helped us all," said Lucille. "But you were the spearhead, right up to and including handing over those horses in order to give that family a life-changing boost that will always seem like a blessing to them. That's what Grannymaw saw and why she said what she did. Whether you like it or not, Virgil Smith, you're the kind of man who—no matter if it's a wreck of a cabin in the middle of nowhere, or the Crossing, or all the way back to Piney Flats—makes a difference wherever he shows up."

"Oh, yeah. I made a big difference behind the walls of Hellstone prison for six years," Braska said bitterly.

"I can only imagine how stifling and smothering that must have been for someone like you. But *trying* to make a difference was what put you there. It's all part of the same fabric. Don't you see? It's not your fault that the grand sacrifice you made fell short. And you have every right to want to hold to account those who failed you. Yet, even with all that, you're not so driven and bitter that you've lost caring about others along the way." Lucille hesitated a beat and her voice shifted, lowering slightly. "As one of those you took time to care about, I just wanted to let you know...well, that I've noticed and I'm grateful."

Braska felt the need for a long, slow pull of his coffee, pondering just how much he should read into those words and that lowered tone of voice. Pulling away the cup, he said, "Once a fella crosses paths with a gal like you, ma'am, it's mighty hard not to do some noticin' of his own. On the other hand, if he was to let slip a kind of secret to such a gal and then she was to turn around and call him something nasty like, say, *Virgil*...well, you can see where that could maybe set things back a mite."

"Oh, yes. Yes, that could be considered a serious

offense." A hint of an impish smile tugged at Lucille's mouth. "And if the fella then retaliated by saying something even worse, perhaps referring to the gal as *ma'am* —why, that could result in outright warfare."

They regarded each other with mock sternness, the flickering campfire light playing across their faces. Until Lucille's expression slowly melted into a beguiling smile. "If I'd known that calling you Virgil was all it would take to get you to look at me like a woman, I'd have used it sooner."

"If callin' me Virgil will keep you smilin' at me like that, then go ahead and use it all you want," Braska told her somewhat huskily.

They sat up and leaned toward each other, faces tilting slowly closer until their lips met. Tenderly, exploringly at first. Then rapidly growing more urgent and impassioned. Coffee cups were cast aside. Braska wrapped Lucille in his arms and hers entwined him in return. Their kisses grew more heated and soon they were tugging at each other's clothes as well as their own, peeling them away in a frenzy. Lucille's bared flesh— the soft slope of her shoulder, the swell of her hips and proud thrust of her breasts—were painted orange-gold in the firelight. The shadows that lay in the valleys between these wondrous curves were pools of soft, velvety darkness that Braska explored eagerly with his hands and lips.

When they coupled, it was with a wild intensity that left them both gasping and spent at its conclusion. Before long, however, they were ready again. This time, it was gentler, slower, almost dreamlike, until another intense climax was reached.

Later, they lay quietly in each other's arms,

enjoying the special warmth and afterglow that comes at such a time.

At length, Braska started to say, "I know how much you admire Grannymaw, and I'll admit she's—"

"Wait a minute," Lucille interrupted. "You're thinking about Grannymaw at a time like this?"

"Only, if you let me finish, about something she said," explained Braska. "When she told me a couple nips of her tonic would make slippin' into my bedroll feel the best ever...well, turns out she was wrong. Bein' here now in this bedroll with you is a whole lot better."

25

Two mornings after Myles Stark shot Marv Kenna in the doorway of the dilapidated Kansas cabin, a wire arrived at the telegraph office in the northern Arizona town of Zemus. It was addressed to O.N. Dodge and read as follows:

MEET ME TAOS 3-4 DAYS. STOP. REGISTER ILKES HOTEL AND WAIT FOR CONTACT. STOP.

The sender was identified as one I. Hunter.

As per prior arrangement, the telegrapher had the message promptly delivered to Mae Walters, widowed proprietress of a small but popular café called Mae's Place. Mae, in turn, wasted no time forwarding the message via her stepson Eugene, a simple-minded mute slavishly devoted to her, to a man occupying an abandoned mining shack in the rugged foothills of some nearby broken land the locals called the *Hopeless Mountains*.

This final recipient of the message was Hector *Hec*

Mallet, older brother of Merl, joint leaders of the notorious outlaw gang that had been terrorizing the Four Corners region after having previously cut a bloody swath of robbery and killing all through Kansas, a slice of Texas, and across the borderlands of northern Mexico. Merl was not present in the shack, but two other men—Big Jess Whorten and Brazo Hacklin—were.

Hec Mallet was a ruggedly-proportioned six-footer with curly black hair, mean eyes, and an oversized nose jutting out above a neatly trimmed mustache. At the moment, his left arm hung in a tightly-cinched sling of black cloth. But the Colt .45 holstered prominently on his right hip offset any sense of vulnerability about the man, sending instead a message of cold danger.

After reading the message interpreted and scribbled down by the telegrapher, Hec crumpled the paper in his good hand, his gun hand. There was no sense passing it to Whorten or Brazo, since neither could read.

To Eugene, he said, "Thanks for fetching that out here pronto-like, boy. Pass the same on to Mae, okay? Also, tell her we'll be heading out soon and be gone for a spell. That means you won't have to be bringing 'round no more supplies or fresh game for a while neither. Not until we signal we've returned. Got all that?"

Eugene, a tall, skinny twenty-year-old, nodded silently, obediently.

"Good boy. Now get on home 'fore it gets dark, and pass on to Mae all that I told you. Right?" Hec patted the lad's shoulder. "Go ahead and grab yourself a handful of rock candy on your way out. From the can there on the shelf, you know where it is."

Once Eugene had gone, Whorten went over to the burlap-covered window and pushed back the cloth to look out. "That kid gives me the creeps," he said over his beefy shoulder. "He not only don't talk or make no sound outen his mouth, he even moves silent-like. Almost a damn ghost or human shadow or some such."

"That's what makes him the perfect go-between messenger," Hec replied. "He couldn't blab anything even if he wanted to. That silence about him is also what makes him such a good hunter, never failing to go out and bag fresh meat for Mae's café—not to mention furnishing us some, too, since we been here."

"Yeah. I noticed that Winchester he packs around seems pract'ly a part of him."

"Don't think he'd ever hesitate to use that rifle on a man, neither, if any ever tried to bother Mae," Hec stated. "That's another thing that makes Eugene such a good go-between. His loyalty to Mae is so strong he'd never cross any of her dealings no matter if a gun was put to *his* head."

Whorten turned from the window. He was a giant of a man—six-six in height, three hundred pounds, a lot of it gut but plenty also carried in massive shoulders and forearms as thick as most men's thighs. His full-bearded face was framed by long, greasy hair and topped by a dusty, dented derby hat that nobody in their right mind would point out as looking somewhat ridiculous. "I know Mae's your cousin and you or Merl told us once before about the boy," he said, "but how was it again she came by Eugene?"

Hec scowled. "She was married—mighty briefly—to

his old man. Turned out the bastard was not only a drunkard, which Mae knew and should've steered clear of in the first place, but he was mule-beating mean to his mute son, who got left to him when his first wife hung herself. Hindsight suggests she probably checked out to escape the bastard because he beat her too—or maybe he did it himself and made it look like her own doings.

"Anyway, Mae soon enough saw the vicious side of what she'd married when he turned on her as well. When she tried to stop him from whaling on the boy, he beat 'em both so bad neither could hardly get out of bed for a week. As soon as she was able, Mae pretended she wanted to make up with the bastard by fixing him a real nice supper. She got him sat down at the table all nice and proper, waiting to be served, then came up behind him with an iron skillet and didn't stop swinging until she'd pulverized his skull to oatmeal. She skedaddled with the boy and they ain't looked back or been apart since."

Whorten gave a low whistle. "Damn! Don't mess with Cousin Mae, eh?"

"You can say that again. All that took place when me and Merl was off ridin' with Bascomb over Kansas way. Had we known sooner about the sonofabitch she got hitched to, we'd've done worse than just bash his brains in. Mae was like a little sister to me and Merl growing up, and we tried to look out for her even though she was always pretty good at taking care of herself."

Brazo, sitting at a rough-hewn table in the middle of the room, squinted through a curl of smoke rising from the black cigarillo clenched between his teeth and said,

"By the pain in her eyes when she herself brought the newspaper showing how those Fergus Hills *bastardos* treated Merl's body, I could tell the closeness you three shared."

The perpetual menace always smoldering in Hec's eyes flamed hotter in response to those words. "Don't worry, that whole stinkin' town of Fergus Hills is gonna pay bad—in *fire and blood*, I'm talking—before my black heart is done beating. I swear it! But first there's the matter of dealing with the lowdown, double-crossing vermin who left my brother to fall into their hands at all. And if *this*"—here Hec held up his fist with the telegraph message crushed in it—"means what it implies, then we are finally on our way toward closing in on that filthy wretch!"

"What does it say?" Brazo wanted to know. He was a wiry individual of average height, dark-skinned in keeping with the Mexican blood of his mother, rakishly handsome with a shock of jet black hair spilling over his forehead and a wide mouth quick to form a dazzling smile. But in his black eyes, there lurked danger that could flash just as quickly, and the Colt carried in a tooled leather holster worn for the cross draw on his left hip was known to flash into action quickest of all.

In response to Brazo's question, Hec recited without looking at the paper, "Meet me Taos 3-4 days. Register Ilkes Hotel and wait for contact."

"From Stark?"

"None other."

"I gotta admit," said Brazo, exhaling a double stream of smoke from his nostrils, "that I never fully trusted your old amigo. But I guess I was wrong."

"It was a gamble whether or not he'd be able to sniff

out any kind of lead to Link," Hec replied. "But, for me, there was never a doubt about trust. You save a man's life and then he turns around and saves yours, that's about as solid as it gets. Besides, if he had in mind to cross us in some way, it wouldn't have taken three weeks to hear from him and he wouldn't be dragging us all the way to Taos to do it. If he'd wanted, he could've had a whole pack of law dogs right here on our doorstep long before this."

"Si. That is so," Brazo allowed.

"What's more," Hec added, "an example of how far he's going to keep us covered is in the way he sent this telegram. It's from I. Hunter, and addressed to O.N. Dodge." In spite of himself, Hec smiled a little at this bit of double-meaning wordplay on names. It was a touch Stark and his offbeat sense of humor had come up with, but they had to call themselves something so it was as good as any. And it *was* clever and a tad amusing.

A little too clever, it so happened, for some. "Who are those hombres?" asked a puzzled-looking Whorten.

Sighing, Hec explained, "It's a ruse, a trick to disguise our real identities. Stark can't hardly fire off a telegram directly to *Hec Mallet* with law dogs and bounty men from hell to breakfast on the alert for any whiff of me, can he? So we worked it out so I'm *O.N. Dodge*—on account of I really am on the dodge. Get it? And because he's on the hunt for some sign of that weasel Link Smith, he's *I. Hunt.*"

Even then, Whorten looked blank for a beat before it finally registered. "Hey, that's pretty slick. Kinda funny, too."

"There's nothing funny about it if the upshot means

getting our hands on Link. Shouldn't be hard to understand me having my personal reasons for that being the
main goal. But, on the purely practical side, I realize
how reclaiming the bank money he got away with is a
big part of it, too."

Brazo nodded gravely. "Si. Avenging both Epps *and*
your brother are important things, jefe. But you are
right to not forget the money. Coming up empty on that
bank job and now having holed up here, licking our
wounds for these past weeks, has run our poke mighty
low. We barely have supplies to make it as far as Taos."

"You really think that's where we'll find Link when
we get there?" Whorten asked.

"I doubt we'll be that lucky all at once." Hec made a
sour face. "But it must be an important step toward
where Stark thinks we *will* find our man, or he wouldn't
have summoned us out of hiding. As far as supplying
ourselves for the trip, well, much as I want to avoid
drawing attention to us for being on the move again, if
forced to, we can resort to doin' what we do best—
finding someplace that's got what we need, and
taking it!"

Whorten grunted. "Yeah. That pretty much is what
we do, ain't it?"

"It is true," agreed Brazo. Then, bringing his gaze to
rest directly on Hec, he added, "But with all due
respect yet also due concern, jefe, what about your arm?
It is not fully healed from the bullet your amigo
removed, and—even though you try to hide it, I can tell
—it remains of much discomfort to you. The ride to
Taos is long and the route we'll have to take in order to
stay as unseen as possible will cover some mighty
rugged ground."

"So you're thinking I can't make it?" Hec asked edgily.

Brazo shook his head. "You set your mind to it, you'll damned well make it. It's just gonna be rugged, that's all I'm saying. Especially if you get that far and Smith ain't even there."

"I already told you—I don't expect him to be there," said Hec. "But I'm counting on him to be *closer*, and I'll settle for that. As far as this bullet-busted wing of mine, we both know it ain't ever gonna heal all the way right again. It'll leave me half-gimped and I'll have to settle for that, too. Hopefully the pain will eventually ease up. In the meantime, thank God my shooting hand is still okay. If it wasn't, I'd learn to pull a trigger with my teeth if I had to, until I caught up with and put a bullet in the rotten cur who ditched my dying brother and stole our money."

Brazo's eyes brightened. "By God, I think you really would!"

"Don't ever doubt it. So thanks for worrying about my arm and my pain, but I'll manage."

"When are we pullin' out, then?" Whorten wanted to know.

"Why not right now? We can get in near three-quarters of a day's travel if we don't waste any time about it," came the answer. "All we have to do is get packed up and in our saddles. So Jess, how about you go get the horses ready and me and Brazo will pull things together in here. We can be well out of sight of these Hopeless Mountains by sundown."

As Whorten started for the door, he detoured over to the can on the shelf and started to reach for some of the rock candy it contained.

"Hey!"

The shout from Hec was so loud and sharp it caused the big man to jump back as if a rattler had sounded from inside the can. His head snapped around and he glared at Hec. "What the hell, man?"

"How many times do I have to tell you to leave that candy alone? It's for Eugene!"

"But we're pullin' out, meanin' he won't be comin' 'round no more. So what difference does it make?" Whorten argued. "No sense lettin' it go to waste."

"I'm thinking that won't necessarily happen. Like I told you, Eugene comes out game hunting regular-like, to bag fresh meat for Mae's café. I can picture him stopping by here to see if there might be any rock candy got left behind. If he comes hoping for that, I want him to find some—not be disappointed." Hec paused, and for a fleeting moment, a soft expression passed over his face. "That boy's known too much disappointment in his life...I want to be sure and not add to it, not even a little bit."

Whorten's glare had faded. He said, "Sure, Boss. I'll leave the candy alone. For Eugene."

Then he went out the door to get the horses ready.

26

MYLES STARK DIDN'T LIKE THE WAY THINGS WERE headed. Didn't like it worth a damn. But the cards were on the table, and he'd even done some of the dealing, so he was left with little choice but to play out the hand.

Double damn.

His first piece of misfortune regarding the matter had been his presence in the town of Fergus Hills on the day the Mallet gang hit the bank there. Compounding this was the fact of him owing his life to Hec Mallet, dating back to the horrendous Battle of the Wilderness during the Civil War. With the dense tangle of Virginia trees and underbrush set ablaze by gun and cannon fire, visibility and awareness of battle lines or even the position of one's own comrades only a few feet away had become nothing short of hellish, bloody confusion due to thick clouds of smoke pouring from muzzles and roiling up out of burning tinder.

Within this, a badly wounded Stark had fallen and, like screaming others about him, was at risk of ending up consumed by the flames if Hec hadn't come along and gone to the trouble of dragging him clear and then carrying him to where medical attention was available. They'd shared only a brief amount of time together after that before Mallet was called back to the fighting. In that time, they'd exchanged names and Stark had issued a deeply sincere, *if ever our paths cross again*, oath to do anything he could to even the score.

In the post-war years that followed, though their paths never actually crossed, Stark certainly encountered the *name* of Hec Mallet again—with growing frequency and notoriety—as the drifting gambler lifestyle he'd adopted took him to various saloons and gaming parlors on the West's frontier where reports of the Mallet gang's daring, bloody robberies were often the subject of conversation. Whenever such brought their past history to mind, Stark couldn't help wondering what might transpire if he truly did run into Hec once more.

In the unlikely setting of Fergus Hills, where he was passing through and had only stopped to get his horse re-shod, he found out. He was lounging in the open doorway of a livery barn, puffing on a long nine cigar while waiting for the farrier to finish with his animal, when two riders passed by and plodded on down the middle of the main street. One of the riders was Hec Mallet. Even after the wear of intervening years and minus the streaks of soot and dirt that had covered a younger face gripped by mid-battle anguish, there was no mistaking him. Not to Stark. The eyes, the distinctive nose—you don't forget every feature of the face suddenly looming over you in the midst of hell, saying *"Hang on, soldier"* and then dragging/lifting you to safety from fiery death.

Stark stood somewhat dumbfounded in the livery doorway. Neither of the riders had taken any notice of him. His eyes continued to follow them as they proceeded to the center of the town's business district, a block and a half on down from the livery, and then swung their horses to the hitch rail in front of the bank. Suddenly, belatedly, it struck Stark what he was witnessing—Hec was here to pull off a robbery.

As his gaze swept the street with heightened interest, he then recognized further confirmation of this. Four other men—two sets of two, one pair from the opposite side of the street where they'd been holding down a bench in front of a saloon, the other pair from a ways farther down where they'd been admiring some items on display through the window of a leather goods shop—also began slowly drifting toward the bank as Hec and his companion dismounted and went inside. One man from each pair followed them in. The remaining two hung back. Lookouts, watching and waiting to be ready with the horses.

Stark's pulse quickened as he took all of this in. Not that he approved of what was about to take place, but he was hardly in any position to intervene—even if he didn't owe a long-standing debt to Hec. Nevertheless, it was hard to dismiss thoughts of the other people he could see moving about on the moderately busy street, innocent citizens merely conducting their daily affairs, and not recall the stories he'd heard about the Mallet gang's reputation for shooting up everything and everybody in sight as they rode away from their hold-ups.

With that image souring in his stomach, Stark had then begun to notice something else occurring up and down the street. Shoppers moving along on the boardwalks suddenly started darting out of sight, disappearing through the doorways of various businesses. Same for freighters and teamsters on the street, abruptly abandoning their rigs and finding a place to get inside. In conjunction with this, others—men brandishing guns—became guardedly visible in semi-hidden positions like the mouths of alleys, the rims high up on false-fronted buildings, and in the shadows of recessed doorways.

Holy shit, Stark realized, there were forces in the town who'd been *ready* for a holdup attempt and now were preparing to spring a trap as soon as Hec emerged from the bank.

Stark felt torn anew. Was this a chance for him to try evening the score on what he owed Hec? To warn him somehow? But Stark was too far away to do anything effective, and what good would a warning do at this point anyway? The trap was already set. And, if Stark was any judge of how the general public felt when it came to the Millet gang, there were those among the waiting gunmen who'd be primed to spill outlaw blood, no matter what. Meaning anyone trying to aid the gang would rate nothing less.

Suddenly, one of the lookouts—a lanky, fair-haired young fella who couldn't have been much past twenty—also took note of what Stark had spotted. And he didn't wrestle with indecision, not for a second. Shouting, "Brazo! It's a trap!" to the other lookout, the lanky one whipped a rifle out from under the concealment of his long coat and began shooting. First he blew a man out of a recessed doorway across the street, then he swung the rifle barrel up and picked off a man leaning out of a second-story window of the same building.

The second lookout, a wiry, dark-skinned Mexican, drew a long-barreled Colt with blinding speed and instantly went to work with it, knocking down a man in the mouth of an alley and blowing another off the low roof of the leather goods shop. Return fire began pouring down on the two men as they simultaneously scrambled to gather mounts and keep throwing more lead of their own.

"Hec! Merl!! Gotta make a run for it!" shouted the Mexican.

The bug-eyed farrier, leading Stark's horse, came hurrying out of the livery barn. "What the devil's goin' on?"

Stark snatched the reins from him, saying, "There's a bank robbery in progress and all hell is breaking loose! I'd advise you to stay back out of the way."

Down in the street in front of the bank, bullets were slicing at all angles through the clouds of powder smoke and dust being kicked up by the pawing, skittering horses. One of the animals screeched in pain as a slug tore out a fist-sized chunk of meat. The lanky lookout took a hit and got knocked down but was back on his feet almost immediately, levering home fresh rounds then blasting away some more.

Hec and the three men who had gone into the bank with him came boiling back out with guns blazing. A townsmen who'd been shooting down from atop the bank building took a bullet and spilled from his perch, crashing to the ground only a couple feet from Hec.

Out in the street, another of the horses screamed and this one fell to a fatal bullet strike. Only a few feet away, the lanky lookout got cut down again and, this time, didn't get back up. More horses screamed and the harsh curses of men mingled with their cries.

Somebody, it might have been Hec, hollered, "Take to your saddles, men...! Scatter...! Scatter!"

Amid sizzling bullets and the thickening clouds of smoke and dust, the outlaws scrambled frantically to comply with this command. From his vantage point, it became hard for Stark to make out distinct shapes in the murky haze—except for a few townsmen who remained shooting from higher positions like windows and rooftops. Continuing to watch, some inexplicable urge caused Stark to go ahead and mount his own horse, even though he held in place before the livery barn.

And then, as if predestined in some cockeyed way, Hec Mallet burst out of the street haze astride a galloping bay horse and came barreling in the direction of the livery barn and Stark, reversing the route by which he'd entered town. Behind him, other riders broke free and streaked off in various other directions.

Bullets chased Hec, burning the air on all sides and gouging the street at the heels of the fleeing horse. They made it twenty or so yards before a round slammed into the left flank of the bay, twisting the beast in mid-stride and throwing it into a drunken stagger until it lost balance and collapsed completely. Hec kicked out of his stirrups and leaped clear, hitting the ground in a rolling tumble.

At that point, there was no indecision or hesitation on Stark's part. He put the spurs to his mount and sent it galloping toward the fallen man.

Hec was back on his feet, shaken and a little wobbly, by the time Stark reached him. Lead was still ripping the air around the gang leader and he was clutching a gun in his fist, ready to return the same. He spun around when Stark came riding up and was starting to train the cutter on him when he was halted by a shout, "Hec, it's me—Myles Stark! Get up behind me!"

There was an instant of stunned disbelief on the outlaw's face, but then he dug a toe into the stirrup Stark had emptied for him and hauled himself up behind this savior, this specter out of the past. Stark wheeled his horse and they went tearing out of town. As they went past the livery barn, the farrier came running out with a shotgun in his hands. "Thievin' bastards!" he hollered as he started to raise the blaster. Hec triggered a quick response and the damn fool— who should have listened when Stark advised him to stay out of the way—flew back with blood geysering from a hole in his chest.

Behind Stark's ear, Hec said, "If anybody gives chase, we're never gonna outrun 'em riding double. But there's broken country to the east. Head that way, we should be able to lose 'em there!"

————

AND SO IT HAD GONE. THEY FOUND REFUGE IN A nest of jagged boulders and ended up spending the night there. After dark, having seen nor heard no sign of pursuit, they risked a carefully concealed fire over which they made a meal from Stark's trail supplies. During this time, Hec had repeatedly and effusively expressed his thanks—not to mention his surprise—for Stark showing up to save his hide. Adding to the aid the gambler was able to provide was the smattering of knowledge he'd learned about bullet wound treatment during the time he was recovering from his battlefield injuries. Based on this, he cleaned and treated the wound Hec had received to his left arm during the shoot-out. With the patient biting off the pain with a leather strap clenched in his teeth, Stark dug the bullet out of shattered bone and then got the bleeding stanched and a poultice applied under a thick bandage.

In the morning, still with no sign of a posse prowling anywhere near and the wound showing no sign of fresh bleeding, they struck out for the gang's hideout down in Arizona. In a situation like this, which had never actually happened before, Hec explained how the gang had a long-standing plan in place for all to follow. Members would scatter individually or, at most, in pairs and fan out for as far and long as it took to make sure they were in the clear before reconverging at a pre-established safe haven—in this case, the abandoned mining camp in the Hopeless Mountains.

"Those tricky bastards in Fergus Hills had a pretty tight mousetrap set for us, I got to give 'em that," Hec allowed sullenly. "But it appears, at least as far as the lack of chase given us two, they fell kinda short on having any kind of posse ready to go after get-aways. Let's hope the rest of the boys fared out as good as I did —thanks to you."

When they made it to the hideout a day and a half later, after stealing a horse and saddle for Hec from a remote ranch corral—without, much to Stark's relief, having to kill anybody to do it—they began to learn the fate of other gang members. Big Jess and Brazo were already present, unscathed. They reported having seen young Rick Epps go down in a hail of bullets, so there was no hope of him showing up. That left brother Merl and a sixth and final gang member named Link Smith unaccounted for. Brazo said he had seen the two of them bolt off together down a side street and it looked like each sagged a bit in their saddles, as if wounded to some degree.

Another day and a half passed with no sign of or word from either of the missing men, leaving Hec increasingly anxious and agitated. Until the morning when a teary-eyed Mae herself made the trip out to the cabin to confirm the worst fear and support it with a newspaper showing a photo reproduction of Merl's bullet-riddled body propped up for public display. The accompanying account stated how the dead outlaw had been discovered, left behind along a lonely trail. It also related that none of the stolen money—which Hec himself could verify had been in Merl's possession when they broke from the bank—was recovered. The account further identified one Rick Epps as another fallen member of the gang, left dead in the street of Fergus Hills. The remaining robbers, it concluded, were so far still on the loose.

After wailing through a bout of initial grief, Hec had quickly switched to an angry rant aimed at the still-missing Link Smith, whom he accused of abandoning the dead or dying Merl and then taking off with clear intent of keeping the bank money all for himself. Brazo and Whorten let him carry on for a while but then got him to calm down some by suggesting that maybe, just maybe, Smith had done all he could for Merl but was left wounded and alone, still out there making sure his trail was covered, and might yet show up. This appeased Hec somewhat. But once another two days had passed with no appearance by Smith, all bets were off—everybody agreed the missing man was on the run and claiming the money for himself.

Stark had remained at the hideout up until that point for two reasons: One, to continue monitoring Hec's wound to make sure no infection took hold, and two, to also monitor the additional reports coming in about the holdup and associated shoot-out in order to see how much notice his rescue of Hec had drawn. If a thorough description of him resulted, it would affect what measures he might have to take—like perhaps altering his appearance—when he was ready to strike out on his own again.

Luckily, both concerns turned out to be for naught. Hec's wound was mending okay, and no mention of Stark's action was part of the gossip overhead in Mae's café or included in any of the newspaper updates she sent via Eugene. Given this, it was decided that all witnesses would have been at a distance down by the bank and must have figured the rider who scooped up Hec was simply one of the other gang members. The only one who could have definitively said otherwise was the livery farrier—and he was past providing any testimony on the matter.

So, with these concerns satisfactorily settled in his mind, Stark had announced his intention to be moving on. There was no opposition to this, not per se. But that was the point where Hec added a hitch to his leaving.

"You don't owe me nothing more," he started out. "You've paid back any obligation you ever had, and then some. So I'm asking this as a flat-out favor. Smith was only riding with us for less than a year, see. More like eight months or so. He was sharp and tough, good with a gun, and always held up his end without any problem. But, at the same time, I think we all kinda saw he was never deep cut for the outlaw life—not like the rest of us."

Looking on and listening, Brazo and Wharten nodded their heads in silent agreement.

"Thinking back, like I been doing a lot of," Hec went on, "I recall more than once him mentioning regret for how he'd run out on his family, a wife and kid, and how he hoped some day he might find the guts to go back and try to patch things up. That was up in southern Nebraska, some place called Piney Flats." Hec paused and eyed Stark shrewdly. "You starting to get an idea what I'm driving at?"

Stark replied, "You're thinking he might have seen taking that money as the chance to go back and make a big enough impression to maybe achieve the patching up he longed for."

Hec nodded. "You got it. I know, it's a long shot. But it's something...some slim possibility of *maybe* getting a lead on where that double-crossing little bastard took off to. We don't have the slightest damn whiff of an idea where he might be headed otherwise."

"But what do you expect me to do?" Stark had asked. "I don't see folks being very likely to open up to me, a stranger, coming 'round asking questions about some local fella."

"You won't have to *ask* nothing. Just do what you do. Gamble," Hec told him. "Sit in at different gaming tables and keep your eyes and ears open. Way Link told it, his family had a good-sized spread in the area at one time. So he oughta be fairly well known thereabouts. Him ditching his wife and kid the way he said was

bound to have stirred plenty of gossip among the old
hens in the town. Double if he showed back up again.
And when hens cluck, their husbands end up having to
listen to some of it and then they do their own blabbing
among each other in the saloons and stores and
whatnot.

"See how it might work? If you end up catching
wind of anything, just notify us and we'll come running
to take it from there. We can't go do any lengthy
snooping on our own up that way due to our descrip-
tions and mugs being plastered on too many Wanted
posters from our hell-raisin' days in Kansas just to the
south. But if you're able to confirm Link is back in that
area, we'll, by God, risk a trip there for the chance to
nail him!"

In the end, Stark had agreed to give Hec's idea a try.
What did he have to lose? Maybe he'd get lucky enough
to win some money at the gaming tables in Piney Flats
and do a favor at the same time. As far as possibly
causing some grief for Link Smith, he had no qualms
about that. The man meant nothing to him other than if
he'd double-crossed his comrades—outlaws though they
may be—then he should be prepared to suffer the consequences.

But that was before Stark had crossed paths with
Link's brother, Braska. In that quirky way fate sometimes works, the handful of nights Stark had spent at
different gaming tables in Piney Flats had netted him
some decent winnings but nothing in the way of *new*
news about Link Smith—though his past deeds were
spoken of a few times The sequence of events
regarding Braska, however—first at the Buffalo Wallow
and later at the Palace—changed everything. Out of

those he learned the older brother had his own interests in running down Link and seemed to have formed some idea he could be found in New Mexico. Where he was planning to go after him.

Stark's subsequent intervention at the Kansas cabin involving the two ex-deputies and the Travers family hadn't truly been the result of him following the deputies, but rather him following Braska and Lucille to learn their more specific destination. He gained that before departing the cabin and then had used his split from the pair, going off with the Travers for as far as it took to find a telegraph office from which he set up the Taos meet with Hec.

Stark's reasons for making Taos an interim stop rather than sending Hec directly to Tulamoro, where Braska suspected his brother could be found, came from the complication of torn loyalties the gambler found himself struggling with. He'd reached an agreement with Hec and felt bound to honor that. But at the same time, damn it, he'd grown to genuinely *like* the stalwart, decent man he recognized in Braska. Stark still didn't give a hang about Link, he deserved however it ended up for him. But if in fact he *was* in Tulamoro trying to re-connect with his wife, then Stark had to somehow perform a balancing act to keep Braska and Hec from colliding over that which each was hunting.

Yeah, Myles Stark didn't like the way things were headed. Not worth a damn...

27

For five days, Braska and Lucille progressed down the eastern side of Colorado. Cattle country. Grassy, rolling terrain rising to a few low buttes here and there, occasional rocky ridges. Sometimes the ground would swell high and the air would be clear enough to catch a faint sight of the Rockies sawtoothing the horizon way to the west. Except for one brief afternoon shower, the weather stayed tolerable. Hot in the daytime, chilly at night.

On the third night after parting from Stark and the Travers family, they swung into a little town called Sharon to replenish supplies. They ended up spending the night, checking into a hotel and treating themselves to a table meal, hot baths, and a soft bed to sleep on. They also treated their horses to a livery stall complete with good rubdowns, double scoops of grain, and some rich alfalfa.

The morning following that first night they'd made love started out more than a little awkwardly. After all, the whole dynamic between them had undergone a pretty significant change. While it was true that neither was exactly an innocent babe, it was also true that neither had a particularly wide range of prior intimacies. Lucille ran off and devoted nearly two years to the shyster who eventually jilted her. Before that, there'd been only a couple of fleeting romances with local boys back home. Apart from losing six years to imprisonment, Braska's involvement with women—largely due to never seeking anything meaningful because of his long-standing plans to go on the drift—amounted only to encounters with friendly saloon gals.

By the time they'd broken camp and were on the trail that morning, however, the level of ease and comfort they'd already established with each other started to kick back in and the awkwardness ebbed away.

It was helped along by Lucille's forthright manner. Moving her horse up alongside Braska and Savvy, talking as they rode stirrup to stirrup at a steady, distance-eating pace, she said, "It was probably inevitable, don't you think?"

"I might be quicker to agree if you didn't sling around such big words."

"Oh, stop it. You're not nearly the cowboy bumpkin you sometimes pretend to be. You know darn well what I mean," Lucille insisted. "Two people, a man and a woman already attracted to one another and with no other commitments, alone together out in the wild...it had all the makings for scandalous behavior right from the get-go."

Braska grinned. "So which of us behaved scandalously first?"

"I did. Even earlier than last night," came the prompt, somewhat surprising answer.

Braska waited. Gave her the chance to build on that.

She did so after a moment's pause, saying, "You see, yesterday, when we parted with Stark and the Travers family, there was a moment where I considered going with them instead of continuing with you. It would have made sense from the standpoint of keeping with my stated intentions when first leaving Piney Flats. I sort of forced myself on you, remember, saying I'd stick until something came along. Well, Greely, Colorado, where the others were headed, fit as a pretty good option. I'd've had company for the trip there and it's a big enough town to expect job opportunities where I could earn and save the money I'd need for finally getting to the Mississippi and New Orleans, like I've been wanting."

"Sounds like it would've suited your aims pretty good." Braska rode staring straight ahead, not looking over at Lucille. "How came you to not go ahead with the notion?"

"Because," she replied quietly, "I didn't want to leave you."

They rode in silence for a ways. Until Braska said, "Look. What happened last night was grand and special. I'll cherish it as one of the best things ever to happen to this cowboy bumpkin. But as to what more can come of it...you know my situation. I'm an ex-con with no aim or prospect except huntin' down my skunk of a brother and then, even if I catch up with him, not bein' sure what I'll do, what it'll accomplish. After that, all I got left is a lifelong yearning to drift, to roam—and six years of bein' penned up only made that yearning stronger."

"And I've got a dream of floating down the Mississippi River to glamorous New Orleans," Lucille came back. "Nobody's saying either one of us has to give up on future hopes. But between now and whether or not we ever reach them, neither should anybody say we need to pass up something—something grand and special, as you put it—in the meantime."

"You were misled and mistreated once before by a snake callin' himself a man. I don't want in any way to be part of causin' you—"

"Stop. Where you and I are concerned, I did what I did and have said what I said with my mind clear and my eyes wide open. I'm neither asking for nor giving any promises. If that's understood and we continue with more of what we started last night...well, then wherever it leads or how it might end shouldn't leave anyone feeling misled or mistreated."

Braska looked over at her. "Does it strike you that what we're talkin' about and the way we're goin' at it is kinda short on bein' romantic?"

"Romance is a word that too often gets brought up too quickly. At this point, cowboy, I think we're talking more a matter of lust," Lucille responded brazenly.

"There's a relief. I'm plumb lousy at writin' gushy poetry and such."

They rode in silence again for a spell. Until, again, it was broken by Braska. Staring straight ahead as before, he said measuredly, "That business about you maybe ridin' off with Stark and the Traverses..."

"Yes?"

"If you'd tried that, I'm pretty sure I would've thrown a rope on you and dragged you back."

Lucille smiled. "*Now* you're being romantic!"

28

LATE IN THE MORNING OF THEIR TENTH DAY OUT OF Piney Flats, Braska and Lucille came in sight of the town Tulamoro, New Mexico. It lay in a shallow valley, surrounded by slopes stippled with sage, cholla and stands of pinyon pine, and cut with scattered rocky ridges. To the east could be seen some low, barren, nameless brown mountains. To the west, the nearer Turkey Mountains backed in the hazy distance by the mighty Sangre de Cristos.

The town itself appeared modest in size, though still somewhat larger than Braska had expected due to its absence from the map he'd started out with. As he and Lucille had gotten closer, though, they'd had no trouble finding people who knew the place and provided accurate directions. In sight of it now, they could see a plaza surrounded by reasonably tidy-looking shops and businesses. The latter were a mix of adobe and wood frame structures. There was an old mission church on the far side of the plaza and a public fountain in the center. The residences fanning out away from this were mostly single-story adobes.

From where he and Lucille sat their horses looking down, Braska said, "Mighty peaceful-lookin' little place."

"Let's hope we can leave it that way," Lucille remarked. When that earned her a sharp look, she added, "I'm just saying that—not without cause, mind you—we've developed what you might call a habit of leaving places in a bit of turmoil."

Braska frowned. "But not without due cause, like you said. And what about that last little town we stopped at up in Colorado? We didn't leave that any worse off than we found it."

"I stand corrected. Maybe there's hope for us functioning in civilization after all."

"That cuts both ways. As long as so-called civilization acts civil in return."

"Fair enough. I can't argue that," said Lucille. "But before we push the limits of whatever civility we find below, can we first test a few of its simpler amenities, like a room with a soft bed and access to a hot bath?"

"And a stove-cooked meal or three taken sitting at a table? Yeah," Braska allowed, "I reckon we can fit that in under the heading of first things first."

———

DOWN IN TULAMORO'S PLAZA, THEY HAD NO trouble spotting one of its larger buildings that bore signs identifying it as a hotel with a restaurant and cantina attached. With that promising to meet their needs, Braska and Lucille swung in at the hitch rail out front. Inside, the thick adobe walls offered refreshing coolness to the near-noon-hour heat without.

The front desk of the hotel was manned by a short, well-groomed Mexican gent wearing a brocaded silk vest and sporting slicked-down black hair, perfectly parted in the middle, so heavily pomaded it also shone like silk. He welcomed the new arrivals heartily to the Hotel de Caza and introduced himself as Pedro de Caza, at their service. Arrangements were made for a room for themselves and for their horses to be boarded at a nearby livery. A tub would be delivered to their room, Lucille was assured, while they enjoyed a fine lunch in the restaurant. Once she had returned to the room and was quite ready, hot water would be promptly provided. As all of this was being settled, Braska, on a whim, signed the guest book "Mr. and Mrs. Elmer Coggins—Piney Creek, Nebraska." When they registered as "Mr. and Mrs. Smith" back in the little Colorado town of Sharon, the smirk it produced on the mug of the hotel desk clerk had annoyed Lucille to no end.

"Come to think of it," Braska reminded her now as they ate lunch, "we almost did have a spot of turmoil there, too. Started by you."

Lucille scowled. "That smirking little pipsqueak. I felt like taking his sign-in register and smacking him alongside the head with it! But I, unlike some people, know how to control myself."

"Uh-huh. But tell me this," Braska said around a bite of enchilada. "What if I'd've signed *Smith* again here, and ol' slick-haired Pedro would've flashed the same look? Could you have controlled yourself a second time?"

"Let's just say," answered Lucille, "it was a safer choice not to put it to the test."

By the time they'd finished eating, it had been decided that while Lucille took her long, leisurely soak, Braska would use the time to go ahead and seek out his sister-in-law Linda. The best way to do that, he reasoned, was by inquiring after her younger sister Trisha, who had lived in the town for some time and was its school teacher.

"Won't the sisters find you showing up out of the blue rather startling, especially if your brother is also here like you suspect?" asked Lucille. "And, if that's the case, might they not—all things considered—try to conceal him from you?"

Braska nodded. "To the last part, yeah, I'd expect so. But as far as me showin' up, that in itself shouldn't seem too unreasonable. They must've heard by now I got released from the pen. And Linda and I always got along well, she bein' the only one besides my mother who wrote me when I was behind the walls—to tell me about Ma's passin' and such. Plus she's holdin' those personal items of Ma's for me. Not that I'm truly lookin' to take possession of them just now, but they give me a solid enough reason for stoppin' by...and if Link *is* somewhere around, I'm countin' I'll be able to pick up some hint of that, even if Linda and her sister try to hide it from me."

———

BACK IN THE ROOM, WHILE BUCKETS OF STEAMING hot water for Lucille's bath were being delivered and poured into the big copper tub previously put in place,

Braska got himself spruced up a little at the washstand off to one side. He washed his face, combed his hair, took from his bedroll the clean shirt that had been laundered—along with other articles of his and Lucille's clothing—back in Sharon. As he reached the point of feeling suitably presentable to go visiting, Lucille's bath was also ready and she had just stepped into the tub. The sight of her in all her splendid nudity, preparing to sink into the heaping mound of bubbles, gave him serious pause halfway to the door.

"What are you looking at?" Lucille said.

"That's kind of a ridiculous question, ain't it? I'm lookin' at you, of course. But I'm also lookin' at that tub —and wonderin' if there's room in there for two."

Lucille cocked an eyebrow. "That's a real intriguing question, cowboy, and one I'd be happy to help find the answer to some later time. But, for right now, my plans are strictly devoted to a nice, long, relaxing soak *alone*. And you've got work to do. So scat. Get to it—before my water starts growing cold."

———

DOWN IN THE HOTEL LOBBY, BRASKA FOUND THE manager, Pedro, fussing around behind the registration desk with no other staff or guests present. When he looked up and saw Braska approaching, he smiled attentively.

"Are your accommodations satisfactory, senor?"

"Very much so," Braska assured him. "While my lady is turnin' herself into a prune in her bath, I thought I'd stretch my legs a little and take a look around your town."

Though his smile stayed in place, Pedro's eyes flicked for just a moment to the Colt riding on Braska's hip. "You will find our village a very quiet and peaceful place," he said. "Especially during these middle afternoon hours."

"Siesta, eh?"

Pedro shrugged. "It is not quite the tradition as down in Old Mexico, but a similar thing, yes."

"Always sounded like a right fine notion to me. Unfortunately, I've always found myself in places where I never got the chance to practice it much," Braska told him.

"I see you are from Nebraska. Cattle rancher?"

"Cowhand, yeah. Mostly. Me and my lady are lookin' for a change, though. Headed down Galveston way. Want to have a look at the ocean, among other things."

"Ah, yes. I too have longed to see the ocean someday. Water stretching as far as the eye can see. It is an amazing thing to imagine."

"But ahead of all that, and sorta gettin' back to the mention of Nebraska," Braska said, working around to what he hoped to glean from the hotel man, "one of the reasons I stopped here in Tulamoro was to pay a quick visit to a couple of hometown gals who I understand live hereabouts. The McBain sisters?"

"McBain?" Pedro echoed, not seeming to recognize the name.

"That'd be the name of one of 'em. Miss Trisha, who's lived here the longest. The other, Linda, who only moved down not long ago, probably goes by her married name of Smith."

Pedro's face brightened. "Senorita Trisha, of course!

Yes, I should have remembered she came from
Nebraska. I have only met her recently arrived but
equally beautiful sister a few times. She stayed here
briefly when she first arrived, until she found a place of
her own. Senorita Trisha, however, has long been a
shining light in our community. She is the teacher of
our children, you know, and soon to be married to the
brilliant son of our alcalde!"

Braska's ears perked up at this. Soon to be married?
So much for what he'd been told about Linda's reason
for moving down here being to console Trisha following
the breakup of her engagement. Unless Pedro was not
current with that development. Considering how he
also ran a restaurant and cantina in such a small setting,
however, it was doubtful he was very far behind in
news or gossip of any significance. All of which only
gave impetus to Braska's suspicions about Linda's rather
abrupt decision to head this way.

"Ernesto—Ernesto Renosa Jr., that is—is another
shining light of our community," Pedro went on excitedly. "Not only is he the son of our beloved alcalde and
part of a bloodline that has been at the heart of
Tulamoro since it was little more than a mission and a
handful of goat herdsmen, but he went on to train as a
physician in the great city of San Francisco! Then,
when he could have set up practice and acquired
wealth and esteem anywhere he chose, he came back
here, home, to provide much-needed but long-lacking
medical care for the whole area. Now we will all be
further rewarded when he takes the hand of lovely
Senorita Trisha—such a handsome couple they make!—
and continues the Renosa bloodline for another
generation."

"Wow. Sounds like a mighty big deal all around."

Pedro made a gesture with both hands. "Their wedding will be a festival such as this valley has never seen!"

"When's the big day gonna be?" Braska asked.

"The exact date has not been announced. But very soon. Preparations are already underway."

"Since me and my lady are just passin' through, it sounds like a whing-ding we'll be sorry to've missed," said Braska. "But in the meantime, ahead of the big whirl, I still want to pay my regards to the sisters. Can you give me directions to whereabouts I could find one or both of 'em? I'm a little more familiar with Miss Linda, but either will do."

"In that case," Pedro replied, "it is easiest to direct you to Senorita Trisha. Her school is just behind the old mission. You cannot miss it, and classes should soon be letting out for the day."

29

Outside, Braska paused to build a cigarette. He remained in the shade thrown by an awning that jutted out across the front of the hotel building. Leaning against a support beam, he stood smoking and letting his eyes make a leisurely sweep of the plaza. It was indeed, as Pedro had said, a quiet and peaceful scene in the hot afternoon sun. No breeze stirred and hardly anybody was moving about.

Through an open window somewhere, somebody was softly strumming a guitar, and over in front of the livery stable corral, a small flock of chickens were noisily clucking and fussing. The busiest activity in sight was that of two toddlers sitting on the ground beside the public fountain, making mud pies from the puddle of water they apparently had splashed out for that purpose. A shaggy red dog lay nearby, watching over them and looking like he wished they would take their play somewhere out of the sun.

Yeah, a quiet, peaceful little place for sure, Braska

mused. He hoped he'd be able to ride off and leave it that way. But he had a gnawing hunch there were some things hidden by this facade that might not allow him to. He dropped his half-smoked cigarette in the dust and stepped on it as he started in the direction of the mission and the school that lay behind.

As he was going around the end of the old church, he was met by a flood of chattering, laughing youngsters coming in the opposite direction. Kids, a mix of boys and girls ranging in age from about six to twelve, released from school and on their way home. Braska stood still, let the flood swirl around and past him, then continued on. The school, when it came in sight, was a single-story adobe building on a patch of grass about a hundred yards in back of the mission. It appeared well maintained, with a couple maple trees for shade, a teeter-totter, and a sturdy post and cross-beam construction with three play swings hanging from it.

Standing in front of the building, with three lingering students, little girls, milling about her, was a tall, willowy young woman with long wheat-colored hair. Trisha McBain had still been a gangly teen when Braska last saw her, but she had matured into quite a beauty. It occurred to him she may not remember him from a hill of beans.

Approaching across the playground with what he hoped was a disarming smile, he said, "Good afternoon."

Trisha returned his smile while the little girls shifted shyly around behind her. "Hello there. Is there something I can do for you?"

"I hope so. For starters, hopefully you'll remember a

fellow Nebraskan from up Piney Flats way. My name is Bra—er, Virgil Smith."

A couple of emotions flickered across Trisha's face. Not recognition, but recollection. And something more that quickly came and went until suddenly all there was a dazzling smile. "Why of course! Linda's brother-in-law from the Bar S ranch!"

"That's right. Kinda far off my range, I know."

"My goodness! Does Linda know you're here?"

"No, not yet. I just got into town a little bit ago. Wantin' to pay my respects to her—and you—I asked Pedro at the hotel and he said it'd be easiest to find you here at the school."

"Of course. Give me just a moment." She turned to the little girls and quickly explained how an old family friend had shown up so she'd have to postpone their discussion until tomorrow but promised she would give them full attention at that time. She obviously had a great rapport with the children, and so, though they looked disappointed, they accepted her promise and took their leave.

As the girls wandered off, Braska said, "Hope I didn't interrupt anything too serious."

"Oh, you most certainly did." Trisha heaved a dramatic sigh. "There is nothing more serious than affairs of the heart, don't you know? You see, all three of those little darlings are madly in love with Tommy Tarloff, who pays none of them the least bit of attention because he is too busy collecting horny toads and digging for the perfect earthworm to go fishing with."

"Uh-oh. I ought to be shot for gettin' in the way of young love."

"No, you ought to be rewarded for saving me from trying to come up with an answer to soothe their tormented little hearts. At least I'll have tonight to hopefully think of something to tell them—or, perhaps by tomorrow they will all have fallen in love with somebody else and at least Tommy will be in the clear."

"Until he reaches an age where he *wishes* he had three gals interested in him."

Trisha rolled her eyes. "*That*, thankfully, should be far enough down the road to be out of my hands."

"In the meantime," Braska said, "Pedro informed me how your own love life sounds to be in pretty good shape and that wedding bells are due to be ringin' soon in the old church."

"My. Pedro seems to be informative about a lot of things. Maybe he ought to start a newspaper to go along with his other business ventures." Trisha smiled. "But that doesn't make him inaccurate. Yes, very soon I will be Mrs. Ernesto Renosa Jr., wife of Tulamoro's very esteemed—and also very handsome, I might add—doctor."

"Very lucky, too, I'd say."

"Gallantly spoken, Mr. Smith. Thank you." Trisha paused and her expression turned more somber. "But, inasmuch as you came knowing Linda was here, you also must know that things under the heading of romance and marriage did not turn out so well for her and your brother."

"Yeah, I heard all the unfortunate details from your other sister Betty, among others," Braska told her. "Leaves me powerful disappointed in Link. On a lot of fronts, but none more than the way he ran out on Linda and his little girl. One of these days, I mean to catch up with him and...well, never mind about that."

"You don't think he's here, do you?" Trisha's eyes had gone wide and the question came a little too quickly, a too-anxious ring to it.

"If I thought that, that he was here tryin' to make amends or some such, that might be a different story. But that ain't hardly the case, is it?"

"No. No, not at all." Another hurried response.

"Look, I didn't come by meanin' to stir up bad memories and feelin's," said Braska. "Linda was the only one besides my ma who wrote me when...you must know about the whole prison thing, right? So it was Linda who wrote to tell me about Ma's passin' and some after that. That meant a lot. I wanted to see her and thank her for that, and Betty also mentioned about some personal items of Ma's that Linda was keepin' for me. Those are the reasons I came by."

"And Linda will be delighted to see you. You can be sure of that."

"I hope so. Then how about takin' me to her or directin' me where I can find her?"

"I'd love to," Trisha said. But then, with an embarrassed little laugh, she added, "Only, right at the moment, I'm not sure where she's at."

When that drew a puzzled frown from Braska, she went on to explain, "You see, when Linda and Alicia got to town, there was nothing available for them at the boarding house where I stay. But they were able to rent an apartment from an elderly gentleman, a widower, just down the street. Mr. Clemenza, their landlord, loves to go fishing, and his affinity for it has spilled over to both Linda and little Alicia. They go with him two, sometimes three times a week. I happen to know that today was one of those occasions. When I saw them last, they were talking about packing a picnic basket and making a whole afternoon of it. So I'm sure they're not back yet, and I have no idea where Mr. Clemenza's coveted fishing spot is."

"To a dedicated fisherman, his favorite fishin' hole can be like a sacred thing. I wouldn't want to go invadin' on that, even if you did know."

"But you indicated you checked in at the Hotel de Caza. So you're staying for at least the night, correct? I can be sure to let Linda know you're in town and have her contact you there."

"Reckon that'd work," Braska allowed. "But instead, how about all of you—Linda and Alicia, yourself, and your fiancé, too, if he'd like—join me this evenin' for dinner at the hotel restaurant? I can make reservations for, say, six?"

Trisha considered briefly, then said, "Why, yes. Yes, I think that would work fine. Pedro's cook staff serves delicious meals. I'm not sure what Ernesto's schedule is, but if at all possible, I know he would enjoy meeting someone from where Linda and I call *back home*."

"It's settled then. I'll go back to the hotel and make the reservations."

Braska drifted away from the schoolyard and Trisha went inside to perform whatever was required before closing up for the day. Instead of going back around the same end of the old mission as before, Braska decided to stroll along the rear side of the weather-beaten yet still grand old structure. He wondered how far back it dated and marveled at the thought of all the surrounding changes it must have witnessed and endured in those unfolding decades. War and strife, slaughter and salvation, rejection and redemption. Yet here it remained, scarred but still strong and proud like an old warrior.

A broken-down stone fence ran along the back of the church and, within it, was a cluster of small trees. An orchard, long untended. Braska fashioned a cigarette and, stepping over a collapsed section of the wall, walked in among the scraggly, mostly leafless trees. Streaming smoke, he moved idly from one to another and tried to figure out what fruit they had once put forth. Pears? Plums? He couldn't tell.

As he stood there in the dappled shade, his attention was abruptly drawn by hurried movement out on the street—or lane, more properly described—that ran in the back of the mission. Crossing left to right in Braska's field of vision, the lane led from the schoolhouse and stretched before an open, grassy lot with no other buildings until it came to quite an imposing estate house set back at an angle off the rear corner of the mission. Trisha McBain was walking briskly along this lane, her movement being what had caught Braska's eye. As he continued to watch, she turned and passed under the arc of a gated walkway then on toward the ornate front door of the home. The place was an immaculately maintained two-story adobe with a red tile roof and a low privacy wall across its front lawn.

A little girl, who couldn't have been much younger than the lovelorn trio Trisha had been counseling back at the school, sat on the rich green grass of the front lawn, playing with a kitten she was teasing with a piece of bright red yarn. Trisha stopped and spoke with her for a minute, then gave a quick hug and went inside. The little girl continued playing with the kitten.

Braska drifted through to the far side of the orchard, positioning him for a closer look at the big house. It wasn't hard to figure this must be the home of Tulamoro's alcalde. And, studying it a little tighter, he formed a hunch that Ernesto Jr. likely had his doctor's office set up here. A long wing off to the right certainly could accommodate such. And there was some sort of sign affixed up beside the front door, glossy black on white lettering, that Braska couldn't quite read from this distance but was willing to bet confirmed his hunch of proclaiming a doctor in residence.

Not that there was anything wrong about any of that, Braska told himself. It only made sense for the young doc to set up shop in his old man's place, where there was plenty of room and amid what he would one day inherit anyhow. His decision to bring his skills back home in order to serve the poor and underprivileged who'd been left lacking for so long cut Junior a lot of slack in Braska's eyes.

Speaking of eyes, Braska's gaze fell once again on the little girl in the front yard and a new hunch suddenly grabbed him. Could it be that he was looking at his niece Alicia? That would stand in sharp contrast to Trisha's story about Alicia and her mother being gone fishing, of course, but who else would this girl be? And what of some of Trisha's slightly quirky reactions when Braska was talking to her—not to mention the beeline she'd made for the big house just now?

Braska ground out his cigarette butt against the stone wall and told himself to calm down, not get over-eager and jump to conclusions just because he *wanted* to uncover some fishy doings here in Tulamoro. He already had the falsehood about Trisha's allegedly broken engagement to build on, no need to—

Further pondering was cut short by the sight of two women emerging out of the doorway Trisha had entered through just minutes earlier. One was Trisha reappearing, the other was Linda.

30

"I HUNG BACK AND FOLLOWED THEM AT A distance," Braska was explaining to Lucille after he'd returned to their hotel room. "Luckily, the lane ran mostly on the back side of houses facing in toward the plaza, so there wasn't anybody about to notice me and be suspicious of what I was up to. And the sisters didn't go far before they went inside a large, wood frame house—either Trisha's boarding house or, more likely, where Linda rents her apartment."

"So what do you think it all means?" Lucille asked. Out of her bath now, she was clad in a clean blouse and her split riding skirt, smelling fresh and looking lovelier than ever.

"The only reason people lie is to cover up something, hide the truth," Braska answered tersely.

"And what you think they're covering up is the presence of your brother here in Tulamoro?"

"What else would they have to hide from me? Or to keep from tellin' the truth to their sister up in Piney

Flats about why Linda suddenly decided to come down here? It seems like an obvious thing, at least as a possibility. But, at the same time, it's what I *want* it to be—for reasons of gettin' my search over sooner and easier. So I gotta be careful not to be too quick jumpin' to conclusions."

Lucille said, "But if Link is here and Linda was drawn down to rejoin him, then why the need to keep him in hiding—and I don't mean just from you? If he was hereabouts and his presence generally known, even under a different name or whatever, don't you think talkative Pedro would have gotten around to mentioning it in some way? If for no other reason—in case you haven't noticed—than a new Anglo in town would be bound to stand out."

Braska scowled in thought. "By God, that's a good point. If Link found out Trisha was here then showed up and was able to convince her to get Linda to come down...what would be his goal? If it was for them to get back together and make a fresh start, then it'd make sense to go off somewhere where his reputation wasn't likely to follow. Then again, this very place could be considered remote enough to fit that bill as good as any. But if he was gonna settle here, then why—like you say —would he keep to hidin'?"

"What about the doctor?" Lucille said.

Braska looked at her. "What do you mean? What about him?"

"That's where Linda was when Trisha went to get her, right? Did Linda come out looking ill or anything?"

"Not that I could see."

"And if it happened that she was, that would have

made a perfectly reasonable explanation for Trisha to suggest you delay seeing her right away—rather than concoct the whole story about her being off fishing."

Braska frowned. "So what do you figure Linda *was* doin' at the doc's? And why would it make any..." His voice trailed off and his frowned deepened. "Wait a minute. Are you thinkin' Link might be in there—not just strictly hidin' out, but bein' out of sight on account of needin' the doc's close care?"

"Remember what Marshal Coggins told you about the big shoot-out the Mallet gang was in a while back? How it left a couple of them dead and the rest report-edly tore up pretty bad. And nobody having heard anything about them since? The timing of that wasn't too far off from Linda's sudden decision to come down here, right? Link showing up badly injured would have given him a sympathy angle to use on Trisha and certainly on Linda as a means to coax her into at least coming to see him."

"But that bank robbery and shoot-out was weeks ago."

"A serious bullet wound, especially if not treated right away, could lead to infections and complications that might drag on for months. And before you start questioning the involvement of Trisha's fiancé, remember two things: One, a physician takes an oath to first do no harm. And two, a man in love would surely be willing, if asked by his bride-to-be, to make certain exceptions that he otherwise might not."

Braska cocked an eyebrow. "Damn, gal, you have got one connivin' mind for calculatin' behavior in folks."

"Thanks...I think. But let's not get carried away,"

Lucille cautioned. "Everything I just suggested is speculation. It could be off by a mile."

"And it could be right on the money," Braska argued. "The thing now is to do a little more proddin' over dinner tonight and see if we can get any reactions that give cause to lean in harder. It's certain the lyin' and odd behavior is hidin' something. And the sooner we find out what, the better."

"You think they'll make good on showing up for dinner?"

"I don't see how they can dodge it. They don't have time to make a getaway—not that Trisha ever would anyhow, with all she has at stake here. And it ain't like they got any reason to think I'm suspicious of anything in the first place. No, havin' bought time to make sure they got their stories straight so's not to say anything that'll *make* me suspicious, I'm pretty sure they'll show."

"In that case," Lucille declared, "if I'm going to be attending a dinner where two other women are present —especially two young, attractive ones—then I darn well want to be dressed in something better than this riding attire."

"You look just fine to me."

"Thanks again, but you don't get it. It's a girl thing that no man would ever understand. What it means is, I'll have to go check some of those shops out around the plaza and see if I can't find something more suitable."

Braska smiled. "Like you said, I guess I don't get it."

"Be glad you don't have to. I shouldn't be long, I expect the choices will be limited." Lucille eyed him up and down. "While I'm gone, you might want to consider re-introducing your face to a razor. And that shirt you changed to earlier is okay, but your britches and boots could stand a good brushing."

"I never knew so much fuss had to go into takin' a meal. I thought all you needed was an appetite."

"Consider it part of my conniving ways," Lucille said over her shoulder as she started for the door. "I'll be back shortly."

When she was gone, Braska went over to the small mirror hanging on the wall above the washstand and leaned his face close. Yeah, what he saw there was in need of a shave, no argument. From his saddlebags, he pulled a bar of soap and his razor, took them back to the washstand, and poured some water from the pitcher into the basin. It was only room temperature, not hot, but it would do. He'd shaved under far worse conditions —everything from trying to get a lather out of icy creek water to making do with the tepid slime and dull razor issued—under tight guard—on shave days back at Hellstone.

Braska undid his gun belt and pulled off his clean shirt. He was just beginning to work up some thick suds when he heard the click of the door opening behind him. He dropped the soap and turned, his right hand sweeping to the Colt he'd placed near the edge of the washstand.

Lucille stepped into the room and quickly pressed the door shut again behind her. She leaned back against it, her face drawn and ashen and her expression one of half-bewilderment, half-fear.

"What's wrong? What is it?" Braska demanded.

Her troubled eyes locked on him. "I'm not exactly sure. But it's bad, I know that much."

Braska hurriedly dried his hands, shoved the gun in

his waistband, and went to her, saying, "I know how hard it is to rattle you. What happened out there?"

"Just as I was starting out the front of the hotel," Lucille answered, "four men came riding into town. I paused in the shadows of the awning and watched. They swung their horses to the cantina, dismounted, and went on in...one of them was Myles Stark."

"Myles? What the devil's he doin' here?"

"I don't know. But seeing him was just the start of, as you put it, rattling me. Because one of the other men was none other than Hec Mallet."

Braska spat out a curse.

Lucille continued, "I'm confident of recognizing him due to those Wanted posters we saw nailed up outside that hotel back in Sharon. I recognized another of the riders, too, a big, bearded hombre—Big Jeff or John, something like that."

"Big Jess Whorten," Braska grated.

"The third one was a slim, dark-skinned Mexican with shifty eyes. I don't remember if we saw a poster of him or not."

"Sounds like it's probably Brazo Hacklin. Makin' 'em all that's left of the Mallet gang...all but Stark. What the hell he's doin' with their like, I can't begin to figure."

"None of the others paid any attention, but Myles spotted me before I ducked back inside. Our eyes locked for just a second and he made a kind of jerky motion with his head, like he was warning me to get the hell out of sight—not that I wasn't already on my way."

Braska swore again.

Lucille clutched his arm and gazed anxiously up at him. "What do you think it means?"

"Only one thing it can," Braska said. "They're here after Link, same as me. And that damn Stark led 'em!"

"You're thinking they may be here to retrieve Link, take him back into the fold if he's now healed enough to travel? But—"

"No," Braska cut her short. "I don't think they're here with any good intentions toward Link at all. Just the opposite. Think back to all of what Elmer told me about that Utah robbery—how the gang got away with the money but got shot to ribbons takin' it. Then, a little later, Merl Mallet—one of the gang leaders—is found dead out on some getaway trail. Well, a standard practice for such business dealin's is for the gang boss to ride off with the take and hang on to it until it's split time back wherever the whole bunch goes to ground."

Lucille's eyes widened, starting to see where he was headed. "So Merl, being *one* of the gang leaders, might have been the one holding the money when he high-tailed out of town. But with him dying from wounds before he made it very far, if another gang member happened to have been riding with him until he went down, then *he* would have had access to the booty."

"Be mighty temptin' to a lot of folks, especially somebody already ridin' the owlhoot trail." Braska's tone was flat, tinged with bitterness. "And if Merl's getaway partner was Link, packin' some bullet holes of his own, maybe he saw it as a chance to break away and use his wounds as a sympathy play to try and get Linda back—while also havin' the stolen money as a sleeve Ace for financin' a fresh start."

"It hangs together, I guess. But it's all based on still more speculation." Lucille's brows pinched tight. "And none of it begins to address how Myles fits in."

As if on cue, a soft rap sounded on the door and a hushed but insistent voice easily recognized by both Braska and Lucille spoke on the other side. "Hurry up, let me in," urged Myles Stark.

31

GUN IN HAND, BRASKA STEPPED FORWARD AND pressed himself against the wall to one side of the door. He motioned Lucille to move back the other way. Then, saying nothing, he reached with his free hand to twist the knob and suddenly jerk the door open wide. As it swung inward and away from him, he twisted around and leveled his Colt dead center on the man standing in the doorway. "Anybody else moves in that hallway behind you, you take the first bullet," he warned.

Myles Stark stared into the bore of the Colt's muzzle for a split second, then lifted his eyes to meet Braska's glare. "You pull that trigger," the gambler said calmly, "you damn well *will* have hombres boiling into this hallway behind me—the whole Mallet gang. What's left of 'em."

"Thanks to you leadin' 'em here," Braska ground out through clenched teeth.

Stark responded, his voice still calm, "I'm supposed to be visiting the privy out back, so I've only got a few minutes. You willing to give me a chance to explain and maybe once again save your hide—not to mention Lucille's—or are you bent on barging into the middle of an explosion bigger than you have any chance to walk back out of?"

Braska hesitated a beat, then motioned him in with a wave of the gun and kicked the door shut behind. "Let's hear it," he said.

Stark moved to the middle of the room and then turned to face both Braska and Lucille, who moved over to stand close beside Braska. "Long story short," Stark told them, "is that I owed a debt to Hec Mallet. A big one, from way back. Part of repaying that was to ride up Piney Flats way, your brother Link's old stomping ground, and see if I could maybe catch wind of him showing back up in those parts. You see, Link was riding with the gang on that Utah bank holdup that went bad. Him and Merl were seen making it clear of the big shoot-out together.

"Well, we all know Merl didn't make it very far. But Link apparently did—so far that nobody's seen hide nor hair of him since. Same for the bank money Merl was known to have on him when they rode off together...so you can understand why Hec has a powerful interest in catching up with Link. Not only for abandoning a dead or dying Merl but for keeping the money all to himself as part of it."

Braska's mouth peeled back into a grimace. "And you're the bloodhound, fed by information culled out of me through false friendship, leadin' him in for the slaughter!"

"That seems to be how it's turned out," Stark admitted sullenly. "I'll admit your brother means nothing to me and I have no qualms about him having to pay the consequences for his actions. You know as well as anybody he did wrong to a lot of people. Mixing with the likes of the Mallet gang and thinking he could pull more of the same with them, that put him in way over his head."

"He ain't drowned yet," Braska declared.

"Is he here in Tulamoro?"

"Not that I'd tell you if I did—but I don't know. We just got in a little while ago."

Stark made a face. "Yeah, and that's a damn shame. You made better time than I figured. I was hoping we'd beat you here by as much as a day. Then I saw Lucille out front and checked the sign-in register for your room number—nice touch on the *Mr. and Mrs. Coggins* bit, by the way. I got a kick out of it. But I'd be getting a lot bigger kick out of knowing the both of you were still about fifty or sixty miles to the north."

"Real sorry to disappoint you," Braska drawled. "But since we ain't...how do you expect this to play out?"

Stark's expression soured even more. "I wish I knew. Hec's plenty wild under the best of circumstances. This business, especially with the loss of Merl being at the heart of it, has him wound tighter than ever. On the belief I provided that Link might be holed up here trying to get back together with his wife, Hec's sworn to turn this town upside down if he has to in order to shake out the answer. Him, Big Jess Whorten, and Brazo Hacklin are down in the cantina, swilling tequila as a prelude. I don't think it will be long before they're ready to start in."

Eyes and tone icy, Braska said, "And you'll join in with 'em?"

Stark met his gaze. "I won't go against them. Not Hec. I already told you—him I owe. But I have no feelings for your brother or this lousy town."

"In that case, if I was to burn you down right here then I'd be makin' the odds more favorable, wouldn't I?"

"Not really. Not against you." Stark smiled crookedly. "You see, for what it's worth, I *do* care about you and Lucille. You think I intervened all those previous times just to help gun you down in the end? I won't go directly against you either, same as I won't against Hec."

"You're not making any sense!" exclaimed Lucille.

"But I am! The sense I'm making," Stark insisted, "is for you two to slip out the back and get the hell away from here before Hec and the others ever know you're near. Face it, Smith, this time you can't save your no-good brother—not if he's here, not if they catch up with him somewhere else! And if you go down trying, think what Big Jess and Brazo will do to Lucille if they get their hands on her!"

Lucille slipped her arms around Braska and he could feel her trembling.

"I have to get back," said Stark, his voice suddenly weary sounding. "You can stop me with a bullet if you want, but it won't save you. Your only chance is to take my advice and ride fast and far away from here."

———

ONCE THE DOOR CLOSED AND STARK WAS GONE, Braska and Lucille stood momentarily silent and motionless. Until Braska pulled gently out of her arms and gazed intently down into her eyes. "You gotta know that the last thing I want is to see you get hurt. So the safest bet is for you to take Stark's advice and make dust outta here. But as for me...I can't. I've got to stay and face these mongrels."

"And you've got to know," Lucille replied without hesitation, "that the last thing I'll do is cut and run on you. So, since I'm staying, what can I do to help?"

Braska's mouth pulled into a wry grin. "I should've known it was a waste of breath to even try."

"Yes, you should have."

"Okay then. You'll still need to kick up some dust. I want you to hotfoot it to that doc's place—you can't miss it, back behind the church. Warn him what's comin' down and do whatever you have to, even if it takes wavin' that pea shooter of yours in his face, to make sure he takes it serious. Then it'll be up to you and him to get as many people as you can—includin' Link, if he's there like we figure, plus the sisters and my niece—to safety. Maybe fort up in the old mission. Because when Hec gets ready to cut loose, he won't hesitate tearin' apart everything and everybody in his path to try and get what he's after."

"What are you going to be doing?" Lucille asked.

"First thing, I mean to get my hands on a shotgun. Then I'm gonna pin down Pedro and see if there's such a thing as any fightin' men in this nice, peaceful village willin' to back my play."

"That's a mighty skimpy battle plan."

"It's a work in progress. You could help if you run across any fighters while makin' your sweep—send 'em this way."

"I could help by staying here and *being* a fighter beside you," Lucille insisted.

"You asked what you could do to help, and I told you," Braska said irritably. "Now do you think standin' and arguin' about it is doin' me any good?"

Lucille's eyes flashed. "All right, you stubborn ass. Have it your way!"

She started for the door in a huff, but Braska caught her arm and yanked her back. Pulling her tight against him, he leaned his face close to hers and said in a ragged whisper, "Once before, that time when I was fixin' to knock heads with Marv Kenna out front of the Palace, you surprised me with a quick kiss for luck. I sure wouldn't mind if you stuck around long enough to give me another one of those."

Lucille's gaze melted. She reached up to press his face softly between her palms and lifted her lips. This time, there was nothing quick about the kiss that followed.

32

"Jesus Christ, Stark," grumbled Big Jess as the gambler came back into the smoky cantina, "you didn't blow the door off that privy, did you? You was gone long enough. Some of the rest of us might have need of usin' it, too, you know."

Stark shrugged indifferently. "Guess all those trail beans caught up with me. Had to get rid of 'em sooner or later."

"Oh, great." Wharten wrinkled his nose. "In that case, maybe you *shoulda* oughta blowed the door off. Air the joint out so's the next poor slob who wanders in don't get gassed to death."

"Yeah, like you're one to talk," snorted Brazo. "I have had the misfortune of following you into more than one privy, amigo, and if you can survive your own stink, then trust me, you are in danger from no one else's."

From where he leaned against the bar with his bad arm still wrapped in a sling and fist wrapped around a bottle of tequila, Hec Mallet growled over his shoulder,

"Knock off the tomfoolery you bunch of jackasses. You forgettin' we're here on serious business? And didn't you notice this whole town ain't nothing but one big shithole? What difference does any single outhouse make—if we leave even that much left standin' when we're done!"

Wharten's mouth spread in a wide grin. "Now you're talkin', Boss. We've gone and cut the trail dust out of our mouths, we're ready to go to work. Just say the word."

There were half a dozen other customers in the cantina, seated at tables playing dominoes or just nursing drinks. All were elderly men with deeply seamed faces, droopy gray mustaches, and weary eyes. Two of them rose as hurriedly as their aged frames were able and started for the door.

"You can start," Hec said to Wharten, "by stoppin' those two. Nobody leaves or does anything else unless I say so. Set 'em back down!"

Wharten moved to block the doorway and planted a broad palm in the chest of each man, shoving them roughly back. "You heard the man—plop your bony asses back on your chairs."

"Please, senior!" protested the bartender, a narrow-faced man with muttonchop sideburns and one arm that ended below the elbow. "They are old men. There is no need to—"

Hec cut him short with a back-handed slap across the mouth, barking, "Shut up!" Then he grabbed him by the front of his shirt and dragged him half onto the bartop. Pushing his face close enough so that spittle dotted the man's face when he said more, Hec added, "What there ain't no need for is you to run your mouth and try tellin' me my business. Understand? Unless, that is, I ask you a question. Then you damn well better talk and tell me everything I want to know!" With that, he shoved the bartender back hard and sent him staggering back to the row of bottles on a shelf behind him, causing them to rattle and two or three to drop and smash on the floor.

Wharten and Brazo tittered with laughter, greatly amused by all of this.

A curtained doorway cut in the wall behind the bar suddenly parted and a plump, wide-eyed young woman burst through. "Uncle! What in Heaven's name is all the commotion about?"

"Nothing, Rosina," the barkeep quickly assured her. "All is fine, you go on back to—"

"No!" As he issued this latest interruption, Hec's gun appeared in his hand. He extended his arm across the bartop, aiming the cutter at the 'keep while his eyes locked on the young woman. "You try boltin' back through that curtain, chiquita," he rasped, "and your uncle will lose his other arm with one pull of my trigger. Just look in my eyes if you think I'm bluffing!"

The girl stood frozen, her chin beginning to quiver.

Brazo took a tentative step toward her, extending an empty hand and coaxing her in a gentle voice, "Come, little one. No harm will befall you so long as your uncle and others who may be called upon show the sense to cooperate."

"If this is a robbery," said the girl, "then take what you want. There is no need to hurt anyone."

Wharten chuckled nastily. "Oh, you damn betcha we'll take what we want, honey. And you showin' up just added to the list."

"Shut up, you fool!" snapped Brazo. Then, with a lightning-fast lunge, he grabbed the girl by one arm and yanked her to him.

One of the old men thrust to his feet. "You filthy gringo swine!"

Stark, standing near, clapped his hands on the man's shoulders and pressed him back down, firmly but not as roughly as one of the others would have. "Give it a rest, old timer," he hissed close to the man's ear, "don't cut your string shorter than it already is."

Hec wagged his gun at the barkeep. "You. Come around from behind there. Hurry it up." As the man was complying, Hec cut his eyes to the girl and asked, "Anybody else back there where you came from?"

The girl shook her head.

"Don't lie to me!"

"N-no. No, I swear."

Hec swung his gun in a flat arc. "All right then, everybody up and outside. C'mon, clear 'em out! We're only gonna learn so much from this bottled-up bunch of mostly walkin' dead. I want to gather a crowd so's there are plenty of alert ears to hear what I got to say, hear what our demands are. And then there'd better be some loose tongues among 'em or there'll be hell to pay if we don't start gettin' what we came for!"

IN A BACK ROOM OF THE HOTEL, GROWLING, "THIS damn thing is such a relic I fear it'd blow up in my hands and do more harm to me than anything I aimed it at!" Braska cast aside the ancient, dusty shotgun Pedro had dug out for him. "Ain't you got nothing else in the way of weapons around here?"

"In a drawer out at the front desk," said an anxious-looking Pedro, "I have a very large pistol. A Colt's Dragoon, I think it is called."

"That'd make a pretty good hand cannon, but it wouldn't gain me much over what I've already got," Braska said, referring to the .44 on his hip and a duplicate of the same he'd pulled from his possibles pack and tucked at the small of his back for backup. He was carrying his Henry repeater too, which would give him plenty of firepower if things broke into a running battle. A good, reliable street sweeper still would have been welcome, though, as a quicker, surer way to even the odds in an initial face-off. "You ever even fire that Dragoon?" he asked.

"Me? No." Pedro shook his head. "It belonged to my brother who runs the cantina next door. He used it once in a duel over a faithless senorita. The man he faced was faster and a truer shot. He put a bullet in my brother's arm that shattered his elbow. My brother lost the duel, lost the senorita, and ended up losing his arm. Since then, the men in our family do not look to firearms as a way to help our problems."

"Reckon that makes sense. Man's got to know his limits," Braska allowed.

He wondered if he ought to be applying that to himself. Pedro hadn't given much hope of him finding any townsmen who'd be willing to back his play. Tulamoro was the kind of place, the hotel man explained, where young, spirited men who might be up for a fight were quickly gone, eager to leave as soon as any opportunity presented itself. What was left were elders and middle-agers, mostly farmers and herdsmen who worked the nearby fields. Their hands were suited to tools of labor, not guns, plus they had families to think of.

"In that case," Braska said grimly, "then those fine family men—and you and yours, too, amigo—better clear out quick and find some good hidin' spots. 'Cause these bad hombres who just hit town ain't gonna wait much longer to show how much hell they're bringin' with 'em. And homey little families and dedicated daddies won't slow 'em down a lick!"

Moments after those words were spoken, a rapid-fire volley of shots sounded from out in the plaza.

The muscles at Braska's jaw hinges bulged visibly. "I'd say Hec and the boys are clearin' their throats and gettin' ready to talk mean."

33

OUT IN THE PLAZA, WITH THE LATE AFTERNOON sun hanging low, casting pools of thickening shadow between buildings and smearing the sky along the horizon a pale rose tint, the people from the cantina had been marched out and ordered to stand in a cluster before the fountain. Stark stood near, guarding over them. Wharten and Brazo, in the meantime, were circling around to the various shops and houses that ringed the area. At gunpoint, accompanied by harsh commands and frequent shoves as well as occasional smacks with a pistol barrel, they were ordering out all occupants and sending them to stand with the group at the fountain. As the assemblage grew, its make-up could be seen to consist primarily of women, children, and more elderly men. When the buildings had been emptied and the group stood milling in place, numbering thirty-four total, only three or four men not sporting gray hair were among them.

All during this, Hec had been pacing back and forth

about a dozen yards out from the front of the cantina. As he made his long strides, he held his drawn six-gun at his side and slapped it idly against his thigh. The arm in the sling he held close to his body in a way that indicated it was giving him some discomfort.

"That's everybody close around, Boss. Less'n you want us to go scrounge out some of the outlyin' houses," announced Wharten as he moved up on one side of the group while Brazo edged up on the other.

Hec stopped pacing. "No, this should be sufficient for starters." His narrowed eyes raked over the group while they looked back with a mix of bewilderment and fear on their faces. Only some of the children appeared unafraid, a few of the youngest even smiling a little in the belief this might be some curious new game.

"Why are there only ancient men among you? Where are the able-bodied ones?" Hec demanded suddenly.

There was a hesitation. Then, coming as a bit of a surprise, it was a stout Anglo woman wearing a baker's apron and a polka-dot headscarf over short-cropped hair who answered. "Our men are out in the fields working. They seldom come in until dusk."

"Well now. That's real industrious of 'em. You must be proud...how about some kind of law? Who keeps the peace for you fine industrious folks?"

This time, it was the bartender who answered. "We have only our alcalde. What you call a mayor. He handles any serious disputes that arise. But he is visiting family out of town."

Hec threw back his head and laughed. "Ain't that the way it goes? When honest folks like you need a law dog, there's never one around. For hardluckers like me and my pals, we can't hardly help stumblin' over the nosy bastards."

"Who are you men? What do you want here?" asked the woman in the headscarf.

Hec's smile remained in place but pulled very thin. "I'm glad you asked that, lady. But here's the thing— don't never ask nothing again. Not *none* of you, is that clear? I'll do the askin', you do the answerin'. And you better answer quick and better not lie, or it'll plumb piss me off!"

All eyes locked on him and the plaza seemed to go extra quiet, like there was a collective inhalation and holding of breath.

"You!" Hec pointed his gun at one of the non-gray men, a painfully thin individual with a heavily pimpled face and a huge Adam's apple. "Step out here."

The man shuffled forward, his entire body shaking with fear.

"What's your deal?" Hec wanted to know. "You ain't that old—why ain't you out workin' with the other men?"

"I-I'm very s-sickly," the man stammered. "I-I pass out sometimes, an-and am too weak t-to—"

"Too weak to do *anything*?" Hec prodded.

"I-I try. B-but—"

Hec told him, "It's a hard life, you sorry sonofabitch. And just tryin' don't amount to nothing for nobody!" And then he put a bullet in the middle of the man's forehead.

As the unfortunate wretch crumpled loose and lifeless to the dust, an eruption of screams and wails broke from the women in the crowd. Startled children puckered into tears and buried their faces in their mother's long skirts.

Hec pointed his gun skyward and triggered two more rounds. "Shut up! Shut up, you blubberin' cows, or I'll shoot any who continue screechin'!"

The howling faded quickly to sobs and mournful mewling sounds.

Then Brazo called out and pointed. "Jefe, look what is coming."

Following the line of Brazo's finger, Hec watched as an elderly man in a priest's robe came scurrying from the front of the mission. A wild mane of snow-white hair flowed back from his face and he was lifting the hem of his attire to keep from tripping in his haste.

Hec grinned wide. "Well, halle-hot-damn-lujah! A Holy Joe! I shoulda thought about rootin' him out in the first place."

The priest hurried past Brazo and rounded one end of the crowd. Voices assailed him. "He shot Alfred, Father!" "It was horrible!" "Killed in cold blood—for no reason!"

The priest stopped short, staring down aghast at the murdered man. He swept a tormented gaze in all directions until his eyes came to rest on Hec. "What in the name of the Lord is happening here?" he said breathlessly.

His grin turning into a broad smirk, Hec replied, "In the name of the Lord, Padre? Not a doggone thing. You see, me and Him got whole different slants on how things oughta operate. So what's goin' on here ain't got a damn thing to do with Him, and He ain't got nothing to do with me."

"But there's a dead man at our feet! One of God's blessed children."

Hec cocked an eyebrow. "Way it got told it to me, this sufferin' mutt got a mighty stingy servin' of blessings. All I did was put him out of his misery and clean up the half-assed job God did to start with."

"That's blasphemy!" the priest gasped.

"Oh, you stupid old fool," Hec groaned. "Can't you see I don't give a damn about that drivel! If you ain't caught on to that, then you'd better catch on quick to this: Me and my friends came here lookin' for a man, and I was just about to start askin' your flock where to find him. So now you can help out. You can either tell me yourself or, if you don't know, you'd better convince *somebody* to cooperate, or I'll commence sendin' more of 'em through those pearly gates you set so much store in!"

"Hot air and hogwash, Mallet! By the time you get done flappin' your gums, half that bunch will be on their way to those gates on account of dyin' from boredom!"

This new voice cut hard and sharp into the plaza and eyes began darting in all directions, looking for the source.

But Hec felt a prickle run through the hairs on the back of his neck and knew with a certainty. He wheeled around and found himself staring into the black eternity of Braska's Henry muzzle aimed square at a point between his eyes. Braska stood granite still in the half shadow of the hotel doorway, the Henry butted solid to his shoulder. Hec had turned with his Colt held at a twenty-degree angle above his waist, not high enough to shoot effectively without raising it higher.

Braska smiled a wolf's smile. "Whatya think, Hec? Ten inches. That's how far you gotta raise that cutter in order to do any good with it. You figure you're fast enough before I can drill a slug from this Henry plumb through that melon sittin' on your shoulders?"

Hec tried to swallow down the sudden dryness that filled his mouth. "Who the hell are you?" he rasped.

"The name's Braska...or maybe it'd mean more if I added Smith."

"Smith!" The name spat out like a foul taste.

"That's right. I'm here after Link, too. Only you know how it is with big brothers—I might be lookin' to knock him around some myself, but I'll be damned if I let him fall to the likes of you."

"You'll be damned all right, you bold bastard," Hec snarled. "Even if you put me down, there's still three guns backin' me who'll cut you to ribbons and then do the same to your brother when they find him!"

"Maybe so," Braska allowed calmly. "But you won't be around to get no satisfaction out of it."

Big Jess hollered, "Throw yourself to the ground, Boss! Soon's you're clear we'll blow that scoundrel to Hell and gone!"

Hec's expression tightened for a second, like he was considering it. Then, changing his mind, a sly smile tugged one corner of his mouth. "I got a better idea," he said. "Train your guns on the Holy Joe and his flock instead. If big brother don't lower his rifle in five seconds, open up on 'em. Let's see if this hero is willin' to sacrifice a bunch of innocents for the sake of his lousy, double-crossin' brother!"

Now it was Braska's face that pulled tight at this threat, this unexpected twist.

But then a voice drawled, "I don't think I'm of a mood to allow that."

Hec's eyes narrowed. He didn't dare look around. But he didn't have to, he recognized the voice well enough. "What the hell are you up to, Stark?"

"Plain enough," came the answer. "Far as you and Smith, I'll stand neither for nor against either of you. But these pet rattlesnakes of yours, Hec, are a different story. No way I'm going to hold off and let them cut down any more innocents."

"Never mind him, Boss!" called Wharten. "Me'n Brazo will—"

From a window of the hotel off to Braska's left, there suddenly issued a loud roar and a long tongue of red-gold flame. The ground just beyond where Hec stood was torn by a deep gash that spewed up dirt and a swirl of dust. This sent a jolt of startlement sweeping through all within the plaza.

But for those trained to the gun, it only lasted a moment.

Eyes blazing, Hec started to swing up his gun hand. But Braska's finger on the Henry's trigger was faster. The long gun barked and a red-rimmed third eye appeared between Hec's brows. His head snapped back, spraying gore and skull fragments out the back as he fell away. His gun hand continued to swing upward, and by the time a death twitch of his trigger finger fired a round, it smashed harmlessly into the face of the hotel.

Out in the plaza, Stark, recognizing Brazo as the faster and more dangerous of the remaining Mallet men, immediately put a bullet through his heart. As he went down, though, the wiry pistolero got off a shot of his own that sent a slug ripping along the gambler's rib cage.

The sudden twisting reaction this caused, however, served to jerk Stark safely out of the way of a shot aimed by Wharten. By the time the big man got his sights reset, it was too late. Simultaneous return fire from both Stark and Braska pounded into Big Jess. He was lifted up on his toes, sent into a staggering spin, then toppled to a dead heap.

In a matter of seconds, it was all over. Then there was only the sound of sobs and anguish coming from the huddled mass before the fountain, where some had dropped to the ground out of fear and mothers had wrapped themselves protectively around their children.

Jacking home a fresh round out of habit, Braska started out from the hotel doorway. A hushed voice at his shoulder stopped him. "By all the saints in Heaven..."

Braska turned to find a wide-eyed Pedro de Caza standing there with his Colt Dragoon clutched tight against his chest. A curl of smoke rose slowly up out of its muzzle.

Braska grinned crookedly. "Pedro, you surprisin' rascal...I thought the men in your family never turned to firearms as a way to solve your problems?"

Pedro met his grin with a mournful, somewhat uncertain look. "Si. That has long been so...but the thought of you, a stranger, going to fight for our village alone against those bad men, made me feel deep shame. So I took the big pistola to the window. And then, when I heard the evil one say to kill our priest, I—I badly wanted to kill him instead...but, shamefully, my hand was shaking so bad I only killed the ground beside where he stood."

Braska clapped a hand on his shoulder. "That was a fine shot, amigo. Don't you ever feel bad about it. It did everything it needed to do."

34

THE AFTERMATH OF THE PLAZA SHOOTING LEFT much to be done. Healing, mourning...and arriving at answers to the matter of Link Smith.

In the minutes immediately following, men from the fields came pouring in, drawn by the sound of the gunfire. They were first overwhelmed by joy and relief at seeing their loved ones traumatized though basically unharmed, save for poor Alfred. Then they were assailed by a wave of excited voices, all trying at once to relate what had happened. Until the priest finally got things mostly calmed down and took over the telling of events. This of course led to much praise and heaping-on of gratitude to Braska and Stark for their actions—and an even more enthusiastic level of the same for hometown hero Pedro.

Lucille showed up in the midst of all this, accompanied by Linda, little Alicia, Trisha, and a tall, handsome young man who proved to be Ernesto Renosa Jr., Trisha's fiancé. The latter's medical skills were promptly called into play when Braska directed him to the bullet gash Myles Stark had received to his rib cage. Luckily, due to having overhead the shooting, the doc had come prepared with his medical bag so was able to get right to work on the wound.

At the first opportunity, Lucille pulled Braska to one side and wrapped him in an embrace. "Looks like your skimpy battle plan was sufficient. But when we started hearing the gunfire, I winced at every single shot —fearing you might be on the receiving end. It was dreadful and I never want to have to go through anything like that again."

"Thanks to your kiss for luck—and some help from Pedro and Stark once again—I *wasn't* on the receivin' end of any of it," Braska consoled her. "And, goin' forward, I'd as soon keep it that way too."

Lucille gazed up with an even deeper anguish in her eyes. "Braska...Link *is* here, just like we figured...for weeks now, he's been under Ernesto's intensive care... but he remains in awfully bad shape."

————

IT WAS DARK BY THE TIME STARK WAS PATCHED UP and things had sufficiently settled down in the town. Once Stark was made comfortable and left well attended in a room at the hotel, Ernesto led a procession consisting of Braska, Lucille, Trisha, Linda, and Alicia back to the big estate house where his office and treatment facilities were set up. In the interim, Braska had had the chance to meet his niece for the first time, and there'd also been the opportunity to speak at some length with Linda alone. In that time he learned that the bits of speculation he and Lucille had pieced together turned out to be surprisingly accurate.

When the moment came to go in and see Link, only Ernesto entered the room with him. An elderly lady with iron-gray hair pulled into a severe bun was already present, sitting still and silent in a chair at the side of the bed. Ernesto bade her leave with a faint gesture and she glided out as silently as when she'd been sitting motionless. Ernesto then stepped back and left Braska to approach the bed alone.

There was a row of candles on a shelf above the headboard, giving off a mildly perfumed scent and casting the patient in a pale gold glow. Although his brother's condition had been described to him directly and plainly, Braska found he still was not prepared for what he gazed down upon. Link's body made barely a rift in the pure white sheets that covered him. So slender he was, so gaunt of face, so hollow-eyed. So pitiful looking. And all along his left side, where there should have been some extended width to the rift, that of an arm and leg...nothing.

An errant breeze from somewhere caused the candles to flutter, and the shifting patterns of light that played briefly across Link's face caused Braska's mind's eye to suddenly flash back decades. To the sight of that same face, narrow and skinny at that point before its growth spurt of youth, on nights with different light patterns playing across it from the lightning pops of thunderstorms sometimes raging outside their bedroom window. Link had been afraid of storms back then, but their stern father told him he must overcome such unnecessary fears and stay in his own bed to show he was a brave little man. Despite this, however, Braska would motion him to sneak over and slip under the covers with him until the worst of the storm was over. Their father never caught on, but even if he had and a scolding or punishment resulted, Braska would have counted the grateful look each time on that scared, skinny face as having been been worth it.

"Hey, big brother." Link spoke now, his voice barely above a hoarse whisper. The expression on his face wasn't one of gratitude or anything else at the moment. Just a look of exhaustion, a look of being nearly drained of all emotion, all everything.

In that moment, a similar thing happened to Braska. The feelings and emotions that had been driving him these past days and weeks—the anger, the disappointment, the determination to find his brother and shake out of him the *why* for all the wrong turns he'd taken... he was instantly emptied of all that. None of it mattered anymore. All he could focus on was his baby brother at the brink of death. Half of him already physically gone due to amputations necessary because of infection spread by half a dozen bullet wounds to his arm and leg. What was left, still fighting recurring bouts of fever and now the threat of pneumonia. If that set in, Ernesto had warned solemnly, there'd be almost no chance of him pulling through, not in his already severely weakened condition.

Link spoke again, saying, "Linda told me you were in town and would be comin' 'round to see me." He paused for a flicker of a smile to come and go. "I figured I owed it to you to hang on long enough so's you could give me a good chewin' out."

Braska shook his head. "That ain't what I'm lookin' to do."

"It should be. I got it comin'."

Now Braska showed a brief smile. "Okay. Maybe later on, if you insist. Right now, I'm a little tired."

"Uh-huh. I heard some snatches of talk...when they didn't know I was listenin'. True that Hec and some of the boys managed to track me down?"

"Don't matter. They're gone now."

"Yeah. Another mess of mine that fell to you to clean up."

"Never mind that. Doc says I can't stay too long so's not to tire you out. But I'll be back in—"

"No! Don't leave." A pale, bony hand shot out from under the sheet and wrapped weakly around Braska's arm. "This might be my only chance to tell you...to try and explain."

Braska looked around to Ernesto. The doc hesitated a moment, then gave a single nod.

Braska sat down in the chair recently vacated by the nurse. He put his hand over that of Link's and said, "Go ahead, baby brother. Talk to me."

EPILOGUE

LINK LASTED THROUGH THE FOLLOWING DAY AND into the middle of that night before he breathed his last. During that time, he had a chance to say what amounted to his final goodbyes to his wife and daughter. And, in two fairly long sessions with Braska, he related as best he could—without excuses or any attempt to deflect blame—what he saw as the reasons behind his veer away from the life's course that had seemed so well plotted for him.

It essentially boiled down to being unable to bear the weight of self-imposed guilt he heaped on himself for accepting the sacrifice Braska had willingly made for him. The wife and child obligations, the workload and responsibilities of running the ranch, carrying on the Bar S brand—all those tasks he welcomed and proved time and again he could handle. But all the while, deep inside himself, was the gnawing question of whether or not he deserved to reap any pleasure or satisfaction from any success or accomplishment, knowing it was all *really* owed to Braska taking his place rotting in a stinking prison cell.

Eventually, the inner question grew into doubt, and the doubt into an anger *at* Braska rather than gratitude *for* what he had done. Next came an overall bitterness toward the tasks and obligations that now seemed *forced* upon him, and that's when Link began lashing out and driving people away and making a downward spiral of bad decisions that brought about his abandonment of Linda and Alicia and the Bar S, and the subsequent collapse of it all in his wake.

By the time he started coming to his senses, he was running with the Mallet brothers gang and Link knew he'd hit rock bottom. Almost from the first moment of that realization, he'd wanted to try clawing back out. But he felt trapped. Once you were in with a bunch like the Mallets, you didn't just ride away of your own free will.

Then came the disastrous Utah bank robbery that left the gang badly shot up and scattered. When Link found himself seriously wounded on a getaway trail with Merl Mallet, who soon dropped dead from his own wounds, he saw it as his chance to not only break away but to do so with the stolen money Merl had been carrying as the means to finance a new life. If at all possible, he wanted that re-start to once again include Linda and Alicia. He knew of Trisha's presence in Tulamoro and was counting on—if he could make it that far—his injuries generating enough sympathy from her to serve as a covert link to Linda.

To a degree, that all worked. But what he hadn't counted on was the serious consequences from the extent of his wounds left untended for the length of time it took him to reach Trisha. Had she not turned out to have a skilled doctor for a fiancé who was willing to bend some rules for her in order to provide discreet and immediate care, Link never would have lived long enough for the reunion with Linda.

As brief as that turned out to be.

And the even briefer—though ultimately cathartic and meaningful—reconnection with his big brother.

———

DURING LINK'S FINAL HOURS, OTHER MEANINGFUL things also took place.

A sheriff from the neighboring town of Cimmaron was called in to officially verify the deaths of Hec Mallet, Brazo Hacklin, and Jess Whorten for purposes of claiming the various Dead or Alive rewards issued on them. The sheriff also took charge of the stolen bank money—which had hitherto remained untouched along with Link's other gear in a storeroom of the Renosa house—and assumed responsibility for getting it returned to the Fergus Hills authorities.

The bodies of the slain outlaws, at the insistence of Tulamoro's priest—in spite of their foul conduct, and reminiscent, in Braska's mind, to a similiar stance taken by Grannymaw Travers—received a Christian burial in a remote corner of the town cemetery.

It was initially decided that the reward money should be split three ways among Braska, Stark, and Pedro. Stark refused taking any due to his past association with Hec. Braska took only a modest amount for a road stake, then directed the balance to be divided between Linda and Lucille. Linda to apply hers to whatever future she could build for her and Alicia, Lucille to apply hers to her dream of going to New Orleans and arriving there in style.

This, of course, meant a parting of ways between Braska and Lucille. While her path had long been clearly focused and now finally possible, his—after first taking Link's body, by agreement with Linda—to the Smith burial plot on the old Bar S property, was as aimless as the wind.

"Let's face it," he told her on their final night together, "we always knew that our time together, as fine and special as it's been, was gonna run its course sooner or later. No promises asked or given, remember?"

"And wherever it led or however it ended, we said no one would be left feeling misled or mistreated," Lucille quoted in a soft whisper.

"You want bright lights and a big city," Braska said. "I want as much wide open wild as I can find. Not forever, but for as far as I can see into the future at this point. I don't know where or when that thirst'll get quenched, I just know it's been pent up too long and I gotta ride to find out."

So the next morning—after taking time to say a quick farewell to Stark, who was taking his own sweet time convalescing under the care of Dr. Ernesto and a particularly attentive dusky and lovely senorita from the village—Braska rode off on the first leg of his long-delayed wandering. With Link's shrouded and casket-encased body secured behind him on a travoise, he would first make the stop at the family burial plot up in Nebraska. And then he would point Savvy west toward...somewhere.

A LOOK AT BOOK TWO
DIABLO GOLD

Wayne D. Dundee returns with *Diablo Gold*, a thrilling tale of lost treasure, deadly outlaws, and one man's fight for survival in the brutal frontier.

In the turbulent years following the Mexican-American War, the ruthless Diablo Lobos terrorized the Arizona-Mexico border, amassing a fortune in stolen gold before meeting their bloody end. But legend whispers that a portion of their treasure—priceless relics from the time of the conquistadors—was never recovered. Many have searched. None have succeeded.

Now, in the aftermath of the Civil War, fresh clues reignite the hunt, drawing Braska into the deadly chase. What begins as a favor to an old friend soon turns into a desperate battle against greed, betrayal, and a new breed of outlaws willing to kill for the chance at untold riches. Caught in the crossfire, Braska must rely on his wits, his guns, and his unshakable will to protect the innocent and survive the storm.

Because in the ruthless West, sometimes hot lead is worth more than gold.

AVAILABLE JUNE 2025

ABOUT THE AUTHOR

Wayne D. Dundee is an American author of popular genre fiction. His writing has primarily been detective mysteries—such as the Joe Hannibal PI series—and Western adventures. To date, he has written several dozen novels and forty-plus short stories, ranging from horror, fantasy, erotica, and several "house name" books under bylines other than his own.

Dundee was born March 24, 1948, in Freeport, Illinois. He graduated from high school in Clinton, Wisconsin, in 1966. Later that same year, he married Pamela Daum and they had one daughter, Michelle. For the first fifty years of his life, Dundee worked his way up from factory laborer to various managerial positions. In his spare time, he was always writing. He sold his first short story in 1982.

In 1998, Dundee relocated to Ogallala, Nebraska, where he assumed the general manager position for a small Arnold facility there. The setting and rich history of the area inspired him to turn his efforts more toward the Western genre. In 2009, following the passing of his wife one year prior, he retired from Arnold and began to concentrate on his writing full time.

The founder and original editor of Hardboiled Magazine, Dundee's work in the mystery field has been nominated for an Edgar, an Anthony, and six Shamus Awards from the Private Eye Writers of America.